THE
SHADOW
SOUL

ALL WORKS BY KAITLYN DAVIS

A Dance of Dragons
The Shadow Soul
The Spirit Heir – Coming Soon!
The Phoenix Born – Coming Soon!

Midnight Fire
Ignite
Simmer
Blaze
Scorch

THE
SHADOW
SOUL

A Dance of Dragons #1

KAITLYN DAVIS

To my family for their unconditional love,
my friends for their overwhelming support,
and my fans for their incredible enthusiasm.
Thank you from the bottom of my heart.

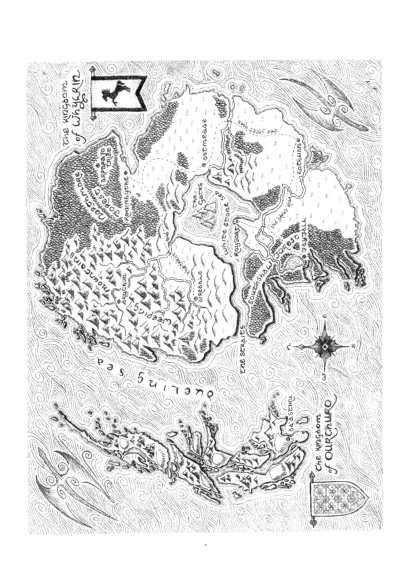

1

JINJI
~NORTHMORE FOREST~

A shadow was just the absence of light, a spot the sun could not reach. It was empty. But floating below her, drifting and dancing along the landscape, her shadow seemed full—not a reflection, but an impostor.

She pumped her leathery wings. The shadow did too.

She dipped closer to the trees. The shadow condensed, its points sharpening to match the outline of her body.

She arched up, farther into the cloudless sky. The shadow expanded and lost focus, rippling over the pointed trees below.

Enough, *she thought, gliding with the wind.* Time for food. *She focused on the horizon, spotting a deeper blue against the sky. Her mouth watered.*

Keeping her eyes on the ground, she watched as forest gave way to rocks that cut deep into the sea, a molten sapphire speckled with white. She swerved left along the shore, focusing on the cerulean expanse of the reef, searching for movement.

There.

The lazy undulation of a fin.

She dove, jaws widening.

A black shape flicked into her peripheral vision. She turned.

Bright white eyes opened in the darkness. Jaws clamped around her neck. She reached out with her claws, sinking razor-sharp nails into the invader's flesh.

They fell as one, smacking into the water, a mass of light and dark, plummeting below the surface. The jaws tightened. Her vision condensed. Air slowed.

They continued to descend deeper and deeper into the shadows, to the part of the world the sun could not penetrate, where the darkness gained a life of its own…

Jinji awoke with a start, gasping for air and clutching her aching chest. Her lungs screamed. Her mind fought to escape the daze. She blinked, but the darkness would not recede, even as her memory ignited.

It was the same dream. A dream she had only had once before but would never forget. A dream that was somehow more.

Another blink and a soft orange light leaked into her vision. She looked up through the smoke circle in the roof, toward the sky.

Dawn.

Jinji stood, throwing her furs to the side and stepping quietly past her mother and father. Soft dirt muted her steps, and her parents didn't stir as she crossed the small expanse of their home. Lifting the pelt aside, she stepped into the morning mist and began to run. Her feet followed the path along the longhouse, past the rest of her sleeping tribe and into the forest beyond. No thought was necessary—she had taken this path too many times before.

Besides, concentration was beyond her. Jinji's thoughts had drifted out of the world and into her memories, all the way back to her brother.

Janu, her heart cried softly, remembering him.

The last time she dreamed that dream had been on the eve of his death—what did it mean that it had happened again, a decade later on the dawn of her joining?

Jinji stopped.

She had reached the clearing, her sacred haven. A place shared only with her closest friend Leoa. Away from the game and too close to the outside world for anyone else in her tribe to discover—this place was their secret. The only place two girls could talk away from the attentive ears of the elders and the only place she could go to truly escape.

Jinji fell to her knees and opened her eyes wide, searching the air for something only she could find. She looked along the ground, over the flecks of dew spotting the grass, along the twining roots, up the rough bark and over her head toward the clouds.

There.

A shimmer. A dull glow. And now that she saw it, the light brightened and Jinji smiled. The spirits were still there for her.

For as long as she could remember, Jinji could see them. Everywhere. In everything. Minute strands of green, red, yellow, and blue, twining together to create the world. Earth, air, water, and fire spirits hidden in plain sight for no one but Jinji to see, and sometimes they tried hiding even from her. But not today. Not when she needed them.

Jinji studied the weaving strands, looking through the intricate patterns she would never begin to understand. And there she saw what she had truly been searching for: the space between the elements, the pure white wisps binding the colorful strands together—the mother spirit, the source of everything.

Jinjiajanu.

That was the name her people gave it. Her brother and she were named for it. But as far as Jinji knew, she was the only one who could manipulate it.

Closing her eyes, Jinji cupped her hands into a ball, envisioning the pearly glow between the strands of air she had trapped.

Jinjiajanu, she thought. The image changed to that of a face that was stolen ten years before.

Jinjiajanu. Bring Janu back to me—bring my other half back.

She opened her hands, facing them out toward the open air, keeping her eyes closed, using her memory to draw a picture in the wind. His tanned skin, the color of freshly exposed bark. His deep brown irises set in wide eyes and framed with full lashes. His smile, always mischievous and often taking over the whole expanse of his face.

She imagined him taller and broader than he had been as a boy, with muscles hardened from long hunts. The frame of a sixteen-year-old man. The frame of her twin as he would be if he were standing with her today.

After a minute, Jinji dropped her hands and let her eyes ease open. No matter how many times she wove the illusion, her heart stopped at the sight and a lump caught in her throat.

Janu. How I miss you.

Jinji rose and standing next to her, vivid as a real man but unnaturally still, was her brother. Her fingers brushed his, passing through his hand, as she knew they would. He was, after all, an illusion made of spirits. But still, she always tried to touch him, hoping to meet resistance just once.

Jinji could manipulate jinjiajanu, but no one could bring the dead back to life.

"Janu," she said softly, pleading. "What are you trying to tell me?"

But there was no answer. She could make his lips move, could make it look as though he were alive, but this wasn't her brother.

Jinji let the illusion fall and, in the blink of an eye, it had disappeared. The elemental spirits snapped back into their proper place, and their subtle glow faded out. She was alone once more with only the trees to keep her company.

A knot hardened in her stomach, a sense of fear she couldn't dislodge.

The last time she dreamed of the shadow, she had woken in a fright and turned to rouse her brother only to find him missing from their shared pallet. Immediately, she shook her father awake. Using his authority as chief, he woke the hunters and charged into the woods. But the minute she had turned to see Janu missing, Jinji knew that he was gone forever. When the hunters returned holding the carcass of a great bear followed by her father cradling a pouch that dripped with blood, she had fallen to the ground—devastated but not surprised. She heard her mother wail and felt the ground rumble as she dropped, but Jinji's eyes saw only a great shadow waiting to swallow her whole.

And now it had returned. On the day she was meant to be joined with Maniuk, to be named the future leaders of their people, the Arpapajo tribe—the last remaining oldworlders.

Dread rippled down her limbs.

What did it all mean?

"Jinji? Are you there?"

She turned to see her dearest friend, Leoa, push a tree branch aside and step into the clearing.

"I thought maybe…" Leoa trailed off, shaking her head and glancing at the ground before meeting Jinji's eyes again. Her friend's face warmed, nervous creases smoothed out, and a grin lifted the left side of her lip. "What are you doing?"

Jinji took a deep breath, trying to relax. "Thinking of Janu."

Leoa nodded, understanding dawning in her eyes. She stepped closer, placing her warm palm on Jinji's shoulder. "He would want you to be happy. Maniuk was his friend."

Jinji nodded.

Maybe that was it. Maybe she was just nervous, just wishing for her brother on such an important day in her life, just afraid that the joining would give her another man to lose.

She sighed and her shoulders slumped as she pushed the shadow from her mind and glanced at her friend again. The knot in her stomach still curled uncomfortably tight, but there was no use in trying to untie it now.

"Are you here to take me back to my mother?" Jinji asked, already thinking of all she needed to do before the ceremony began, especially of her braid.

Leoa shifted and it was then that Jinji noticed the stark white skins on her friend's arm, almost as pure as jinjiajanu in color.

Her gown.

The edges had been tied into hundreds of knots decorated with dried berries. Feathers of all hues were woven through the fabric, shimmering in the sun, changing colors with each minute move of Leoa's arm. Twine had been specially dyed just so the ancient ceremonial patterns could be woven in, patterns Jinji didn't even truly understand.

She had seen her mother painstakingly work on every inch of the garment, had watched as she laid it on the drying rack to bleach in the sun every day and brought it inside to clean and embroider every night.

Everyone in their tribe would eventually wear exquisite leathers to their joining, but none would ever be as fine as the one Jinji's mother had prepared. Yet the sight of it just made the knot in Jinji's stomach tighten.

She looked up just in time to catch the concern in Leoa's eyes.

"What's wrong, Jinji?"

"Nothing."

"Is it Maniuk? Did something happen?" She stepped closer, but Jinji moved away. It was ridiculous to be so concerned with a dream, absolutely ridiculous.

"No, of course not. He's a friend. He'll be a great leader."

"And so will you."

Jinji nodded absently. She had been born to lead her people; it was the only thing she knew how to do. No, that was not the cause of her anxiety.

"I know what's wrong," Leoa said with a smirk and stepped toward the edge of the clearing to lay Jinji's dress neatly on the grass. She held out her hands and cleared her throat. "You're going to miss me. That's what this is all about."

Jinji smiled. "Yes, Leoa, this is all about you."

"I knew it." She straightened her hands again, urging Jinji to take them. "But I know just the thing to help." She impatiently shook her fingertips one more time. Knowing not to disobey her friend, Jinji obliged and held on.

The smirk on Leoa's face widened. From years of experience, Jinji knew exactly what that look meant.

"One," Leoa said.

"Two," Jinji laughed, her mood already lifting.

"Three," they said in unison, completing the routine. And then they were off, spinning in circles like the center of a great storm. Jinji gripped Leoa's hands tighter and shuffled her feet to the left, trying not to fall. Their weight pulled them apart, but still they held on, straining to stay connected.

The world was a blur, rushing behind Leoa's face in a daze of colors that Jinji couldn't unwind. Her smile widened, pushing against her cheeks, straining her muscles so that they hurt in a good way—a way they hadn't in a while. And suddenly, the joining seemed far off. She was a child with her best friend, feeling girlish and untouched. The pressure of growing up had fallen from her shoulders, thrown off by the force of her sudden glee.

And then it was over.

In a heartbeat, Jinji's fingers slipped free of Leoa's, and she was thrown to the side, landing on the ground with an *oomph*.

But giggles invaded her senses before the pain took any toll, and she rolled to her side, shaking uncontrollably with an innocent joy that pushed itself out into the world because there was simply no way to contain it. So she let it go and unknowingly let her fears go with it.

"That was fun," Leoa said when the silence returned.

"It was," Jinji said, glancing over her shoulder with a contented sigh. Like always, Leoa had known exactly what she needed.

"Are you ready now?"

"I am," Jinji said and slowly sat up. She brought her hand to her hair, running her fingers through the long, ebony tresses, already missing them when she had reached the end. But before Jinji could make another move, her palm was slapped away.

"I'll do that," Leoa said, taking over the job of weeding out the knots, "just enjoy it. You're finally getting your braid." Her friend's voice was wistful, but to Jinji, this was the worst part of the joining.

Her braid.

She would miss the wind flowing through her hair, the way it moved with the spirits. She would miss the feel of it floating around her face when she dove deep down into a stream. But mostly, she would miss the feeling that it was hers alone, a part of her that belonged to no one else—not yet.

Her future belonged to her tribe. Her past belonged to her brother. Her essence belonged to the spirits. But her hair, as unimportant as it seemed, still belonged to her.

But soon it would belong to Maniuk, to their family, and to her people. No longer would it flow freely down her back, curling in soft tendrils down her spine. No, after sixteen years of freedom, it would be bound for the rest of her life. One strand for Maniuk, one strand for their future children, and one strand for the tribe—three parts braided together to show she had matured into adulthood and had left her carefree childhood behind. It would never be cut or undone, not unless it needed to be.

Jinji had only seen her mother unbraided once. When Janu passed, she had cut one strand of her braid off to be burned with his body, a symbol that their bond had been broken. She let her hair free until the cut strands had grown even with the other two portions and were ready to be braided again, a sign that her heart had healed.

Jinji touched the tips of her silky locks. No, if she was going to be braided, she hoped it would be forever.

"You're usually quiet," Leoa said, continuing to run her fingers through Jinji's untamable hair, "but usually I can tell what's going on in your head."

"I'm just thinking."

"I should be used to that by now. All this thinking you do, it always seems exhausting. More exhausting than all the talking I always do. I wonder what would happen if we changed places for once."

"I would grow hoarse, and you would grow bored."

Jinji was sure Leoa's pause was from rolling her eyes.

"Then I'll keep talking…" She tapped her fingers along Jinji's back, something Leoa always did when she was thinking, or more accurately, scheming.

"Hmm," she said after a minute—an idea had sparked to life, something Jinji probably wouldn't like. "Maniuk is so handsome, don't you think? Have you seen how far he can throw the spears?

How easily he can wrestle the other men to the ground? So strong, a great warrior, and well," her voice dipped lower, "I'm sure a great lover, too."

"Leoa!" Jinji tried to turn, but her friend gripped her shoulders, keeping her straight so her hair remained still.

"Don't tell me you haven't thought about it, with the joining so close. I know he has. I've seen him watching you."

"We're friends," Jinji growled, her face burning.

"Well, soon you'll be a lot more than that, and I want to hear all about it, but for now, the braiding."

"Is my mother coming?" Jinji asked, surprised they were not returning to the village before beginning the preparations.

"She knew you wouldn't want everyone around to watch. That's why she sent me to find you."

Jinji smiled, sending her thank you to the spirits since her mother was not there to hear. The last thing she needed was the scrutiny of the elders, picking over her flaws, telling her how to sit and stand and walk and speak. No, it was much better this way.

"I'm glad."

"Me too. Now," Leoa started and then separated the first third of Jinji's hair, placing it gently over her right shoulder, "for your joined."

"Taikeno," Jinji whispered, repeating the word in their native language, the one that had been stolen from them hundreds of years ago when the newworlders had taken over the land. But still, there were some things that could only be said in Arpapajo words. Some things only the ancient words could really express.

Leoa took the next third and draped it over Jinji's left shoulder. "For your children."

"Ka'shasten," Jinji responded, closing her eyes and saying it like a prayer.

Leoa gathered the remaining locks, tugging gently on them while she said, "For your people."

"Arpapajona." Jinji bowed her head, bringing her palms together, trying to catch the words and fuse them into the spirits around her.

As she wove the three parts together, Leoa began to hum. Following the rhythm, Jinji let her hands dance, weaving the words and the spirits together in an invisible braid, copying her friend's movements in a personal prayer.

Taikeno.

Ka'shasten.

Arpapajona.

Jinji repeated the words again and again in her mind, turning them into a song. A song of hope for a future that was happier than her past.

And then it was done.

Leoa tightened the strands, tying a series of intricate knots at the base of Jinji's braid to keep it tight and strong.

Just like that, she was a woman.

Waiting one more breath, Jinji opened her eyes.

And screamed.

Jumping up and backing quickly away from the spot, she stumbled over Leoa's feet until they had both fallen to the ground again.

Eyes.

She had seen bright white eyes staring out of her shadow.

"We must go," Jinji urged, breathlessly struggling to stand on her feet. Was that a yell she heard off in the distance? Were cries riding on the wind? "Do you hear that?"

Leoa gripped her hands, keeping her steady. "What? There is nothing. You're scaring me."

Jinji paused, took a deep breath, and listened. She heard nothing. Leoa was right.

Looking down at her feet, Jinji let her eyes run over the edge of her shadow, looking deep into the depths for some sign of betrayal.

But it was all a dream. It must have been a trick of the light. An illusion she had woven without realizing it.

Everything was fine. Everything was as it should be.

Her breath slowed as she tried to relax. *Everything will be all right. The past is the past—I will not let it determine my future.*

She would not let the shadows drive her crazy—she had moved beyond that, past the craze that Janu's death had left her in. She was better now. Stronger.

"Come here," Leoa said, holding up the dress.

Jinji stepped closer, turning around and slipping off the furs that she currently wore. They were brown, covered in dirt and grass stains, blending into the spot where they fell.

She raised her arms up, letting the fresh dress slide down over her body. It was still rough and unworn, scratchy against her skin. But it was beautiful. And it made her copper skin glow.

Leoa tugged on the strap around Jinji's waist securing it tightly before stepping back. Jinji turned, meeting her friend's smile with a weak one of her own.

"Let's go—" Leoa began.

But she never got the chance to finish, because the imagined scream Jinji had heard on the wind turned into a real one, piercing both of their ears like a dagger.

Their eyes met. After years of friendship, of sisterhood, no words were needed. The fear in their gazes said it all, spoke more than words could, and they ran.

Another wail cut through the forest.

Then a growl and a grunt.

The howl of a warrior cry.

Then silence.

Leoa ran faster, her long legs carried her farther than Jinji's petite frame could match. Before long, her friend had become a phantom dashing farther and farther out of Jinji's sight.

The fringe on Jinji's dress pulled against branches, tangling her in the forest as if the trees themselves were trying to stop her. The wind pressed against her limbs, strong gusts that acted like a wall holding her body. Her feet dipped deep into soft mud that should have been hard and dry.

But Jinji pressed on, speeding through the small stream at the edge of their home until she spotted a figure in the distance, just beyond the entrance to the great longhouse.

She sighed, slowing her steps. It was Leoa.

If her friend had stopped running, then there was nothing to fear. Jinji had gotten them both worked up over nothing.

"Leoa?" She called.

Her friend turned just enough for Jinji to see a long stick protruding from her chest, a red spot seeping through her skins.

"Leoa!" Jinji screamed. Her eyes widened in horror and her heart pounded, but she was stuck. Her feet felt too heavy to move, as if everything was happening in slow motion. Janu's face flashed before her eyes. This could not be happening. Not again. Her limbs were stiff, her mouth dry, her brain just repeated *no, no, no* unable to comprehend anything but agony.

And then a whisper filtered through the wind, "Jinji," and Leoa's arm reached out.

Her instincts kicked in. Jinji dashed to her friend, her sister, catching her just as her knees gave out and her body fell. They landed together, sliding slowly to the ground as Leoa's weight pulled them down. Jinji hugged Leoa to her chest, wishing that the beat of her heart would somehow spread to that of her friend's.

But she felt the body in her arms slacken, felt it drop an extra inch into her lap, heard one last gasp of desperate air, and knew.

Her arms lost their grip and Leoa tumbled onto Jinji's lap, lifeless and wide-eyed, shock written across her features.

"Ka'shasten," she whispered, ignoring the tears that blurred her vision. *My family.* "Pajora jinjiajanu." *Be with the spirits.*

Her voice cracked and she screamed.

And then her vision went red. She was not a little girl this time. She was a warrior. And she would find out who did this.

Jinji stood. Her eyes scanned the trees, searching for the bow that loosed the arrow, searching for any movement. But the village was still.

"Who are you?" She screamed.

A shuffling noise drew her attention. Just beyond the longhouse, someone was moving.

Jinji crept closer, pressing her body against the curved wood of the house, using it as a shield, hiding from the invader.

Heart pounding, she peered around the corner.

But it was a man she recognized.

"Maniuk," she hissed, trying to catch his attention. His spear was poised at the ready, a bow was slung over his shoulder, and the knife at his waist dripped red.

Part of her was proud. He was already a great warrior, and he would be a great leader when this fight was over.

But another part was afraid. Where was everyone else?

Maniuk didn't turn to her call. All of his attention was focused on the trees opposite them. She followed the line of his head, unable to see his eyes, and scanned the woods.

There was nothing there.

"Maniuk," she called again. Chills ran along her limbs. It was not the time to be fighting alone.

Suddenly he jerked into action. His arm lashed out, releasing the spear in a low arc that sailed through the center of their small village until with a thud, it landed.

A body fell forward, scratching against bark as it dropped.

But it couldn't be.

Jinji stepped back.

Maniuk?

He would never…

But there was Kekohi, one of their own, an Arpapajo, facedown with the spear through his chest.

Jinji's trembling hands rose to cover her lips, holding in the cry.

And then Maniuk turned around.

White.

His eyes were white, drained of all color, of all spirit, empty and somehow full at the same time.

The shadow had found her. It had come for her.

She stepped back again and again, moving away from the monster before her until her foot caught, and she stumbled.

Looking down, Jinji saw what she had missed earlier. The feathers along the arrow piercing Leoa's chest were raven black with red painted tips. They were Arpapajo, not newworlder. They were Maniuk's—Jinji had plucked those feathers herself.

He moved closer.

Jinji didn't try to run. She had no weapons, no hope of outpacing him. She had nothing left to run for.

Three feet from her body, Maniuk stopped. He slipped the knife from his waist and held it before him, arm out, almost as if he were offering it her.

Her eyes narrowed, traced the bulging veins up his wrist to his shoulder, until she stared into those absent yet knowing eyes.

The knife rose higher, up and up, over the height of her head, until it rested at his throat.

"No," she reached forward.

But in one quick motion, it was over.

Jinji didn't look away. Instead, she searched those eyes, and the instant before Maniuk's life was gone, she saw what she had been looking for. The shadow disappeared and Maniuk, her taikeno, was back. A deep despair flashed in his irises, and they froze that way as death took him.

He dropped to her feet.

Jinji knelt down, put her palm to his cheek, and closed his eyelids. "We would have done great things together," she whispered, brushing her fingers up through his hair, "I'm sorry I brought the shadow to you. I'm so sorry, my taikeno."

Jinji lowered her head until her lips pressed softly against his. Their first kiss. The one they should have shared at their joining. The one that should have been the first of many, yet would be their last. The only kiss they would ever know.

Suddenly adrenaline punched through her veins. This couldn't be the end, there had to be someone alive. Her mother. Her father. The children.

She jumped over his body and paused at the edge of her home.

To her left, the longhouse where her tribe slept each night. To her right, the longhouse where food was stored. Across from her, the smaller hut where she lived with her parents. And behind, the ceremonial grounds—today, the burial grounds.

It did not take long to decide where to check first, and before she realized she had moved, Jinji was pulling the furs of the longhouse aside.

The stench hit her like a punch in the gut, and she stumbled. Red splashed over the dirt floor, against the wooden slabs of the walls, dripping from the beams.

The only way to keep moving was to turn her mind off. She walked emotionless down the rows of bed pallets, checking each cut throat for a pulse, not caring as her hand stained maroon.

The children looked asleep, and she was happy for that, happy they had drifted away in ignorance, without experiencing the slow terror that was spreading along her nerves.

None.

There were none alive. And barely any sign of a struggle.

It was too much.

Jinji burst from the door and gulped in fresh air, heaving and coughing until spit dribbled from the corner of her lips—spit and tears.

Lifelessly, she moved back to Leoa's body and lifted her by the arms, dragging her over to the longhouse.

Jinji did the same for the bodies of the warriors she found sprinkled through the trees. She did the same for Maniuk, because she knew in her heart it wasn't really his fault—it was her fault, her burden to bear.

And when all of the bodies were safely tucked inside, she turned to her family's hut, knowing without a doubt what she would find.

She saw her father first, face down in the dirt. She turned him over, hand trembling above the wound that had opened his chest, and threw his furs over his stomach before pulling him to the rest of their people.

And finally, her mother, hand tucked under her cheek— peaceful and unaware.

And then it was done.

Before she could think, Jinji moved to the great fire always burning in the center of their village. She pulled a stick free and placed it against the dried wood of the longhouse, watching it spark, flare, and spread wildly.

Jinji stepped back, letting it burn her eyes.

Better to blaze than to drown.

Everyone she knew. Everyone she loved. An entire people wiped out. An entire culture gone.

But no, not everyone.

She was still here.

Alone.

Jinji looked down at the red stains covering her white dress, oozing wider with every second. Suffocating. The dress was suffocating her. It scratched her throat, sucked close to her body, constricting her breath, closing in on her lungs.

She screamed, ripping the dress down the seams, pulling the skins her mother had spent hours preparing apart, until she was standing completely bare in the sun.

Like a ghost, she turned around. Her eyes were vacant. Her arms hung lifelessly by her side. Her feet shuffled forward, barely lifting off the dirt.

Jinji went inside her home, reached for the box she always kept by her sleeping mat, and lifted the lid. Her brother's clothes. Tiny as she was, Jinji still fit in Janu's boyhood clothes. She still wore them sometimes, when she needed to feel like she was not alone. So she slipped them on, sliding her legs through the breeches and her arms through the leather shirt, both worn soft by time.

Reaching down again, Jinji gripped his hunting knife and grasped the end of her braid. Barely there an hour, and already all was lost. Her prayer had failed.

Slowly, she sliced through her thick hair, back and forth, back and forth, mechanically.

The braid dropped to the ground.

Her body shivered.

She reached back up again, eyes wide and wild, fighting the tears that were bound to come.

Crazed, Jinji kept cutting, grabbing any loose hairs she could, forcing herself as bald as she could go, as though cutting it all off could somehow bring them back, or at least bring them peace.

When it was done, she lay down, curled on her side with her legs pulled firm against her chest, so she could cry away from the world—whatever was left of it.

And deep in her heart, she wished for one thing, a wish she had longed for years ago—that she had died instead of Janu.

Before, it had been a selfless wish, a wish that her twin could live a long, happy life. She would have died to give him that chance. But now, she was acting selfishly. She was alone, and she wished beyond all things that she were the one with her people in the spirit world.

Her eyes closed and she cupped her hands, imagining the spirits and the jinjiajanu she had trapped in that small place.

And as she wished, she wove, tying the elemental spirits around her body in an intricate illusion, so for at least a little while she could pretend that she was the twin who had died, instead of the twin who was alone—the last remaining Arpapajo in this hopeless world.

2

RHEN
~RONINHYTHE~

"Faster, Ember," Rhen called, urging his horse onward, leaving only the echo of a carefree laugh behind him on the breeze.

Free again.

Rhen grinned, relishing his narrow escape. Adrenaline punched through his veins, fiery and intense, urging him to run as fast as possible. That nobleman had been inches away from gutting him. Of course, he couldn't blame the man. Rhen had spent the night in his daughter's bed, and it was a father's job to protect her virtue after all. Lucky for him, the old man's sword arm was a little slow.

He did, however, feel slightly uneasy. It really wasn't the girl's fault that he had slipped into her room just before dawn. He had a reputation to protect—and he needed a reason to be run from the city. But the fist's worth of gold arriving at their door later that afternoon should be payment enough, Rhen assured himself.

That was assuming Cal, his loyal friend and future Lord of Roninhythe, was on time with the delivery.

Rhen rolled his shoulders, loosening the knots court life left, ridding his body of the weight of nobility.

Despite the cost, there was no question in his mind. Now, riding Ember—carefree for a few minutes of peace—everything had been worth it. There were few things he wouldn't do to just be Rhen again.

Not Whylrhen, son of Whylfrick.

Not Whylrhen, Prince of the Kingdom of Whylkin.

Not Whylrhen, blood of Whyl, the great conqueror who united the lands.

No, just Rhen, a nineteen-year-old man with no strings attached.

As the walls of the city faded into the horizon, Rhen slowed Ember, patting her soft muddy-red hairs until her breath calmed, and she understood that the urgency had passed. Aside from his mother, she was the only female who had ever held his heart, and though she was old, she had never failed him. Not as a foal, when she had kicked down the stable door, saving his older brother Whyllem from the blazing flames. And not as a mare, when she had saved his life time after time, never demanding more than a light scratch along her neck.

Well, sometimes demanding more…okay, often demanding more, but Rhen was soft when it came to his horse.

He dropped the reins, trusting Ember to keep the pace, and reached into his saddlebag to grab the plain brown tunic resting inside. Stripping off the bright red silks of the crown, he let his bare chest soak in the sun before donning the less noticeable, but also less comfortable, common shirt. His boots and pants were still of the noble variety, but he wouldn't be able to fully hide his station without leaving Ember—and that just wasn't an option.

She neighed.

"Alright, alright," he said, grabbing hold of the leather straps again. "I suppose you deserve it." He pulled back, bringing Ember to a slow halt, and jumped from the saddle.

"Here you go," he said, slipping an apple from his bag. She greedily stole it away from his hand in one bite. A minute later, she stomped her foot, twisting her neck to look at him with distinctly pouting eyes. Rhen rolled his own eyes and reached for another.

Stroking her neck, he felt a sigh rumble down her nerves and knew she was satisfied.

"Okay, Cal, what did you find?" He muttered to himself, unrolling the parchment he had stashed in his belt just before sneaking out of the castle.

Whylrhen, the note began. Rhen sneered at the use of his formal name before continuing. *I feel it is my duty as your friend and loyal servant to first advise you on the idiocy of your current plan to pursue…*

Rhen sighed, skimming over the rest of the first paragraph. *Irresponsible. Dangerous. Foolhardy.* Blah. Blah. Blah. Did his best friend write this or the king? The similarities in the phrasing were almost uncanny.

He ran a hand through his hair, looking up at the endless sky for a brief moment, disregarding the paper in his hands.

All Rhen had ever wanted to do was protect his family. His father always said there were more than enough men who wished to be king. What a kingdom really needed were less people looking for glory and more people looking for honor.

Well, his eldest brother would be king and his other brother would be the right hand of the king. But what few people knew was that Rhen planned to become the left hand of the king—the unseen hand, the one that lived in the shadows, catching secrets on the wind.

To the world, Rhen would always be the third son—the useless son, the extra son, the afterthought. He was known as a womanizer, a gambler, and a fool—a reputation he did nothing to stop. No, quite the opposite. It was a reputation he was usually proud to build and strengthen. Better they think that than know the truth. That he was smart. That he was always listening. And that he was creating something his father had forbid, something he had banished after—

Rhen shook his head, blinked, stopped his mind from finishing those dark thoughts. That was history. And there were more important things happening here and now that required his absolute attention. Awenine, wife of his eldest brother Whyltarin and future Queen of Whylkin, was with child. There would be a new royal heir soon, a royal heir who needed Rhen's protection.

And for the first time since Rhen had chosen this path, there was something stirring, something waiting to be heard. There were no coincidences. Secrets were being whispered on the winds, if only he could just reach out far enough to catch them…

Ember pressed her forehead against his arm, nudging him into action as though she had felt his mood shift. He patted the white patch between her eyes, thanking her, and then lifted his body back into the saddle.

"Follow the road," he whispered into her alert ear and lightly kicked her belly to emphasize the command. She kept walking, and Rhen turned back to the letter, skipping down farther until Cal's words finally grew interesting.

I asked my father about your information, and he said he has heard nothing of the sort. His squire, however, said differently. Just as you described, the merchants and their crews are talking. Rumors of the spotting of unflagged ships on the horizon have begun to spread around the docks, though no one seems to take it too seriously, as there haven't been pirates in these waters since Whyl the Conqueror united the lands.

In other news…

Rhen paused, chewing on his bottom lip, ignoring the hair that had fallen over his eyes.

Nothing new, and yet, the word was spreading. Weeks ago while visiting the royal shipyard, Rhen had overheard sailors talking about spotting unflagged ships—ships that belonged to no kingdom and no king. Later that day he returned, looking distinctly less royal, and weeded out more information. Unidentified ships had been spotted along the northwest shore of the kingdom, a shore almost completely uninhabited due to the miles upon miles of steep cliffs blocking access to the ocean.

But there were only two kingdoms left in this world, the Kingdom of Whylkin and their neighboring Kingdom of Ourthuro. Secret ships could only mean one thing—the Ourthuri were looking for something, something that hinted of war.

Unless Rhen could stop it.

He kept reading.

In other news, the game has been lacking of late. The butchers have been complaining that no meat is being brought into the city, that they are losing their income. Unless the oldworlders are hoarding animals in their little wooden huts, someone else is taking them or something else is killing them. I probably shouldn't be telling you this, as it will only spur you on, but I find it my duty as a friend to keep your trust—even if you end up killed.

Perhaps my last piece of information will dissuade you from that course of action though. Unexplained deaths have been a recent phenomenon— bodies found with their throats slit, suicides we presume—though gossips have been labeling them as something far worse. I wouldn't have believed them, but Henry, a knight in my father's guard, and his wife recently passed the same way. And he was a strong fighter, an honorable man. He would not have done it to himself or to her.

So again, I would advise against chasing down these mercenary, and currently quite imaginary, ships on your own. Stay in Roninhythe and we can explore these mysterious deaths together; a noble cause I assure you.

You are a prince and someday you will have to understand that. But until that day, I will do my best as a friend to make sure it is something you do not forget.

Rhen snorted—as if he could ever forget. No, Roninhythe was not where he needed to be. Disappearing game sounded like a good lead—perhaps the unflagged ships had dropped off unspotted infiltrators. Cal had mentioned the oldworlders, which meant Rhen's destination was the Northmore Forest—home of the Arpapajo and another day's ride away.

"What do you say we move a little faster?" He asked. Ember's ears pricked at the sound of his voice and before he had fully gripped the reins, her slow walk had turned into a gallop.

There were few things Rhen loved more than the air whipping past his face as Ember raced through the countryside. In that time, the two of them were one. Her eyes were his eyes. Her legs his legs. Their minds were so connected that he didn't even need to speak to give her directions, she just understood.

Sometimes he would close his eyes and just let the smell of the grass fill his senses. Or open them so wide that tears leaked out the side from the wind. Heart thumping to the beat of her feet, all other sounds faded away and every dark memory seemed to disappear.

They covered miles in what felt like minutes, but the drowning sun betrayed the real time. Shadows elongated and the air cooled until eventually, Rhen could barely see a few feet before Ember's nose.

"Alright, girl," he said sadly, wishing it were not time to stop, "let's settle down for the night." He had spotted a tree line ahead, just before the light disappeared, and the last thing he wanted was to lead Ember straight into raised roots or a wide trunk. There was no use risking injury.

He slipped from the saddle and unhooked the buckle under her belly, letting the heavy leather seat fall from her back. Then without giving her time to protest, he pushed on her behind, signaling that it was time to lay down. She often preferred sleeping upright, but tonight, with the last remaining winter nips still on the breeze, Rhen would need her warmth. And after a long run, she would need her sleep.

Once Ember settled, Rhen curled in next to her side, and the two of them let sleep come quickly.

But it didn't last very long.

Just before sunrise, Rhen woke with a long gasp and coughed, flipping over onto his hands and knees while his lungs rebelled against his body. Within seconds, Ember had smelled it too, hopping to her feet and letting out a long screech that scratched its way down Rhen's spine.

Smoke.

Plumes and plumes of smoke.

"Easy, girl," he jumped to his feet, wrapping his arms around Ember's neck until she calmed. "You know I won't let anything happen to you." She curved inward, using her head to complete the hug while Rhen continued to pat her short hairs.

He looked down her long body toward the forest, and farther still to the large black tunnel drifting from the treetops. It was moving with the wind, which just happened to be smacking the two of them in the face.

Excellent.

Quickly, Rhen reached down and resecured the saddle. He walked before Ember and gripped her nose, making her look at him. Fear was written across her dark black pupils.

"I know what this is putting you through," he said as she winced, "but you must trust me. Fire is something that will never hurt you, not when you are with me."

She pulled against his hand, her vision going back to the forest for a quick second. She kicked the ground, complaining, letting him know just how unhappy she was.

His heart sank. There was no need to remind him of her fears. Though her name was Ember, fire was the last thing she was made of. Her skin trembled, remembering the barn and the fire that had almost claimed her life.

But there was no choice. He had to find the cause of the flames, and he had to put them out. Because fire was exactly what Rhen was made of.

Jumping up into the saddle, he urged Ember forward, bringing them closer to the trees but to the side away from the smoke. They would follow it like a great river, along the edge and just out of reach.

Cutting through the forest was slow moving as they maneuvered around low branches and tall bushes. He held the reins steady, keeping Ember's movements controlled and not frantic.

Even from afar, the smoke permeated his senses, making his breath feel tight and his eyes burn. It seemed endless, as though the smoke came from the ground itself, bursting forth from the soil to wreak havoc on the world.

After what seemed like an eternity, a bright flame flickered in the distance. He spotted it an instant before Ember.

Flinging his feet to the side, Rhen landed almost upright a split second before her forelegs lifted from the ground and she jumped away, backing from the bright orange blinding her eyes. He let her. Better Ember act on her fear, better she feel some control.

Besides, he had work to do.

Rhen stretched out his hands, reaching his palms before him, and crept closer and closer until he felt the pull. His fingertips burned, still feet from the flames, but they called to him. His body zinged, energy bouncing from limb to limb. He let it build—let the need go crazy. And then, as though sucking in a large breath of air, he pulled with his mind and the fire listened, crashing into him like a wave.

As a boy, Rhen had loved playing with flames. He would stand by the candles in the great hall, poking at them with his fingers, letting his palm absorb their heat, until one day his mother ran over with a scream and pulled him away. *You cannot do that*, he remembered her exclaiming quite vehemently as she checked his chubby hands for burns. But there were none. Because it never burned him, and until that boyhood moment, Rhen had never realized that it was strange, that it wasn't normal. Ever since that day, he had kept these powers to himself.

The fire spoke to him. He couldn't create it—he had tried that many times to no avail. He couldn't even move it or shape it or aim it. All he could do was absorb it and let the flames fill his body until he felt like all he needed to do was open his mouth to breathe smoke.

But at times like these, he was grateful for the gift, or curse, whichever it was.

So he stood, letting the heat crawl under his skin, letting it bubble under the surface, until the onslaught passed and he could feel the breeze on his cheeks again.

Rhen opened his eyes.

Like giant claws, the trees rose from the ground, bare and blackened, stripped of leaves and life. But the fire, at least, was gone.

He spun.

"Ember!" But he didn't see her behind him where the forest turned green again.

He whistled, body stiff and alert, until thunderous hoofbeats reached his ears and Rhen relaxed. Moments later Ember emerged, but she stopped beside an untouched tree, not stepping one hoof into the blackened soot of the burnt forest floor before her.

"Come here," he commanded.

She stepped back.

Rhen crossed his arms.

She shook her head.

He stomped.

She did too.

"So dramatic," he rolled his eyes and stepped forward, giving Ember the victory, scratching the soft patch in her forehead until she finally showed her forgiveness by padding into the ash.

"I'm sorry," he whispered before swinging into the saddle.

Moving opposite the wind, the two of them pushed onward. *It's worse than a battlefield*, Rhen thought as he looked around. Tree trunks rose up into sharp, blackened points and then stopped. A field of topless trees, of stake-like spires, stretched out before them. All color was gone from the world. Little clouds of ash followed Ember's footsteps, blackening her russet coat.

But worse was the eerie quiet. No birds chirped. The wind licked his face, but there were no swaying branches or whispering leaves. When they came upon a splashing stream, it sounded as roaring as a great river, as though the crashing waves were the size of a man instead of a toad.

Rhen had never ventured this far into the Northmore Forest. No one did, aside from the missionary his father sent once a year to ensure the Arpapajo were still adhering to the laws of the land and speaking the king's tongue. There was no need. They lived a secluded life apart from the rest of the world, and as far as Rhen was concerned, they should keep it that way.

Everyone spoke of the strange people, still dressed in poorly sewn animal hides, running around with stone-tipped arrows and paint on their faces. It was a bedtime story to frighten young children into sticking close to home.

Yet out here alone without the forest to cover his movements, Rhen almost felt as though he were being watched.

The hairs on his forearm rose, and he darted glances from side to side, searching for movement.

He might be a prince, but no one in these woods would know what that truly meant—and even if they did, he wasn't sure that they would care.

I better not die out here, he joked and tried to calm his rising nerves, *Cal would never let me hear the end of it.*

And then he spotted green in the distance.

The origin of the fire.

Rhen pressed Ember forward, forgetting caution as his excitement and nerves compounded into a sudden burst of energy.

But as he neared, his confusion grew. It almost seemed like a village. Was it possible the Arpapajo had burned their own home down?

He searched the ground but there were no bodies in sight. A pile of smoking wood, burnt down to little more than rubble, caught his attention. It drew a line in the fire—one side black and one side green. Had it been a house?

The start of the fire for sure, but it was now completely unrecognizable.

Rhen dropped to the ground, noticing a great wooden structure behind the collapsed heap. A second house?

He moved quickly, searching the length of the twisted branches and bark for some sort of door. A breeze blew in, lifting a slip of tanned hide and Rhen caught it with his hand, flipping it over his shoulder as he entered.

Dried fruits hung from the ceiling. Carcasses that were half-cleaned and now buzzing with insects were piled along the wall. A putrid smell filled his nostrils and he retreated quickly.

There was nothing human in there.

He spun in a circle. If this had been the food house, maybe the other had been a living house? He turned one more time, trying to differentiate a wooden structure from the trees behind it.

Nothing.

Nothing.

And then all of a sudden a smaller hut materialized from the woods, almost invisible against the forest.

He ran, pushing back the now obvious skins of the door.

Blood was the first thing he saw. At his feet, a great red circle spread against the entrance of the home, dried into the dirt and stained that way. He followed the line, and farther into the room was another spot, also dry but on a raised wooden expanse that must have been a bed.

If there was blood, there must have been an attack.

And if there was an attack, there must be foreign invaders.

Which meant one thing: his kingdom wasn't safe—no, his family wasn't safe.

Rhen whipped around, bringing his fingers to his lips to whistle for Ember when a shape caught his eyes. A smaller bed sat to the left of the entrance and it looked…

He crept closer, slowly, trying not to make any noise.

His heart pumped wildly in his chest. He flexed his fingers, reaching his hand out to grab the animal skin, cursing himself for being unarmed.

He pulled back and brought his hands around a thin throat, making to choke the body before his brain caught up with his muscles, and he realized it was just a boy. Not a mercenary, not even a fighter, just a child.

Rhen sat, his body heavy with surprise.

The boy hadn't even stirred at his touch.

He leaned down, bringing an ear to the immobile chest, and there was a soft thud of a beat—very faint and very slow, but still there.

Rhen scooped the boy into his arms, taking just a moment to loosen the small fist from a crudely created rock knife, and then sounded his whistle loud and clear. By the time the two of them emerged, Ember was waiting—dare he say it, impatiently.

But her look softened when she noticed the small figure in his arms, and she knelt to the ground, making it easier for Rhen to climb on without jostling the fragile body he held.

"Back to the stream," he told her.

Ember stuck to the unburned forest, keeping out of the sun as best she could, moving as carefully and quickly as possible.

Within minutes, they reached the same stream as before, but this time the edges were lined with soft grass instead of ash. Clean water was exactly what they needed, not something blackened with soot.

Rhen slipped from Ember as she knelt down and settled the boy on the grass. Digging through his things, he pulled out a canister of water and gently opened the boy's mouth. Being careful not to pour too much, he tilted the bottle. Reflexively, the boy swallowed, opening his mouth for more. Rhen obliged with another small dose, but then stopped. He didn't want all of that water coming back up and out the boy's mouth.

Next, Rhen dipped his hands into the stream. Without drying off, he patted the boy's cheeks, his forehead. Going back for more water, he wet the boy's hair and arms, and then repositioned the body so the child's feet slipped into the water, hopefully absorbing it.

Rhen leaned down. Already the heartbeat sounded stronger.

He poured some more water into the child's throat before sitting back up.

There was no blood, no wound, and no foreseeable reason why the boy had gone so long without food. He seemed old enough to take care of himself, maybe ten or twelve. Scrawny still, but surely able to hunt in the absence of adults.

No, this seemed like something else. Perhaps the result of a mental incapacity.

But Rhen thought back to the blood, the ash, the burnt pile of wood. Perhaps it was just a lack of will.

Rhen understood that—the feeling of failure when a loved one died, of helplessness, of wanting to drift away never to be found again. But he had overcome it, with help.

Rhen looked at the boy again. His skin was dark, born that way and not just tanned from the sun. His hair was black and chopped so haphazardly that it stood out at all different directions. He had lived with wooden huts instead of stone castles. With animal skins instead of fine silks.

So different from the people Rhen had grown up with.

And yet, still the same somehow. Still fragile, just like someone else Rhen remembered—someone he so often tried to forget.

He reached for the water again.

If this child was truly alone, then Rhen was the only one left who could save him.

A thunderous boom sounded through the trees.

Rhen dropped the bottle.

It fell, rolling along the ground, sinking closer to the water. He dove, catching the canister just before it fell into the stream, but half of the contents had been emptied. He turned it, looking through the top to judge the remaining amount, when something just behind the bottle caught his attention instead.

A footprint.

No, he corrected himself, *a bootprint*. Something that could never belong to an Arpapajo.

Invaders had been here.

Rhen looked at the boy, torn. He really shouldn't leave, not when the child was still so weak. But his skin had brightened. He looked better. And those prints could be the key to saving a lot more than one boy. They could be the key to saving the kingdom.

He had no choice.

Decision made, Rhen stood.

Scooping the boy up one more time, he gently placed him under a tree, hidden from the riverbank in case anyone approached.

"Keep him safe," Rhen whispered into Ember's ear. She stomped a hoof, letting Rhen know she would not let him down.

"I'll be back soon," he said, but still grabbed his sword and scabbard, belting them tightly around his waist.

Sloshing through the water, Rhen moved to the opposite side of the bank to examine the print further.

Most definitely a boot.

He looked close by, scouring the ground until a second print identified itself. Rhen stepped closer, repeating until he had a solid trail to follow. Crushed branches and chopped bushes created a line through the normally untouched forest, a track that was easy for Rhen to find. He was used to stone, something that left a much more invisible path. Compared to that, this was simple.

Before long, Rhen happened upon a camp. A few tents were set up. Weapons lazily rested against a tree. A fire was still warm though the flames had died. And behind, stacks of logs were piled up, tied together in tight bushels like those resting beside the fires in his family's castle.

The loud noise must have been a tree falling, but why? Why so much wood? Unless they were planning to make camp for a long time—or for a much larger crowd—an army, perhaps.

His mind spun.

This was more proof than Rhen had ever hoped to find, more information than he was prepared for. The king had to know, immediately. Biting his lip, Rhen reassured himself that his father would believe him. With news such as this, with stakes so high, surely just this once, everyone would believe him…

Rhen moved to turn.

But before his feet had even shifted, something heavy slammed into the back of his skull.

The last thing Rhen thought before he crashed to the ground, slipping into the darkness, was *Damn it, Cal, why must you always be right?*

3

JINJI
~NORTHMORE FOREST~

Blue. There were so many shades of blue.

The deep midnight of a heart in mourning.

The gray shadow behind closed eyes.

The hot white when they first open.

The oscillating flashes of blinks, until it's just one bright hue against the clouds.

Jinji saw them all, lying there, staring up through the trees because her body had forgotten how to move. Even if she had strength left in her muscles, there was none left anywhere else. Her spirit was spent, was broken.

So she kept watching the clouds drift, even as her eyes began to sting and tear and dry again, she kept looking up. Because the other option was to close them, and every time she did, all she saw were shadows—darting between flames, circling in blood, hiding behind big, brown eyes.

The shadow had taken everything, but it still hunted her. In her dreams, in her sleep, even in her waking eyes—it was always there.

Something nudged Jinji's foot, but she didn't stir.

Then something wet and slightly scratchy brushed her hand.

Hot breath tickled the hairs on her arm.

Just let me be, Jinji thought, ignoring the sensations. She wanted to join her family in the spirit realm, to drift away unnoticed by the world.

And she had been so close.

What happened?

And then Jinji really looked at the blue sky above her, noticing it as if for the first time. How was she outside? Why wasn't she still in her pallet, blanketed by the memory of her parents and of Janu?

And that little twinge of curiosity was enough to finally push her into movement. After days of indifference, something had broken through the hurt.

Slowly, carefully cajoling her muscles back to life, Jinji lifted her head and looked into two bulbous black eyes.

She jerked back—her entire body shocked into movement.

A very large animal was looking at her, leaning over her, but Jinji wasn't afraid. If it had meant to hurt her, it would have. Instead, the creature leaned its head forward, slapping a soaked tongue against Jinji's cheek.

She rolled away, standing quickly. Blinded from the head rush, she wobbled on unsteady feet until she felt soft fur under her fingertips and held on for balance.

"Thank you," she whispered and opened her eyes.

Jinji ran her hands over the soft hairs and felt the animal sigh. At the sight of a large leather seat, Jinji remembered what it was called—a horse. The newworlder who came to give the children language lessons always rode one.

"Who traveled with you?" Jinji asked, continuing to pet its neck.

The horse stomped, dipping its head in the direction of the water. Following the line, Jinji looked along the ground. Sure enough, she saw footsteps into the stream and out the other side.

Large footsteps.

The footsteps of man.

Suddenly, Jinji's hands dipped to her legs, feeling for her animal skins.

She let out a breath—they were still there. Her eyes searched for any maltreatment, but there were no rips or tears in her clothes, no aches in her body where there shouldn't be.

Her parents had warned her about males in the new world, especially about ones who could not control their urges. It was the reason she had never traveled to the great cities her father spoke of—she was not allowed to until she joined, and then Maniuk would—

No, Jinji thought as her chest clenched tight and her mouth dried. Maniuk would not be taking her anywhere. Nor would her father. Or her mother. Or…

Water. I need water.

Jinji ran, fell next to the river, and dipped her hands deep into its cooling currents, splashing her face.

A moment later, Jinji realized the curtain of hair normally falling over her shoulders was not there. Goosebumps rose on her neck and she reached back, grasping the air.

Her braid.

She had chopped it off.

The memory slowly returned as she rubbed her fingers over the mess that remained, chopped and ripped, her own personal battlefield.

Hesitant, she leaned over the water. It had been so long since she had seen herself without long, flowing locks—the sight of her face free of the frame of black would be a shock, but she needed it.

They were gone.

Her prayer had failed and she had to face it.

As much as she wished to fade away, to leave this place, she had been kept alive for a reason. And right now, remembering her people, that reason was vengeance. She would find the shadow, and she would destroy it.

Taking a deep breath, Jinji forced her eyes to the water to look into her braidless, tribeless, but not purposeless reflection.

The image of Janu stared back at her.

With a yelp, Jinji fell onto the grass. An electric shock pulsed through her body, setting all of her hairs on end. Disbelief.

Reservedly, she sat up and leaned over the water again.

The image was slightly distorted by the moving current, but it was unmistakable to her eyes. The slightly flatter, higher cheekbones of her brother. His slightly wider eyes and thinner mouth.

Almost the same as she, yet completely different in Jinji's eyes.

The blue spirit strands flowing through the water appeared in her vision, almost as if they could read her mind. Searching through the spirits, she peered closer and closer, until the white spaces, the mother spirit of jinjiajanu was there. She grasped it, and almost instantly felt the illusion woven across her facial features.

Using only her mind, she felt along the tightly knotted strands circling her face, and she remembered—remembered lying in that bed dressed in Janu's clothes, wishing beyond everything else that he were there instead of her.

In their own way, the spirits had listened to her prayer. They couldn't let her trade places with the dead, but they could for a time, let her pretend.

She felt her clothes again.

Her savior, whoever he was, must have thought her a boy.

Well, she was happy to keep it that way. And feeling the knots tied tight across her face, Jinji realized that this illusion was built to last—was permanent. Nothing would unravel until Jinji decided it was time to reveal her true face, to let the mask of her brother's features fall away.

Now was not that time.

Releasing her connection with the spirits, Jinji stood and looked over the water one more time. The sight of her brother gave her strength and made her feel less alone, even if it was just an illusion.

Masked by Janu's face, she felt ready to find this man—her unknown protector.

The Arpapajo were gone, but not forgotten. They lived through her, and venturing into the new world was the only way Jinji would ever be able to find the answers they all so desperately needed. So that was exactly what she planned to do.

And maybe, after all of the mysteries had been solved and the shadow was gone, maybe then the spirits would let her drift away—maybe then they would let her truly enter their world.

With a sigh, she turned and waved to the horse.

"Follow," she said and the horse stepped forward. Satisfied, Jinji turned toward the tracks.

The sun was starting to lower in the sky. They would have to move fast.

Wasting no time, Jinji splashed through the water and ventured farther into the woods.

The more she walked, the more footprints she saw and the more signs of life. Bushes carelessly chopped. Branches thoughtlessly broken. Something had been in her woods.

After a long while, when the sky had already started turning pink, Jinji heard what she was searching for.

Laughter.

Deep, boastful, taunting laughter. The sound of men who thought they had won without even realizing the fight had yet to be fought.

Behind her, the horse neighed and stomped its feet. Jinji reached for the leather straps hanging from its body, calming the poor animal down before securing it to a low-hanging tree branch. The time had come for them to part ways, at least for a little while.

Using the growing darkness as a cover, Jinji moved closer to the noise. In these moments, her body felt as one with the forest. The dirt seemed to soften under her feet, muting any sound. The trees opened wide, letting her move swiftly between them. Even the animals quieted, as though they were in on the mission.

Normally, she hunted for game. But not tonight.

As the sun disappeared, a fire brightened into view, flickering through the woods like a beacon for her to follow.

Jinji crept as close as she dared before stopping behind a large tree trunk and peering around the edge to survey the scene.

There were five men—four smiling, and one distinctly more sullen.

My rescuer, Jinji thought dryly, taking in the straps binding his ankles and the harsh angles of his arms, which must be bound behind his back. His skin was pale, reminding her of her joining dress, bleached by the sun rather than baked by it. His hair was light brown, fused with red, almost like a bird's feathers—a color Jinji had never seen on a man. Even sitting, he seemed rather large, stockier than the boys she had grown up with.

But more than anything, Jinji found herself drawn to his eyes. They were green, like the forest, filled with a deep despair that Jinji understood. Hopelessness. The feeling of failure.

Even though the two of them could not be more different, Jinji felt as though she looked into her own reflection. Her eyes, brown as they were, told the same story. And that sense of shared loss made her want to help.

But how?

Jinji shifted slightly, taking in the other four men. It was their laughter that had rung through the trees.

They were not particularly large or threatening, more like foxes than bears, but still she was outnumbered. Jinji looked at the red tint to their cheeks, the jugs in their hands, the wide smiles plastered on their lips. Something was odd about them, like they had leaned too long over a fire and breathed in too many fumes. Their eyes were vacant, open, but unaware.

Perhaps it would be easier than she realized.

Jinji reached for the knife at her waist, but grasped nothing. She looked down, wincing at her idiocy. Her brother's skins. She was in her brother's skins, not her own. Her knife was a long distance away, back home laying useless on the floor.

Using the firelight, she searched the ground, but a branch would not be nimble enough to wield against four foes. She could knock out one maybe, but four? No.

Jinji turned back to the camp. They had to have weapons.

She crept in a circle, moving behind the trees and just out of sight. The men looked unarmed and relaxed. But surely they kept protection with them.

And then a bright light caught her eye.

She looked closer.

The hint of flickering fire gleamed from the dark.

A newworlder weapon. Jinji had only seen them a few times; like hardened water they shimmered. *Metal*, she thought. The newworlders fought with metal and not rock. *But*, she sighed, *it will have to do.*

It looked like her knife, slightly longer with a curved edge rather than a straight one, and a cuff circled the handle.

But it was a few feet out of reach. She would have to make herself known before grabbing it, would have to expose herself. If one of them held a weapon she couldn't see, Jinji would be dead. And she would never avenge her people.

Oh what she wouldn't give for a spear—something she could throw from the shadows. Slamming a fist against her leg in frustration, she searched for another option. But there was none.

A drumming sound caught her ear, pounding closer and closer.

From her peripheral, Jinji saw her rescuer look up with a gleam of hope, the smallest hint of a smile.

A squeal sounded through the darkness.

All four captors looked up from the fire, brows furrowed.

The horse, Jinji realized. Her knot hadn't been tight enough—thank the spirits.

The thunder got louder, quicker.

The men stood and turned toward the darkness on swaying feet, searching for the cause of the noise.

Before she had time to second guess, Jinji jumped from the trees and ran the short distance to the gleaming knife, gripping its cool hilt.

She felt eyes on her.

Jinji looked up, right into the crystal green irises of her former rescuer. They were wide, shocked, and then satisfied.

A deep yell interrupted her focus, and Jinji stood swiftly, swinging the knife into the throat of the man reaching for the weapons at her feet. Blooded spurted out, raining on her like a wave as he crashed to the ground.

Before it was too late, Jinji gripped another knife from the pile, this one smaller and more like the ones she was used to.

Another man turned from the darkness, looking straight at her, and she acted out of reflex.

The blade landed with a thud against his forehead, sinking until only the hilt remained. All life left his face before he fell, knees first, to the ground.

The last two men spun, taking Jinji in with surprise. She was small, she knew, but that didn't mean she wasn't threatening. And two of their companions were already down.

They stepped apart, circling her, coming closer at two different angles, and her heart sank.

These men were trained—intelligence reflected in their eyes, their movements. She had never been in a real fight before, not one against people. Animals were different; they tried to run. But these men had turned in challenge.

She brought the curved knife up in front of her face, flicking her gaze from side to side, never taking either man out of sight.

They were creeping in.

The man who had saved her before was wriggling his body, trying to get free of his bindings, was yelling out to her, but she couldn't hear his words.

Jinji's own breath filled her ears, loud and ragged. Her heart hammered with the decision to move left or right. Which man would she face and which would she turn her back on? She had to choose soon before they were both on her, unchallenged.

One.

She flicked to the smaller man, coming in from the right.

Two.

Her attention shifted to the larger man on the left, his eyes more unfocused, and his footing a little more unsure.

Three.

Jinji jumped and feigned right before moving all of her weight to the left. The man was slow, but his bicep rose just in time to block her blow with his forearm. The knife dug deep into the leather strapped to his skin, and though blood seeped through, it was not enough.

She pulled, but the curved side of the knife had dug too deeply and Jinji could not get it free.

The man reached with his uninjured arm, wrapping long fingers around her throat. He was too big. She kicked as his grip tightened. Her breath wouldn't come. His fingers squeezed, lifting her onto her toes as she tried to fight.

Did I survive just to die like this? Could life really be so cruel—to give a glimmer of hope and then take it so swiftly?

Over her shoulder, the other man grabbed a weapon and raised it high over his head.

She tugged at the hand trapping her, but it did not budge.

The other man readied his aim, preparing to lunge the metal straight through her back.

Jinji closed her eyes, prepping for the blow, her family's faces flashing in the darkness. A new sense of failure and loss penetrated her heart.

But the pain never came.

Instead, pounding hooves broke into the clearing and the crunch of shattering bones sounded in Jinji's ears.

The grip on her throat tightened.

She opened her eyes, looking over her shoulder at the broken body under the horse's feet. The man's skull had caved in—his insides oozed out onto the grass.

She looked forward into the fearful eyes of her captor, and knew what to do.

His muscles held her, so Jinji jumped, using his arm as an anchor, and kicked both of her feet against his chest.

A second later, she landed on the ground, banging her already sore head against the dirt.

The man stumbled back, and the body of the horse soared into Jinji's view, ramming into his chest.

The man fell, coughing up blood.

Jinji reached for the knife that the other captor had dropped and stood.

He was already dying, she could see. The strength had left his limbs, the knowledge of his own mortality seeped into his features.

She arched back, brought the knife deep down into his chest, and twisted until the body stilled.

Jinji dropped the weapon and stumbled back, shuffling her feet closer to the stools by the fire until her body fell heavily on top of one.

Her hands were red, wet.

She wiped them on the ground, trying to fight the sudden awareness shocking her senses.

She had killed people. Killed them like they were food. No, like less than food. Animals at least served a purpose; they were not wasted. Their bodies fed the tribe, their skins clothed the tribe, their bones made weapons, and whatever remained was given back to the earth, to other animals that might use it.

But these men, these four bodies were like a weight on the world. Useless and heavy.

And why had she killed them?

Jinji's eyes moved across the dirt, over the fire, and into the wary expression of the only other living person around.

For him.

For a guide.

For answers.

The horse had moved closer, nudging its head against the man's thick shoulder. He whispered something into the animal's ear and it stood, backing a foot away as though standing guard.

He turned, looking through the flames and right at Jinji.

When their eyes met, the spirits jumped into Jinji's vision, reaching out to her in a way they rarely did, making their presence known even in the darkness. And she winced at the brightness.

Fire.

All she saw were strands of fire, swirling and circling his body, spirits alive and constantly weaving new forms around his torso.

It was dizzying.

The bright red threads muted all of the other spirits, almost like he himself was a walking flame. She had never seen the spirits cling to a living being like this—they lived in the earth, in the soil and the leaves and the air and the streams, not in people.

Jinji blinked and the spirits disappeared.

The clearing was just a clearing, the fire just a fire, the trees just the trees. But the man was not just a man, not anymore.

The spirits were guiding Jinji's path now—they had enshrouded her in the image of her brother, they had brought her to this man, they had circled him in fire. They were the only things left in the world that Jinji trusted, and they were telling her to trust him.

She didn't.

Not yet.

But still, Jinji stood and grabbed the knife, cutting his bindings free.

4

RHEN
~NORTHMORE FOREST~

For a third time that day, Rhen thought he was going to die.

The first, perhaps obviously, was when he had been knocked unconscious. *Always check behind you*—the lesson had been drilled into him since infancy, and still he had forgotten in his excitement. *Idiot*, he cursed as the pounding in his skull continued—the pain a constant reminder of his stupidity.

But then he woke, bound and bruised, yet somehow alive. And he cursed his awareness, because he knew his entire family and kingdom were at risk, yet there he was, powerless to stop it.

The second time was when the boy had been seized by the neck, his weightless body dangling from the ground as the two remaining Ourthuri tried their best to kill him. And Rhen, trained as a knight by the best Whylkin had to offer, could do nothing but watch and wait for his turn on the sword.

But then Ember, beautiful horse that she was, swooped in to save them both with the most perfect head-bashing stomp Rhen had ever seen.

And the third was now as the boy knelt, staring at the blood on his hands with emptiness in his eyes. He was young and the Arpapajo were a peaceful people—those four men were most likely the only he had ever killed. And sometimes, that feeling could swallow a man, could make him lose his sanity, could make him lash out at the nearest living being…which just happened to be Rhen, still bound like a babe on the ground.

He sighed, wriggling his wrists one more time.

If his brothers saw him now, Rhen shook his head—he didn't even want to imagine the endless banter, the ceaseless taunts.

Ember knelt, nudging Rhen's shoulder with her forehead as if to ask, "What is taking you so long?"

"Well fought, girl," he whispered, returning her nudge with one of his own. Pleased, Ember neighed softly and stood alert at his side.

When he turned, the boy was staring at him. As their eyes met through the flames, the boy winced, jerking back ever so slightly, but not breaking contact. And then those dark brown eyes, flecked with gold, illuminated by the fire, jumped wildly around Rhen's figure, circling him.

Rhen watched, unmoving, not wanting to break the trance. What did the boy see? What had him so wide-eyed? So intrigued?

For a moment, Rhen's eyes flashed to the fire. But it was at least a foot away, and he had not touched it, despite the pull he felt in his bones. *No*, he mentally shook his head. There was no way the boy could know about that. It was his own paranoia sneaking up on him.

Movement caught his attention. Rhen pulled his gaze from the flames back to the boy, who had stood. His features had hardened, resolute. He gripped the knife, stepping closer to

Rhen, who leaned into the log at his back. Did he need to sic Ember on the boy? Or was he being freed?

Sad, really, that he couldn't tell, but the boy was iron, hard to crack. Either that, or Rhen had simply lost his touch—a very poor spymaster in the making.

No, Rhen sat up and shifted his feet. He had saved the boy, and the boy had saved him. There was trust there, thin maybe, but existent.

And a second later, the binds around his ankles had been slashed. Leaning forward, Rhen moved to give the boy access to the ropes tying his wrists behind his back.

Free at last.

Rhen sighed, rolling sore bones, and stood to stretch his muscles.

"Thank you," he said, sounding loud against the quiet night.

Silence answered him.

Rhen spun to find the boy sitting back down, his gaze fastened on the hilt protruding from one Ourthuri's skull. It had been a nice hit, something to be proud of.

"Did you know these men?" Rhen asked. "Were they the ones who destroyed your village?"

The boy twisted, looking into the dark forest and away from him, but Rhen continued, urged on by the lack of a response.

"Did they fight you? Surprise you? Is there anyone else alive? People who were away, who might have run from the fire? People who fought? Anyone we need to find?"

"Please," the boy said, his voice ragged and scratchy, still high pitched due to his youth, "no more."

Rhen sat still. His mouth had run away again. The urgency to save his own family, to gather as much information as possible, to fill this painful silence—it had stolen his common decency.

It was a boy. Only a boy. And his silence assured Rhen that he was definitely alone in the world.

"I'm Rhen, from the Kingdom of Whylkin. Do you have a name?" He reached out, touching a bony shoulder, but the child flinched away. Rhen pulled his hand back and settled it on his own lap.

He waited, very much against his instincts, until the boy glanced one wet, lost, crinkled brown eye over his shoulder.

"Ji—" he started and then paused. "I am called Jin."

"Jin," Rhen said, stumbling over the strange word before nodding. "Well, Jin, it seems we're stuck together, unless you have some place better to be?" He raised an eyebrow in question, hoping to lighten the mood even the slightest bit.

"No," Jin said, turning his body to reflect his word, placing himself very much in the camp with Rhen.

"Do you know why these men were here?"

Jin shook his head.

"Would you like to hear my theory?"

Jin nodded, still too wary for words.

"Do you know the histories? Did anyone ever teach them to you?"

"I know some," Jin said, his voice meek and quiet. "The newworlder who visited told us stories."

The newworlder who visited? Rhen thought, confused. And then he remembered. The emissary sent on behalf of the crown. Once a year he visited the tribe to ensure they were obeying the laws created by Whyl the Conqueror ages ago, the rules that forced the Arpapajo to give up their own language and customs to conform to those of the land.

A nauseous feeling stirred in Rhen's stomach.

The Arpapajo or oldworlders, as some called them, were a fantasy, a people he learned about but never saw, never interacted with. They never entered his mind once the lesson was over.

But looking at Jin, Rhen had to face his own ignorance.

No matter how many years ago, it was his family, his blood, who had torn their identity away. Jin spoke the king's language very well, but still, it sounded foreign on his tongue, as though it wasn't really supposed to be there.

There were many lands in this kingdom that Whyl the Conqueror united, many cities and peoples he had merged into one, but all of them looked and lived alike—the differences were so few and far between that uniting was almost natural.

But not the Arpapajo.

They were outsiders, myths—at least to everyone but that sole emissary sent by the king.

Rhen felt the urge to apologize stir on his lips, but what could he say? Stealing a way of life was not something an *I'm sorry* would really fix.

And now Jin was alone.

His culture would fade completely away, dust in the wind.

Rhen was staring, dumbstruck.

He didn't realize it until Jin shifted his brows and leaned forward, inquiring, "Your theory?"

"Right!" Rhen jumped into motion. There was nothing he could say to make up for the past. Better to befriend the boy and keep him safe—safe enough to keep the Arpapajo alive.

His hand went to his waist, searching for his sword, but of course it was gone. Sighing, Rhen turned to Jin. "One minute."

He walked to the pile of weapons, searching for the gold hilt of his sword. Being a prince did have its perks, and his weapon was one of them—made from the finest metals by the finest blacksmith. He did not want to part with it.

He scanned the dull gray blades.

Not there.

He stood, hand on hip, searching and feeling like an imbecile as Jin's gaze grew more and more doubtful.

There.

He spotted it across the fire, unscratched.

Picking the sword up, Rhen walked back to his spot next to the boy and drew a large circle on the ground, then a smaller one in the middle of it.

"This is the Kingdom of Whylkin," he said, pointing to the outer circle. "Over here is the Northmore Forest, where we are now." He shaded in a spot on the upper right of the circle. "This," he said, outlining the smaller circle in the middle of Whylkin, "is the White Stone Sea, named because there is a great mountain range in the center of the water composed of a pearly rock, so all of the sands in the sea are bright white. And down here is my home, Rayfort, commonly called the King's City because it is the home of the royal family." Rhen poked a deep circle in the dirt on the lower left bank of the White Stone Sea— the motion mirrored by a stabbing pressure on his heart. His home, the one he wanted—no, needed—to protect. "Do you understand?"

Jin nodded. Rhen took the silence as a sign to continue.

"Over here," he drew a series of small ovals to the left of the circle that represented his kingdom, "are the Golden Isles, or the Kingdom of Ourthuro. And the men who attacked your village, these men you just killed, are Ourthuri—are from those islands. See how their skin is darker, slightly olive, and their hair a thick black? That's one way to tell. But more obvious," he leaned down, picking up the wrist of one of the dead men, "all Ourthuri are marked at birth with their station. These men all have one thick band tattooed on each wrist, a very simple design. It means they were from the outer isles, most likely farmers, or workers of some sort."

He dropped the arm, letting it thunk back into the dirt and paused, taking a second look at the design. It was definitely the simple design of a commoner—not the more intricate dot and striped design of an Ourthuri warrior.

But what would they be doing in Whylkin? Why farmers and not soldiers?

"And why were they here?" Jin asked, thinking the same thing.

Rhen grinned. Finally, the boy was showing some interest, some life.

"I think they were here as a scouting team, to see how difficult it would be to make land without my king knowing. I think they were here to prepare for war."

"War?" Jin scrunched his face. The word sounded ugly on his lips, like something he never thought of, let alone said. Something foreign he didn't understand.

"Yes, war." Rhen said. The word, he noticed, sounded much smoother on his lips, much more familiar. "Ourthuro was once the most powerful kingdom in the world. We call their lands the Golden Isles because the soil is practically made of the stuff. They had riches that no one in this land could ever understand. It was before the time of Whylkin, when our kingdom was divided and composed of many different cities and kings constantly fighting with each other.

"But almost three hundred years ago, one of those kings, King Whyl of Rayfort, conquered the land and united us all under his name, creating the Kingdom of Whylkin—to be ruled forevermore by his blood, the family of Whyl."

The words rolled off Rhen's tongue.

Whylrhen.

His name. His blood.

This tale was his personal bedtime story, the one his mother had told him over and over again until he didn't even have to think to repeat it.

Rhen looked up from his drawing, and Jin looked away quickly.

But not fast enough to hide the bitter edge to his gaze. The boy knew this part of the story—the part where a lot of his people were killed and their culture stripped away.

Rhen skipped ahead.

"Throughout history, the Ourthuri have mounted attacks, trying to regain their former power, but nothing has worked. And I think they are trying again, here and now."

"But why?" Jin asked. "Why?" He repeated, a slight shake in his voice.

Because it's what they do, Rhen thought, but he kept silent. Somehow the answer didn't seem like enough.

"Because power is everything," he said instead. Another lesson drilled into him from infancy.

"Not to the dead," Jin whispered.

Rhen had no reply. Instead, he watched Jin, watched him take a heavy breath, watched him bite his lip, watched him furrow his brows. The boy was smart, smarter than his years. There was more going on inside of that head than he let on—a puzzle Rhen intended to solve.

But not tonight.

Tonight, he intended to sleep off the ache in his muscles.

"We should both rest. We've a long day's journey ahead of us tomorrow." Rhen stretched his arms high above his head, creaking like an old man. *But*, he shrugged, *that's what getting knocked out will do.*

Not a word to his brothers, he sighed, not a word. And definitely not one to Cal—Rhen was in no state for another lecture. The bump on his head was quite enough.

There was a tent across the fire with his name on it—all he was hoping for was a sleeping mat, something soft for his sore, royal behind.

"Where are we going?" Jin asked.

The sound surprised Rhen—the boy was becoming a regular chatterbox.

He eased his weight back down. Sleep would have to wait.

But he understood.

"To Roninhythe, a nearby city, and then probably on to Rayfort so I can speak with m—" Rhen stopped short, biting the word *father* back into his lip. He looked up sharply, but Jin's concentration was elsewhere. Eventually, the boy would have to be told, but not yet. He still wanted to be Rhen, just Rhen, at least for a little while longer. "So I can get word to the king," he said, finishing the sentence softly.

"Is Roninhythe," Jin stumbled over the word, forcing it out, "is it a stone city?"

Rhen laughed loudly—he didn't know what he had been expecting, but not that. The question was so simple, so straightforward when compared to the events of the day.

"Yes, Jin, it's a stone city. There is a large defensive wall around the limits and beside the port there is a great castle towering into the sky."

He smirked as Jin's eyes widened, imagining the scene. The oldworlder boy was about to be in for a big shock. *Just wait until we reach Rayfort*, Rhen thought, picturing his home. Its multiple defensive walls, the glittering town homes of the rich, and of course, the palace—stained glass windows, halls lined with silk tapestries, walls of white rock slabs that blinded in the sun.

Much different from animal skins and the forest.

"How tall?" Jin asked, looking up at the nearest tree.

"So tall," Rhen said, leaning in close, "that you can see this very forest on the horizon even though it is miles away. So tall that the highest tree you have ever climbed will seem small in comparison."

"It seems unnatural to build such a thing," the boy shook his head, disapproving.

Rhen smiled, raising his eyebrows in jest. "To my people, it would seem unnatural to live in the woods, without horses and carriages and stone walls."

"To my people, it—" Jin stopped short, drawing his knees into his chest, shaking slightly.

Rhen winced. Just witnessing the sadness on the boy's face was painful.

"To your people?" Rhen asked, trying to cajole the boy, to let him know it was okay to speak about them even though they were gone.

But Jin shook his head, digging his chin farther into his knees.

Rhen backed off, giving him space. He needed time to heal, time to adjust.

So instead, Rhen stood, completed the stretch he had started just before Jin began speaking, and reached for Ember. She walked over to his outstretched hand, rubbing her soft neck into his palm.

Scratching behind her ears, Rhen listened for the contented rumble of a sigh, the sign that she forgave him for needing to be rescued yet again. And there it was, vibrating against his hand. Ember dipped her head down low enough for Rhen to kiss the white patch on her forehead and then stepped to the side.

He undid the straps on the heavy saddle, rubbing down the disrupted hairs and pulling an apple from the pouch. Ember took it happily.

"What is your horse's name?"

"Ember," Rhen answered, not turning around as he peered into the bag again. His red silk shirt was still there, untouched. A pit in his stomach dropped, and Rhen brought his hand quickly to his chest, sighing with relief when he felt the small bump under the roughly woven shirt.

His ring was still there. His unique royal seal. The only thing on his person that truly denoted his birthright. His safeguard.

57

And the only way to ensure any letter he wrote would go straight to the king.

"Ember…" Jin said in a drawn out breath, "to go with fire?"

At that Rhen did turn, meeting the boy's questioning gaze.

He squinted, trying to read through the silence.

He couldn't know.

Rhen hadn't touched the fire. He hadn't breathed it in like his body had begged him to do. And Jin had practically been dead, lying in a hut, when he had drawn the forest flames in.

There was no way the boy could know.

And yet, some intelligence sparked in those dark eyes, some impossible knowledge seemed hidden in their depths.

"Ember," Rhen said slowly, "because her coat is the color of dying flames, and because as a foal she saved my brother from almost certain death by fire."

"It's a girl?" The boy straightened, excited.

"Relax, she's still a horse," Rhen laughed. Jin tilted his head, confused.

Apparently, raunchy jokes were not part of the Arpapajo culture. *Something to add to the boy's education*, Rhen noted wryly.

Having a traveling companion could be more fun than he expected.

"I'll explain later." He sighed, looking at the tent over Ember's head. "But for right now, we should both sleep."

Rhen stepped forward, lifting the flap of the enclosure.

Yes, he grinned. His prayer had been answered. There was a sleeping mat, not extremely thick, not even very luxurious looking, but still softer than the ground.

He looked back into the night, where Jin now stood scratching Ember's neck. The two were getting along quite nicely, leaving Rhen completely shocked—Ember was normally quite dramatic around other people, a little bit of a princess in a castle made only of princes.

But the sight calmed his nerves too.

Jin was keeping secrets, of that Rhen was certain. And in time, he would uncover them. But for now, it was enough to know that Ember trusted the boy. She was the best judge of character he had ever seen—after all, she almost got sent to the butcher for spitting on the king.

Rhen laughed quietly at the memory. It had been years ago, but his father still referred to Ember as Rhen's *damn horse*.

He blinked, refocusing on the current night.

"Do you want to sleep in the shelter?" He called out.

"No," Jin shook his head. "Tonight, I want to see the stars."

Rhen shrugged.

He had slept under the stars enough times to know it was not as romantic as it seemed in the stories. *No*, he thought as he lay down on the mat. Soft cushions were much more awe-inspiring.

As sleep sought to overtake him, Rhen's overactive mind did its best to keep him awake. There was so much left to do. He had to find Cal, he had to get word to the king, and he had to determine if more Ourthuri had disembarked on his lands.

Where were these unflagged ships? How did they go unnoticed? And how could he stop it?

And just as Rhen was on the brink of a breakthrough, the answer surely on the tip of his tongue, a snore sounded on his lips—loud and thunderous enough to be heard in his dreams.

Dark dreams.

Dreams of a future he hoped beyond all hopes to change.

5

JINJI
~RONINHYTHE~

They had been traveling for days and all Jinji could think was, *Oh the spirits that man is loud.* He was loud when he was awake, talking and talking, until even her short answers caused her voice to run hoarse, and she was in awe that he had sound left in his body. He was loud when he slept, drumming thunder into her ears at all hours of the night, keeping even the animals awake.

Loud.

Loud.

Loud.

And all she wanted to do was quiet him for a mere moment. Even Leoa did not talk so incessantly, dragging on and on. Her friend had known when words were no longer needed, were more of a bother than a comfort.

But not this Rhen, this newworlder who had saved her life only to make her die this slow, intolerable death.

At first, it seemed like a purposeful distraction. The farther they moved from the forest, the deeper the pit in her stomach grew and the louder he seemed to become. Every so often, Jinji would catch him watching her, turning his head up to observe her expression as she rode Ember. And for a while, she even appreciated it. The talking kept her from thinking, from missing, from feeling.

Only two days before, she had turned to watch as the treetops disappeared from eyesight, fading into the green grass of a rolling hill, and in that small, seemingly insignificant moment, her home was gone.

Rhen caught her arm as she slipped from the horse, shock numbing her grip. He continued chatting while her breath grew short, her eyes filled up, her stomach bundled into knots. She couldn't recall a word he had said, but he didn't wait for responses anyway. Instead, he pushed on with words that Jinji barely comprehended, yet were somehow enough help.

But now, he continued, battering her with speech she did not want to hear, and all she wondered was if the distraction were really for him, not her.

"Jin?" Rhen nudged her leg, pointing an elbow deep into her thigh to grab her attention.

She looked down, meeting his wide eyes and preserving her voice.

"Did you hear me? I said you can see the city of Roninhythe on the horizon."

She didn't wait for him to finish and instead darted her eyes ahead, earning a low chuckle.

Her mouth dropped open—that earned a louder chuckle.

There was a stone Jinji used to climb as a child, all the children did—they would dare each other to stand at the top. She could picture it perfectly, dropped in the middle of the forest, almost like some giant creature had casually discarded it amongst the trees. And Jinji remembered staring at the height she had to overcome to end Janu's taunts, wondering how anything other than a tree could grow so tall.

Even so far in the distance, Jinji's breath caught at the sight of this stone city—a patch of gray rising from the green hills, cutting into the sky, angular and unnatural. Ahead of them, a road—also gray, also unnatural.

She looked at the green below Ember's hooves, at the soft warm way the grass cushioned her feet. What would it feel like to walk on something so unforgiving, so tough? Even dirt after a long hot summer baking in the sun had some give, would eventually soften under her feet.

As if called, the elemental spirits danced into her vision, sparkling along the grass in a faded green hue. Looking up, Rhen was still shrouded in a blanket of hot red fire, sparking and spinning around his person.

Above the city, the wind howled, throwing yellow spirits into spirals, weaving webs out and over the walls, spilling back down to disappear from Jinji's vision. The very sight of so much unchallenged air set her on edge. Where were the green spirits, swooping out of the trees to mix with the breeze? Where was the water, dripping down to be caught by the wind, or the heat of a fire, blazing red?

Where was the balance?

It was unnatural.

Jinji shivered, hugging her arms close, for once listening for the rumble of Rhen's voice.

"That road up ahead, we call it the Great Road, it connects all of the original cities to Rayfort, to the king. It was built over the span of one hundred years. For a century, the punishment for disobeying the law was ten years labor on that road. Many were lucky if they survived, and many more considered themselves unlucky for the same fate. But before you test their craftsmanship, which I assure you is quite awe-inspiring, we must stop."

Rhen tugged on Ember's reins, shushing her sighs with long brushstrokes up and down her neck.

"There is something I have not told you," he said quietly, still looking at Ember. Jinji scrunched her eyebrows, waiting. What could he have possibly left unsaid? She knew more history of the kingdom after a few days with him than she had learned in a lifetime.

"I am not who you think I am."

Her fists clenched, her body suddenly tight. A warm pain started in her heart, surprising her with its sting.

He looked up, green eyes piercing hers, deepening the pain. His lips were drawn in a tight line, struggling with what to say.

He couldn't be…he wouldn't just go…

"My name is not Rhen…"

Jinji held her breath.

"It's Whylrhen. And I was not asked to search the forest by the king, I was actually strictly forbidden from leaving Roninhythe."

He looked away, looked back, shrugged.

Jinji tilted her head, waiting for the words he still held back, the ones he was trying to force out. A chill started in her fingers, traveling up her arms, bringing goose bumps to her skin as she looked out to the city. So unnatural, so unfamiliar—what would she do without a guide? Without a friend?

"You see, well…the king is really my father…that is to say, I'm his son." He bit his lip. "I guess that's the same thing really. But what I'm trying to say is, well—"

"You're a prince?" Jinji finished the sentence for him, her voice higher than normal, alarmed.

He nodded, deflated, letting the air out of his body in one big sigh.

Silence hung between them.

Heavy.

Cold.

Jinji looked behind her, searching for the trees, finding none. No familiarity. No comfort. Her breath shortened.

"Are you leaving me?" She asked, forcing the words out, the fear out, as her throat tightened with panic. What would she do? Alone?

"No," he said quickly, putting his hand on her shoulder, squeezing it once. "Of course not, no, Jin, I would never do that to you—not after—you're just a kid. I'm telling you because you deserve to know."

He reached past her into the saddlebag behind her thigh and pulled out a bright red cloth.

Just like the fire spirits, she thought.

"Will you?" He asked, handing it to her.

Jinji reached out, grasping the material. It was soft, thin. She rolled it between her fingers, amazed. Her own clothes, Janu's skins that she still wore, felt coarse in comparison.

Holding it aloft, Jinji realized it was a shirt. Golden threads, the color of the sun on a clear day, were woven through the sleeves. Glittering stones caught her attention and she brought the spot close, gasping at how crystal clear the rocks were.

"Here," he said, tugging on the material, pulling it over his bare chest and handing her the shirt he had just removed. "You might want that."

Jinji looked at the dull brown cloth in her hands, damp with sweat, and wrinkled her nose.

"Why?" She questioned, looking up.

He raised his brows, grinning. A golden speck glistened in his grassy eye, calculating, reflecting some idea sparking in his head.

He shrugged, and it disappeared, decision made. "Never mind," he said, his voice too light, his lips too upturned. He grabbed the shirt, but Jinji held on.

"No, I will wear it," she said, now nervous. He was far too pleased with himself—far too silent.

Shaking his head, Rhen pulled hard, and the shirt slipped from her grasp. In one swift move, he ripped it down the middle, dropping the remains at his feet.

"You know," he said, "in the kingdom you must bow before royalty, on penalty of death. Did the emissary forget to mention that?"

He looked back, smirking.

Jinji slapped the only part of him within reach, his head.

"Hey," he said as he rubbed the spot with his hand, "that actually is punishable by death." He continued massaging his scalp. "For a little thing, you have a good arm. You'll be a good swordsman. I can teach you, you know. I always wanted," he coughed, clearing his throat and looking back to the city. Softer this time, he finished, "I always wanted a little brother to teach…" Rhen looked over his shoulder again, devilish grin back. "But I suppose you'll do, little Jin."

"I'm not so little," Jinji retorted, still unused to being referred to as a boy. Especially by a man who was no more than a few years older than she. "Perhaps you are too large."

Rhen barked out a laugh, loud and sudden, almost echoing on the wind. "No such thing, Jin, no such thing. Just ask the whores."

"Whores?" Jinji didn't recognize the word.

Rhen shook his head, walking forward toward the road in the distance. "You have so much to learn but…" He tugged on the leather straps, prodding Ember along. "I think I'll enjoy teaching you. Tonight, after the docks, we'll go to the Staggering Vixen, I know a girl named Martha who would love to meet you."

He turned, winked.

A blush rose on Jinji's cheeks as realization hit. Her father had mentioned these women, one of many reasons he forbade her from visiting the stone cities.

"The docks?" She asked, changing the subject, trying to erase it from her thoughts. The Staggering Vixen? She was certain that was not a place she wanted to visit.

Ever.

Jinji looked at the looming city again, swallowing a gulp. It was large, probably full of more people than she could imagine. Maybe she would find a new guide…one not so focused on her education…a woman, maybe.

"We need a ship," Rhen said, interrupting her thoughts.

"Why?"

"How else will we travel to the Golden Isles?"

"Across the sea?" She asked, turning her gaze sharply on him. The wide waters, the great blue expanse, she had only seen it once while traveling with Janu. They had snuck away from the village, exploring, and after two days of walking, they had reached the edge of the forest, the edge of the world. Jinji could still feel the breeze brush her cheeks, could still feel the warmth of Janu's hand as the two of them stood, toes inches over the rock, looking down, down, down toward crashing waves.

Her fingers tightened on the saddle, rubbing harshly against the leather.

"We need to figure out what those Ourthuri were doing here, and there's no better way than stopping in to say hello to their king."

A new guide, Jinji sighed, rubbing her eyes.

She needed to find a new guide.

"I'm going to show you the world, Jin. It's a lot bigger than you realize."

That's what I'm afraid of, Jinji thought and tried to relax in her seat. But the city still loomed ahead, growing larger and larger with each step they took, and it was growing harder to understand if leaving the forest would be any help at all.

Would the shadow still find her behind those tall stonewalls? Would it continue to haunt her? Or would she be discarded, left to live alone, always questioning why and how? Was she traveling toward answers or away from them?

Clicking noises drew Jinji from her thoughts. They had reached the road.

Ahead, she saw travelers scurrying to the side, hastily shifting their horses and possessions to make way. As they walked by, Rhen nodded from side to side, but the people were not looking. Their eyes were downcast. Their entire bodies seemed to bend toward the ground. Only the children dared look up, and it was not at Rhen.

No, it was at her. She felt eyes scan her body, pop open, shocked.

"Is that a...?" One boy asked loudly, only to be quieted by his mother, pulled behind her skirts. But still, he peeked around her large belly, eyes locked on the Arpapajo riding the horse.

Jinji looked ahead, tunneling her vision on the city, trying to ignore the gasps chasing down her ears.

The gates were not far off, wooden slabs breaking up the walls of stone, but they were bolted with metal—nature maybe, but trapped and bound. The doors were open, perhaps welcoming to Rhen, but not to her. To her, they looked like a trap, waiting for the right moment to swallow her whole.

Jinji held her breath as they approached. Behind the walls, more stone, more people, more noise, more movement. More of everything except the one thing she wanted—trees.

67

"Your Highness," four men said in unison, kneeling down on one leg, nodding in respect to Rhen. He continued walking, waving, but not pausing for anything more.

Jinji gawked at their metal-coated bodies, chinked and chained together, covered by a slight cloth in bright blue over their chest. On the cloth, some sort of beast that she did not recognize in darker blue.

They did not stand again until Ember had passed fully through the gate, and then as one they moved, alert once more.

But Jinji's attention was already elsewhere, on the rows and rows of homes filling her entire line of vision. They were wooden and something else, something that looked like mud, but she knew couldn't be. They slanted on top of each other, leaning, pulling, held up by a mystery Jinji could not understand. Each one had holes, some sort of material she could see through. Movement flashed, some eyes popped through, meeting her curious stare with one of their own, making her feel not quite so alone in her awe.

The road still held under their feet, hard, but to the side she noticed the mud had returned, catching on people's clothes, the bottoms of their homes, dirtying everything close to it. The people wore clothes that were so different from Rhen's, more like hers, dull and drab to match the dirt.

And it was loud. People screaming to no one, pointing to slabs of food laid out on tables, holding out strips of clothes or items Jinji did not recognize. Girls talking, giggling as their eyes scanned the streets. Children screeching, jumping, running in front of horses in some sort of game. Men boasting, pushing carts, cursing at the crowd.

But like a cloud, silence followed the two of them. Conversations paused, everyone stopped to lower their heads, all the while peeking up under hooded brows to watch Jinji on the horse.

Behind them, noise grew, louder than before, the word *Arpapajo* crashing like a wave into Jinji's ears. Rhen looked back once, his expression concerned, but that was it. His head scanned slowly from side to side, watching everything.

Keeping her eyes ahead, she finally saw the stone castle, the one Rhen had mentioned, stretching into the sky, almost blocking the sun from her eyes. It was impossible. Yet there it was.

And then it was gone from her sight as Rhen turned them down a narrow road, somewhat vacated.

"Are you alright?" He asked, turning to pet Ember and run a hand through his hair, pushing the reddish locks from his brow.

She nodded, not sure how to express the mix of fear and excitement brewing in her chest. Everything was new, everything was an adventure, everything was terrifying. Taking her hands from the saddle, she flexed her fingers, forcing her blood to pump again.

"You'll get used to it, the staring I mean. Everywhere I go, people look and then just when I get close enough to say hello, they turn, eyes to the ground as is proper. Since I was a boy that's how it's been with the common folk and even some of the nobility." He patted her knee. "You'll get used to it."

But would she?

"I'm sorry I took the shirt," he said, wincing slightly, "I thought it might be funny to see your expression. I wasn't really thinking." He shook his head, blowing out air.

Jinji looked at her dark skin, more out of place in all this gray than it ever had been in the forest contrasted against golden bark.

"I stand out either way," she told him. Her chest felt heavy, as though a fist had closed around her heart. Even in the middle of more people than she had ever seen, Jinji was alone. She swallowed the grief down, forcing her shoulder back, steady.

"Besides," she continued, meeting his stare like she would any other stare she came across, "I don't intend to forget who I am."

Rhen paused, considering her.

"Then you're a better man than I am, Jin," he responded, so softly that she almost didn't hear it.

Then he slapped Ember's behind, earning a nip on his shoulder and a very annoyed sounding neigh. But Rhen just grinned, scratching his horse's ears and pulling them all down the street.

A flash of blue caught her eye, far down where the narrow lane opened up again. The noise grew as they approached. The sun returned, as did the crowd. But Jinji's eyes were still glued to the blue, to the water, chopping and crashing against gigantic wooden structures that somehow floated atop it. Men swinging from ropes. Giant white cloths that looked like clouds against the sky. Squiggling fish caught in nets bigger than her entire village.

"These are the docks." Rhen shrugged, as though this were somehow normal.

"And those are…boats?" She asked, searching for the word.

"Not boats, Jin." Rhen patted her shoulder. "Ships. Big, beautiful ships."

"And this is how we get to the isles?" She asked, wary.

Rhen just nodded as a mirthful smirk sprouted on his lips, birthed from a memory Jinji didn't have access to.

He led them forward through the crowds that parted as they neared, to the beginning of a long wooden row standing over the water, lined with ropes and ships. Tying Ember's reins to an open post, he scanned the area.

"This should do." He nodded. "You can walk around if you'd like, but I wouldn't go very far from Ember. She'll keep you safe, just in case any unfriendly people come near. I should be back shortly."

He waited until Jinji gave her consent before disappearing into the crowd. Once he was gone, she slid from the horse, stepping over the creaking wood, until her eyes dropped over the edge and down into the churning water.

Breathing deeply, she sat, letting her feet dangle over the side as her body began to relax. She imagined she were home, toes dipped into the cool water of their little stream, not feet above the deepest waters she had ever been so close to.

Keeping her eyes downcast, Jinji watched the blues intermix—bright and greenish swirls faded into cloudy gray, warmed into sun-kissed turquoise. All were flecked with bubbling white as they splashed over and under each other, fighting for the top spot. Farther down, the ground faded in and out of view as the waters changed, muddied each other, and then cleared.

Blue strands popped into her vision as the spirits awakened in her eyes, spiraling in and out, braiding and weaving, splashing into the yellow strands of air and then sinking to the green strands of plants below the waters.

Balance.

Nature.

Cupping her hands, Jinji pictured the jinjiajanu between the elemental strands, the pure white mother spirit that tied everything together. And then she imagined a rock resting on her fingers, painted with the faces of her family members.

Closing her eyes, she spun the weave, praying to the spirits to listen to her plea for a moment to mourn, a moment to remember.

When she opened them, the image was there, dancing an inch over her fingers, solid. Four faces—her father, her mother, Leoa, and Janu—all smiling, as though saying hello. She would not forget their faces, ever. And to make sure, she had called this illusion every day since she had left the village. Each time, her throat caught and her eyes burned, but she didn't look away.

"Ka'shasten," she whispered, *my family.*

Jinji's heart slowed, her mind began to clear, and for a brief moment, she felt at peace.

And then a shadow passed overhead, skipping over the image, distorting it.

Jinji released the illusion, gasping, and looked up.

A bird.

Just a bird.

And yet, she looked out over the water, following the shadow as it floated over the waves, reminding her of the dream—her nightmare.

A shadow was never just a shadow. Not for her.

"Rhen?" She called, jumping to her feet.

But as she spun around, it was not Rhen standing close by. On the other side of Ember, a few feet from where she stood, two men were in close conversation. Their clothes hung loose on their bodies, dirty and ragged looking. Their skin a deep tan, not born that way but turned that way from hours of exposure in the sun.

They hadn't seen her, were not paying attention.

Jinji leaned in closer, following a hunch that told her this was not a coincidence.

"Dead?" One man asked, shock coloring his words.

"Ay, dead," the other confirmed.

"But how?"

"Another mystery." The second man shrugged. "They found the two of them below deck, one stabbed and the other with a cut throat. No one knows how it happened, or why."

Cut throat?

Maniuk flashed before her eyes, the image of his hand stilled and a blade at his throat. A shadow was never just a shadow, she repeated. This time it was a sign.

"But Georgey? Kill himself? I've never seen a man more at peace on the water, like a fish he was. Always climbing the ropes, securing the sails, never a complaint. He used to say it was as close as a man could get to flying, standing all the way up on the lookout while the wind whipped his face raw."

The other one shook his head. "I guess there was more going on than we knew."

"Ay, something unnatural, something godly, like we're being punished. You heard about the little boy and his sister found just outside the wall not two days ago? I heard rumors her throat was slit too, though the Lord of Roninhythe says the children fell to their deaths."

"Fell to their deaths?" He guffawed, "if they fell, then I'm a Son of Whyl."

The other man laughed. "If you're a Son of Whyl, then I'm the conqueror himself."

"You smell enough like the grave."

They both fell into a loud round of laughter, giving Jinji enough time to crouch down and hide behind Ember's wide body before they noticed her eavesdropping.

"Jin!"

Rhen's voice startled her, coming from the same direction she had just turned from. She straightened her legs, watching as the two men jumped apart, bowing their heads low as he neared. Rhen paid them no attention, walking straight to Ember as they scurried out of the way.

"I found my ship." He smiled, obviously proud of himself. "We leave tomorrow."

"And until then?" She asked, anxiety leaking into her chest.

Rhen winked. "Follow me."

73

Jinji paid little attention to her surroundings as she followed Rhen down the docks and back to the street. The mud was squishy and wet beneath her feet. Her mind was still on what she had just overheard, wondering if the deaths could somehow be connected—if her shadow was after more than what it had already taken, after more than just her ruin.

She might be closer to answers than she ever realized.

If only she could talk to more people, learn more about these deaths.

But—she looked down at her clothes, at her skin—she was nothing more than something to gawk at to these people. A walking myth. Something to stare at, not talk to.

Looking to the side, she eyed Rhen's profile. His straight, sharp nose. His pearly flesh freckled and kissed only minutely by the sun. His red hair, gleaming brighter against the stone around them. He stood out too, but not nearly as much. And he was powerful amongst these people—it radiated off him. If she asked him for answers, he would find them. It was only a matter of opening up and telling him what she searched for.

But her lips tightened, unsure, holding back.

Now was not the time.

And Jinji wasn't sure when or if she would ever be able to talk about what had happened, with anyone, anywhere.

He met her stare, green eyes sparkling like the surface of the water she had just been studying.

"We're here." He grinned. Her lips tugged wide, a natural reaction to his overflowing glee.

And then she looked above, at the sign hanging overhead. She couldn't read it, but somehow she knew what it said.

The Staggering Vixen.

Her gut dropped to the floor, the word *whore* fluttering back to the forefront of her mind.

Rhen tied Ember to a post, flicking a coin into the hands of a skinny boy waiting by the door, who immediately ran inside and emerged seconds later with a bucket of water to place by her hooves. Ember sunk down, licking greedily, and Rhen pushed open the door, letting Jinji enter first.

Holding her breath, she passed him, resisting the urge to close her eyes and walk forward blindly.

But oh, how she wished she had.

As soon as she had crossed the threshold, Jinji was grabbed into an embrace, her face thrust into the largest breasts she had ever seen, while a woman cried out, "What a darling you are!"

Jinji pushed away, careening back and out, immediately crossing her arms over her considerably smaller chest to keep them flattened and contained, as if the mere proximity to the busty women around her would somehow spurn them into growth.

"Martha!" Rhen called behind her, slapping Jinji forward and farther into the room. "An ale for my young friend. And two for me!"

Jinji groaned inwardly as his laughter rang in her ears, loud once more.

6

RHEN
~RONINHYTHE~

Priceless.

That was the only way to describe Jin's face when they walked in, Martha doing exactly what Rhen had expected of her. She couldn't resist goading a young boy on, couldn't resist the attention.

As another chuckle poured from his lips at the mere memory, Rhen wished he could relive the scene again—just once—maybe twice.

But, he remembered, looking at Jin in the center of the tavern, arms still crossed awkwardly over his chest, face still glowing red—there was more fun to be had.

"Sit down," he announced loudly, starting to play up the role of the womanizing prince—his usual fallback, especially in this tavern.

Jin looked at him with utter confusion, so taking charge, Rhen pushed him over toward a booth where the boy sat down stiffly, still not uncrossing his arms.

"Relax, Jin, these women aren't here to bite," Rhen said, slightly caring and slightly goading. The boy's eyes sparked, almost taking him up on the challenge, but then softened.

Breasts interrupted Rhen's eyesight, filling his vision. *Good old Martha*, he thought, *always putting the goods on display*. She was older than most of the women in the tavern, but she made up for it by pulling her corset the lowest and proudly displaying her ample bosom.

"Maybe he's never kissed a girl," she said, her voice high pitched and airy, at least until she had a few ales in her and then it would drop a few octaves, the ladylike persona gone. Rhen had even heard her belch before, alongside the men, no shame—just the way he liked a girl. Unafraid. Real.

Thinking of ale, Rhen reached out, grasping his cup and taking a long, full gulp. Damn, it tasted good. He'd been far too long in the forest.

"Cheers," he said, lifting the cup. Jin paused for a moment, unsure, then followed suit, clanking his glass against Rhen's. He took a sip, winced, and then grinned. "Be careful," Rhen warned, "if you're not used to it, that drink will go right to your head." Jin would most assuredly be an entertaining drunk, but Rhen needed a few things to look forward to on the journey ahead.

Jin nodded, eyes bulging as Martha came back boasting a cup of her own and sat next to him on the booth. Rhen picked his ale up, hiding his smile behind a large gulp.

"Have you? Kissed a girl?" Martha asked, leaning forward and closer.

Rhen watched a blush creep up Jin's dark cheeks, turning his skin a rosy copper as his gaze flashed back and forth between the view before his eyes and the foamy rim of his glass.

Jin just shook his head.

Rhen paused—he could intervene, save the boy—but why?

Martha pressed forward, figuratively and literally, asking, "You've never had a sweetheart?"

Another shake, but this time a shadow fell over Jin's eyes, a darkness crept into his expression. The blush was pushed aside by an ashen hue and his eyes fell to his cup, not looking anywhere else in the room.

Rhen's brows closed together as worry clenched his heart. If Jin had a sweetheart, she was dead now, along with the rest of his people. A memory was playing in the boy's head, flashing behind eyes that had grown distant, and Rhen couldn't help but feel sorry, feel hurt himself watching the pain pierce his new friend's entire being.

Just as he was about to speak up, about to intervene, another voice entered the conversation, and Rhen turned just in time to open his arms for the female that landed in his lap.

"Who's never had a sweetheart?"

"Reana," he said, remembering her name and nodding his head in greeting. She was new; a petite blond Martha had recently found and pulled from the streets. He saw her not two weeks ago when he first arrived in Roninhythe, and already he noticed the change. Her clothes were tighter, her cheeks had been rouged, her appearance fake like the others. But still, it felt nice to have a warm body on his lap, a skinny waist to wrap his arm around, even if just for a few hours.

"Surely not our Prince Whylrhen," she cooed, leaning in closer to his body, not providing quite the same view as Martha. "That poor innkeeper's daughter. Her reputation will never be the same. We heard her father tried to chase you from the city!" She drew a hand flat against her chest in mock distress. Rhen saw Martha's eyes narrow, annoyed that she was no longer the main attraction. "Is that why you came to the Staggering Vixen, instead of the castle?"

Rhen laughed loudly, adding, "Now why would I go to the castle when I have everything I need right here?" He lifted his glass and gripped her waist tighter, earning a soft giggle as she snuggled closer to his body.

Martha jumped in, bringing Jin back into the center of conversation, but Rhen's mind wandered elsewhere. *Cal better have dropped off the gold*, he thought, making a note to bring it up when he saw him later. He hoped the poor girl wasn't ruined for life. He had needed a reason to leave the city, a reason to move so suddenly and so urgently, but the last thing he wanted…

Ugh, he sighed, leaning back in the wooden booth. According to the rumors, he had ruined many a girl along the path of the Great Road. If he even spoke to a woman, the gossip began and a mere conversation would be turned into an affair before the sun fell. It was one reason Cal kept his very proper sister very far away from Rhen.

But there was no better way to sneak around castles and the town at night, no better cover than the story other people would create. If he was caught wandering the streets, it was brushed off as Rhen going after another conquest—not Rhen, looking for information, spying on other lords, working under the cover of darkness. That was a weapon he couldn't afford to lose.

And he knew it.

It was also a weapon he would deploy tonight, he knew, hugging Reana closer to his body, feeling her limbs buzz with excitement as she cast a sidelong glance in his direction, a coy smile plastered on her lips.

He'd chosen her.

Just not for the reason she thought.

The noise around them had grown, Rhen realized, casting a glance around the filling tavern. Night must have fallen. The more stars in the sky, the more men in the tavern—it was just how these things worked. More girls had come out of the woodwork, serving drinks and providing some much needed companionship.

He looked to Jin, whose face was brighter, full of life and laughter. What conversation had he missed while his mind wandered?

Tuning back in, Rhen caught the word *snore* roll from Martha's lips as she clasped a hand over her mirthful mouth.

"Snore?" Rhen echoed, rejoining his group, but all three of his companions burst into fits of laughter, leaving him the odd one out once again. "What?" he asked, looking at each of their faces, but none of them could pause long enough to breathe let alone clue him in.

"I must say," Reana finally spoke, sputtering between gasping breaths, "I've heard many rumors about what our prince can do in the bedroom, but that was never one of them!"

Rhen's eyes widened, turning on Jin in surprise. *That rascal!* The boy looked quite proud of himself, and the smirk playing on his lips spoke of payback.

Of course, the fact that Rhen probably deserved a little payback was of no consequence. A rumor like that could ruin his reputation, the reputation he had spent a lifetime building, the cover he needed to continue his work uncovering other people's secrets.

Rhen reached for his ale, downing the rest of his second glass in one large swig. He knew just what to do.

"You want to know if the rumors are true, do you?" He asked, a blush now rolling up Reana's pearly white cheeks, mixing with her rouge.

She smiled, bit her lip, and nodded just ever so slightly, curiosity lighting her gaze.

"Then, my lady, I'm more than happy to oblige," he said, smirking, and in one motion he stood, throwing the weight of Reana's petite body over his shoulder. She laughed and screamed playfully, thumping at his back with her delicate fists. The rest of the tavern turned at the commotion, and the men erupted into drunken cheers, most only just realizing they were in the midst of a prince of the realm.

His plan was working perfectly.

"Martha, you'll take care of Jin, won't you? Make sure he finds a place to sleep," he asked, then added, "alone?" Jin was not ready for a night with Martha, of that Rhen was completely certain. And the boy had been through more than enough for one day.

"Of course, your Highness," she said, using his formal title, sealing the deal with a nod. She understood that the command was not a jest—Jin would have a place to sleep uninterrupted by the unfamiliar city he'd been forced into.

For good measure, Rhen flipped a gold coin from his pocket and into her palm. Her eyes brightened, and she stuffed the money between her breasts.

He shook his head. The greedy woman—if only all people were so honest.

"Barkeep?" He yelled aimlessly across the room, pretending to be drunker than he was.

"Yes, sir?" A meek voice called back from somewhere in the crowd.

"Two glasses and your best house wine delivered to the usual room," he shifted Reana on his shoulder, earning another shriek. As always, he felt more like an actor on a stage than a real man, but it was necessary.

"Yes, sir," the voice responded, firmer this time.

And then Rhen turned, climbing the stairs at the back of the tavern while catcalls still rang in his ears. He walked sturdily down the hall to the last room on the right, the largest room, and also one of the few rooms with a window.

As soon as they entered, he tossed Reana onto the bed, still playing his role.

Moments later, a young boy, the tavern owner's son, ran into the room, gently placing a tray with two glasses and a jug of wine onto the table. He bowed once before closing the door behind him.

Rhen grabbed one of the glasses, turning his back on Reana while he poured the drinks. He heard her moving on the bed, probably rearranging herself into a more graceful position than the one he had dropped her in. Out of eyesight, he pulled a small vile from his pocket, untwisting the lid and slipping a few drops of a sleeping solution made by the palace apothecary into the second glass, before filling it with wine as well.

He spun around slowly, meeting her eyes with a hungry stare, watching as hers sparked to match it.

But unlike her, Rhen was pretending. There was no heat stirring in his veins, no passion building in his chest. This was business.

He settled on the bed, handing her the laced wine and holding his own aloft. "Cheers," he said, and clinked her glass, trying to embolden his expression before downing the wine in one sip.

As he expected, she followed suit, taking two large sips to finish her drink.

In a few moments it would be done. But, Rhen mentally shrugged, he did have to give her something to dream about.

And there was no harm in one kiss.

Propping himself up on the bed, Rhen leaned over her, pressing Reana's body into the bed below them, loving the way her feminine curves cushioned his weight. He let their breaths mingle, let the stars in her eyes continue to dance, faster and faster. After a moment of hesitation, of letting her electric excitement build, he touched his lips to hers. A contented sigh swelled in his ears.

She wrapped her arms around his waist, hugging him closer, surprising him with her passion, and throwing him off balance. But just as Rhen reached to steady himself, her limbs fell free of their hold, landing with an *oomph* on the mattress.

Wriggling from her embrace, Rhen stood.

Another conquest down, he grinned, staring at the spread eagle limbs before him. With a laugh, he repositioned her legs, dragging her left side back over to her right, hoping her sleep was full of the wonderful dreams the apothecary assured Rhen the potion created. And it must do the trick, because there were women all over the kingdom convinced they had shared a night of passion with the prince, when in reality, Rhen was the best chastity belt a worried father could buy.

He shrugged and walked back to the table, downing one more glass of wine before turning his attention to the window.

It was time to see Cal.

It was time to get a message to the king.

Unlike most taverns in Roninhythe, the Staggering Vixen was three stories tall, a long way to carry a woman, but high enough that he could jump onto the next-door roof—a roof that just happened to sit next to the backside of the castle, directly under Cal's bedroom window.

Opening the glass slowly, Rhen let the wind whip his face, let the salty smell ensnare his senses, and then he crouched onto the pane, balancing there. Slowly, he reached up for the loose brick above the window. A few tugs and it slipped into his hand.

A rope fell before his eyes. Rhen smiled and pulled the rest of it free before returning the brick and jumping a few feet down onto the roof below him.

He coiled the rope in his hand, feeling the points of the claw knotted tightly to the end. The metal was a little worse for wear, but it would do—as long as Cal had gotten word and had cleared the guards from the wall.

Rhen looked up.

No movement.

The castle was divided into two levels, a wide base with platforms and walkways built for war, and a second narrower level where the family lived. As long as the first level was clear, no questions would be asked.

And if there were questions, well, he was the prince—he'd think of something.

Taking a deep breath, Rhen counted to three.

One.

Two.

On three, he tossed the rope high up, aiming for an arrowslit in the wall.

Bull's-eye.

The sound of metal on stone rang in his ears, just loud enough to float on the wind but not so much that it was alarming.

Waiting a moment, Rhen watched the edge of the wall, searching for a moving helmet or the swing of an arm.

All was clear.

He grinned.

With one sturdy tug on the rope, it was time to climb.

And climb.

And climb.

No matter how many times he made the long trek to the top, his arms always burned, his legs felt on fire. And it was no different this time, as he slipped his hands over the top stones and pulled himself fully onto castle grounds.

"Took you long enough, Prince Whylrhen," a voice said.

"Cal!" Rhen turned, greeting his sullen friend with a wide smirk. *Oh Cal.* He was still dressed in court wear, a formal jewel-studded jacket with his best leather pants and boots. Sword still at his waist. His brown hair was tied back into the nape of his neck, and his brown eyes were glowing with worry as they darted wildly around his surroundings. The only still parts of his body were the arms crossed grumpily across his chest.

Always adherent to the rules, Cal motioned for Rhen to follow and harshly whispered, "Come on, the guards will be back any minute. There are only so many emergencies I could think of to drag them away."

"Did you set a pig loose in your father's room?"

Cal rolled his eyes and stepped through a narrow door in the stone, tired of Rhen's jokes already. Little did he know that suggestion was serious—a dirty pig running around the lord's bedchambers, a lord as pristine and proper as his son? The entire castle would be in an uproar.

On the other side of the door was a stone hallway, glowing with line after line of candlelight. Rhen flexed his fingers, fighting the pull of the fires. The heat tickled his skin, called for it. He clenched his fists, holding his hands behind his back, and followed Cal a few feet down into the next room on the right, Cal's bedchamber. It was draped with heavy tapestries depicting knights on horseback, the ancestors of Roninhythe. His walls sparkled with candlelight too, but it was easier to manage, especially with the cool wind blowing through the open windows, forcing the heat outdoors.

Rhen sat down in one of Cal's leather chairs, sinking into the soft cushions, and let his head fall back. This was what the forest was missing. A nice comfortable spot to rest.

"Rough journey? Why were you so late getting back? I was sure something had happened."

"Something did happen," Rhen said, looking up. Cal sat in the chair opposite him and poured two glasses of wine, nodding along—a signal he wanted more information. "I picked up an Arpapajo, an oldworlder. He's a just a boy, but Cal, all of them are gone."

His friend looked up sharply. "All of who, Rhen?" Cal had slipped back to using his nickname—a sure sign Rhen had been forgiven.

"The oldworlders. Wiped out, dead, with their village burned to the ground. All except for one, a boy named Jin who I brought to Roninhythe with me."

"But who would kill them? Who would bother?"

"The Ourthuri."

Cal rolled his eyes for a second time. "Rhen, with all due respect, you can't really think they would travel all the way from the Golden Isles just to kill some natives running around in animal skins waving around sticks."

Rhen jerked back, offset by the harsh description. An ugly shudder ran down his arms. He had probably heard similar things before, he'd probably said them, but Jin's face popped into his mind—the lonely boy, the cunning boy, the curious boy—all different facets of the person he had come to know. No, the Arpapajo had been much more than oldworlders with sticks, of that Rhen was sure.

"Calen," Rhen said, his voice low and harsh—too harsh, he realized as Cal flinched, looking wounded. Rhen took a deep breath, trying to pull back on the anger bubbling in his veins. It was not his friend's fault, not entirely. "Cal," he said, more gently but still with iron, "I saw them. I fought them. The Ourthuri are here."

"Then we must notify the king immediately."

"My thoughts exactly," Rhen said, drumming his fingers on the table, waiting. After a moment, he sat up. "Well, won't you get some paper? I just scaled a castle wall. I wasn't exactly carrying a scroll and quill in my breeches."

"Right," Cal jumped up, moving into action. He placed the supplies in front of Rhen on the table, but Rhen just breathed heavily and pushed them across the table.

"Save me from another lecture from the king, won't you? You of all people know I never paid attention during calligraphy classes, not when the training yard was right below the window."

"Got some good welts on the back of your head for it too."

They grinned at each other, jumping back in time for a moment, looking five years younger and far less responsible.

"My dearest father," Cal said.

Rhen choked on his wine, about to furiously correct Cal, when he saw the teasing glint in his eye.

He's spending too much time around me, Rhen thought, raising his eyebrows.

Cal coughed. "My King."

Rhen nodded, listening to the scratch of the quill on parchment. As a boy, he had nightmares about that noise, but knowing this letter would help save his family, the sound soothed him.

Until it stopped.

He sat up, watching Cal drop the quill back into the jar of ink. "What?"

"I'm just thinking of the best way to tell the king that his youngest son snuck out against his orders to search the forest for enemies. On his own. Without a guard."

Rhen chewed his lip.

"I see…" He said slowly. "Why don't I just tell you the whole story, and you can think of what to write tomorrow, when I'm gone."

"Where are you going?"

Rhen waved his hand haphazardly through the air, pushing the question off until later, and started telling Cal everything that had happened. The fire. The Arpapajo village. Jin. The fight. And finally, the docks.

"This sounds like war," Cal said, grim.

Rhen just nodded. He had said as much to himself days earlier.

"So, naturally, you're sailing across the sea to face the enemy alone once more."

"Naturally," Rhen deadpanned without batting an eyelash.

"I'm serious, Whylrhen," Cal responded, worry quivering in his voice. *Formal again*, Rhen sighed, sitting straighter.

"Cal, enough worrying. I'll be sailing with Captain Pygott on the *Old Maid*—she's an old warship. We both know he pirated her from the royal fleet years ago when the new ships were built, a gift from the king to his retired captain. He's an honest merchant now. There won't be any trouble."

"It's not him I'm worried about."

"The Ourthuri? I'd like to see that old king try to kill a Son of Whyl, really, I would. My father and the other lords would crush him in an open battle."

"But you're missing one point in that argument—by then, you'd be dead."

"Most spies end up in the grave."

"Most spies aren't princes."

Rhen stood. They were back to where they always were— arguing like ten year olds again, like brothers. He loved it and hated it at the same time. Two brothers was quite enough, what Rhen needed was a friend who would jump into the action with him. Not another lecture.

"Will you watch after Ember? I'll drop her off at the stables before I leave tomorrow." Cal nodded—he already expected this charge. "I'll send word when I've arrived safely back home, to Rayfort."

"No need, I'll see you soon enough," Cal answered. Rhen scrunched his brows, trying to think of why Cal would be traveling to Rayfort, the King's City.

Seeing the confusion, Cal jumped into action, pulling a piece of parchment from the stack on the table. "I can't believe I forgot to tell you—Awenine gave birth. You're an uncle."

"Awenine!" Rhen grabbed the paper, ripping it from his friend's hands to inspect the royal seal. It was true. After years of trying, years of heartbreak and stillborn babies, his sister-in-law, wife of his eldest brother Whyltarin and future Queen of Whylkin, had finally had a child.

He was an uncle.

To a baby boy.

A new prince of Whylkin.

Warmth sprouted in his chest, spreading like a bubble, filling him up, and bursting down his limbs. A child in the palace. *It has been far too long*, Rhen thought, pushing the small knot of dread out of his mind.

This was a good thing. A happy thing. And nothing would ruin it—Rhen would make sure of that.

He gripped Cal's arm, shaking it, needing some way to pour some of this happiness out of his body and into the world.

Cal slapped his back. "Congratulations."

"Thank you, dear friend." He held on for one moment longer. "I'll see you in Rayfort for the Naming."

"For the Naming," Cal repeated.

And then, as they had done a dozen times before, the two friends prepared for Rhen's escape. Cal pulled a second rope from the chest beside his bed and peeked into the hall.

Empty.

Rhen followed Cal down the corridor.

Another check, this time to the door outside.

Clear.

Rhen moved past Cal, stepping over the wall and gripping the rope as he silently made his descent. Cal waited at the top, keeping watch for any guards.

As soon as Rhen's feet touched straw, he tugged on the rope, and Cal pulled it back up toward him. When everything was done, they met eyes.

At the same time, both men formed a fist with their right hands and placed their arms across their chests, nodding the formal goodbye of the knights of Whylkin—something they had done hundreds of times before.

Breaking formality, Rhen sent one more wave up to the sky as Cal disappeared behind the stone.

Rhen turned, tired. All of his traveling had finally hit his bones, making them ache, and all he thought about was the warm body in the bed four feet above his head.

Swiftly, he climbed back through the window, reset his rope in the loose rock, and stripped off his shirt, settling in under the covers.

An airy sigh kissed his ear as he sank into the cushions, draping his arm over Reana's body. She wasn't his wife. She wasn't his sweetheart. And though she would never realize it, she wasn't even his lover.

Rhen had none of those things. The older he got, and the more palace ladies that were thrust before his eyes, the more Rhen thought this was as good as it got.

Soft skin under his palm with no strings attached.

Tomorrow, he would be journeying once more. On a ship. In the middle of the ocean. Without a woman in sight.

Sailors were good, crude fun. Captain Pygott was a fantastic storyteller, a very loyal friend. And Jin was an entertaining new companion.

But none of those equaled a woman.

As sleep overtook him, Rhen hugged Reana closer, dreaming that maybe she was something more.

By morning, he would forget that the wish had even existed.

7

JINJI
~OPEN OCEAN~

Eight days on a boat had taught Jinji one thing about Rhen—he had an inherent disregard for clothing.

As soon as they lost view of the city, Rhen had lost need of his shirt. He stripped it off to join the other men in securing ropes, loosening ropes, and moving parts and pieces that Jinji had no understanding of. Within an hour, his pale skin was red and raw, but he seemed to like it despite the pain.

And she had thought that would be it.

But no.

Once again, around Rhen, Jinji had not been so lucky because later that night she discovered where her sleeping quarters were. Not in the front of the ship with the rest of the men, which she had at first been thrilled by...until the captain led her and Rhen to his first mate's cabin, a small wooden hole with one bed and a hammock (as she later learned it was called). Rhen immediately fell into the bed, leaving Jinji in the doorway weighing the options. Try to squeeze in beside him—not happening—or sleep in the odd fabric hanging on the other side of the room.

The second option was the clear winner, so she had slugged over and awkwardly climbed in. Immediately, a wave of happiness had rolled down her limbs. For the first time since boarding this ship, the death trap as she thought of it, the queasy feeling in her stomach had stopped. Instead of rocking back and forth, unsteady and uncomfortable, the hammock swayed with the ship, doing all of the moving for her.

She remembered settling in, tossing and turning until her legs curved at the perfect angle. Moments later, upon hearing a snore, Jinji had mistakenly looked over toward Rhen, only to be greeted by the sight of his bare butt slipping free of the sheets.

Her cheeks had grown hot and her limbs stiff. With a groan, she had flipped on her side to stare instead at the wooden knots on the wall. But out of sight did not mean out of mind, and the awareness of a naked man in the same room with her had left Jinji unnerved for the rest of the night.

Eight days later, she had gotten slightly more used to it. Then again, she might have gotten better at just closing her eyes, feigning sleep, and doing her best to ignore it.

Despite all of this, Jinji had to admit that a part of her was starting to have fun.

Not at first.

Not even at the middle.

But now, whatever part of her story it was, a little bit of joy had nestled into her heart, finally warming a place that had been cold for too long.

The journey from the forest had been heart wrenching, the trek through the city surreal, the first days on the boat sickening. *But now*, Jinji thought, staring at the waves splashing against the ship, *now it feels a little exciting*.

She had found her favorite part of the ship—the front, or the bow she reminded herself. Right behind the great wooden spike protruding from the deck, like an armless tree sprouting from the wood, that was where she liked to stand. Right in the center, the seam, where the water parted ways and glided around them. There, the wind whipped past her face, the ocean sprawled before her, and the entire world seemed to welcome her with open arms.

At the front of the ship, where no one else liked to stand, the spirits would dance just for her. Moving faster than she had ever dreamed, the spirit strands spiraled into a vortex of colors, clashing and crashing just for her eyes to see. The yellows of the air laced with the blues of the sea, weaving into a bright turquoise, a color as beautiful as any she had seen before. When Rhen stood close by, the spirits danced around his figure, as bright red as his skin, and it stood out like a beacon of heat against the cool colors behind him.

None of the others on the ship were shrouded with spirits as he was, no one in the city had been either, and Jinji was starting to understand that there was something he was hiding, a part of him that was special just like her.

And she ached to know what it was.

Ached for something to make her feel not quite so alone. For someone she could share that part of herself with, even if that someone seemed made to annoy her.

Constantly.

The man had turned the entire ship against her. As soon as they realized how easy it was to make the small boy Jin uncomfortable, all of the crew joined in the fun. Jinji had never seen so much of the male anatomy before, and she hoped to never see so much of it again.

"What are you thinking so hard on, Jin?" A voice said, interrupting her ruminations.

Jinji turned, smiling when she realized that it was Captain Pygott standing beside her, greeting her with a warm smile barely visible through the coarse strands of his thick white beard. His leathery skin crinkled around his eyes, blue just like the ocean he lived on. The rest of his hair was secured in a tight braid at the nape of his neck, hidden under the rim of his wide black hat. It was topped with a great blooming feather like one she had never seen before—soft and airy, not coarse and firm like the ones they had used for arrows back home. That it never blew off his head seemed like a magical feat to her, but no one else was so amazed by it.

Unlike Rhen, the captain had a distinct regard for clothing—colorful ones that popped against the sea. Deep purples and bright oranges, all decorated with some sort of bauble that sparkled in her eye. In the sun, he was almost too brilliant to look at, but Jinji thought he might like it that way. He stood out amongst the crew, the clear leader, and they all listened to him.

During the second day on the ship, Rhen had told her that the captain used to sail warships for the king and then one day, out of the blue, he just left, taking this ship and some of its crew with him. The king asked no questions, but everyone else in the kingdom did. Rumors swirled that he had fallen in the love with the queen and was banished from the royal court when the king found out.

Rhen claimed he knew the truth—that the man was old and alone and simply wanted an easier life, but there was still a part of his story that seemed falsified.

Jinji didn't push to know the truth, because no matter what, she liked this captain. He was a kind man and a breath of fresh air. And she loved the way he told her stories, how he helped her escape.

"I'm thinking that perhaps sailing is not so bad as I thought," Jinji said, looking back out at the water.

"I told you those sea legs would come eventually." He moved next to her, leaning on the front banister with his forearms. "Look at that, wide open water with not a cloud in the sky. It's the perfect day to be a sailor, Jin, the perfect day. A hundred little boys in the kingdom are looking out of market stalls, enviously daydreaming that they were where we stand. Remember that."

"I will," she said softly. He had a way of making every moment feel special.

"I was one of those boys once, did you know that?"

She shook her head, looking at his profile while his eyes glittered with reflections of the sun. There was still a spark in him, one that came out mostly when he was spinning tales. A weaver of sorts, almost like with her illusions, but his were webs of words that ensnared her mind in wonder. Over the past few days, he'd told her all about the kings of old—Whyl the Conqueror, the kings before and after him. Stories of knights and princesses, of love and loss, of honor. But never anything personal.

Until now.

"Yes, I was one of those boys, working for a butcher but dreaming of the sea. Day after day, always the same. Yelling over the other vendors, shouting our goods out to the crowd, fighting for the smallest penny. And the smell, the smell was so thick I swore it had seeped into my bones to haunt me for the rest of my life. Until one day, everything changed." He paused dramatically, drumming his fingers on the wood, as though the humming air would tell his story for him.

"What happened?" Jinji asked, losing patience.

The older man grinned.

"One day, I saw a little boy playing in the streets, running through the crowds, looking behind his back every couple of steps—a little boy in a bright red shirt. I knew exactly who he was, so I snatched him up, holding him tightly despite his protests, and waited for the guards to come. That little boy was a prince at the time, but he is the king now, and he was trying to run away. But I stopped him, and the old king granted me one wish. Do you know what I wished for?"

"A ship?" Jinji asked. He laughed.

"No, nothing so grand. A job cleaning the decks, but eventually it turned into a ship of my own."

Jinji looked back out at the water. It was a wonderful story, but it seemed too perfect—too happy to be real. "Is that true?"

"Stories are hardly ever true, but they do sound nice." He shrugged, nudging her shoulder. "Would you prefer the truth?"

Jinji leaned forward, looking out toward the horizon. The truth was hard. It was dirty and painful and it left scars. But it was real—it was human. And sometimes, just sometimes, it could be the best thing in the world.

She nodded.

"The truth is that my father was a captain, and his father, and his father's father, and all the fathers in my family, probably from the beginning of time, were sailors. It's in my blood. People are born to this world with their destiny already laid out before them, with a future already set—they only get to fill in the details. That's the truth, Jin.

"But that little boy was real, it just wasn't the king, it was Whylrhen. He used to love playing on my ship when I worked for the crown, and I caught him trying to run away too many times. Because Whylrhen is like those little boys in their stalls daydreaming of ships, thinking the world is a far more magical place than it truly is. Who are you, Jin?"

The spirits were silent, though she half expected them to suddenly jump into her vision. She was the spirits, that was her path now, that was her destiny. But she couldn't say that—she didn't want to tell that truth. So instead, she simply answered, "I don't know."

"And that might be painful now, but in time you might find it a gift. To not know. To be free. To get to choose. Your future is as vast as this sea before us." He shrugged. "But who am I? Just an old man spinning stories of youth while my crew tries to sail us round in circles."

He turned, cupping his hands before his mouth, "Back to work! What do you think this is, social hour? We have royalty aboard." He looked at Jinji, winked, and then whipped his head in Rhen's direction. "Prince Whylrhen, why don't you show our little friend the crow's nest?"

"Ay, ay, Captain," Rhen said with a salute, and a rather mocking one at that. Captain Pygott shook his head, pretending to smack Rhen when they crossed paths. For his part, Rhen didn't try to dodge the blow, but Jinji saw the captain pull back at the last second, careful not to lay a hand on the prince. His old eyes twinkled, sparkled with affection, almost like those of a father.

"How long have you known Captain Pygott?" She asked when Rhen came closer.

He turned to look over his shoulder, as if the question had spurred a memory, and replied, "My whole life. I used to run away from the castle all the time, and the only place the guards gave me any peace was on his ship. They deemed it safe, I deemed it a sanctuary."

"And how often do you sail together now?"

Rhen's head shifted quickly, his eyes narrowing on Jinji. But then they softened and he shrugged. "Whenever convenient. But no matter, to the crow's nest with you."

Jinji locked the memory in the back of her mind, the anxious vein in his gaze. There was something in their relationship Rhen did not want her know, maybe something to do with the fire spirits constantly circling his body. Or maybe not.

"What's the crow's nest?" Jinji asked instead. She would dig into his reaction later.

Rather than answer, Rhen just pointed high up overhead. Jinji gulped, following his finger until she saw the small basket hanging from the center mast of the ship.

She gulped again.

"Why would we go up there?"

"For the view." Rhen pushed his elbow into her side, goading. "Are you afraid to climb it?"

"No," she responded instantly.

"Then follow me."

He didn't wait for a reply, but instead walked confidently forward, toward the ropes on the right side of the ship, ropes that were tied to the outer edge of the wood, on the ocean side of the banister. Jinji raised her brows, confused as to what they were doing, until Rhen grabbed hold and pulled himself on top of the railing.

"It's all about balance," he said, reaching higher up on the ropes, lifting his foot off the wood as he began to climb.

Does he want me to follow? There was a reason the Arpapajo lived in the woods—they liked their feet firmly planted on the ground. Even climbing trees had never been particularly fun to her. She preferred the solid cushion of a patch of grass or the weightless buoyancy of a pond.

Only birds were meant for the sky.

"Come on, Jin!" Rhen yelled, letting go with one hand as his body sprung wildly out toward the sea, waving her up.

The man was insane.

But she refused to give him any more reasons to make fun of her. If she didn't climb, it would mean endless taunts for the rest of the day.

Taking a deep breath, Jinji grabbed hold of the roughly bound rope, not caring as it itched her palm. She only strengthened her grasp. Pulling with both hands, she lifted her body onto the rail.

The boat lurched.

One foot slipped free of the wood.

Instantly, the image of falling down into the crystal waters below flashed before her, the icy cool prickle, the pain of the crash. She winced, pulling with all her strength, hugging the rope to her until both feet were once again planted.

One breath.

Two breaths.

She kept her eyes closed, steadying her heart until she felt one with the boat. Slowly, Jinji opened her eyes, meeting the concerned faces of the crew. Instead of speaking, she just smiled. They released their gazes, relieved, and returned to their tasks. Gripping the ropes, she reluctantly returned to hers.

Just go one step at a time, she thought.

Up one with her right arm, up one with her right leg, steady with her left arm and then safe again with her left leg settled in.

Making the same movements again and again, Jinji crawled slowly upward, amazed at how naturally the other men on the boat moved across it, like spiders. She never appreciated the skill it took, but now, refusing to look down and locking her eyes only on the small figure of Rhen above her, she understood.

When she neared the cage, Rhen grasped her arms, lifting her free of the rope and pulling her safely into the wooden basket. She panted for a moment, regained her depleted strength, and took in the view.

Blue.

For miles and miles in every direction, a stark and sparkling blue.

She tried to stand, but the rocking of the ship was magnified with their height, and it seemed to tip almost sideways with every other breath. Her legs wobbled, and then she dropped back to the floor.

"Stay seated," Rhen said, pushing down just slightly on her shoulder when she tried to lift herself up for the second time. He sat too, sighing as he dangled his feet over the edge and leaned back into the railing. His large frame took up over half of the small space.

Their arms touched from shoulder to elbow, causing a heat to rise under her skin. Jinji grabbed her legs, pulling them into her chest and shifting her weight, careful not to touch his body anymore. It was too intimate, she realized, after spending so many hours locked in the same room as him. There had to be a distance between them, otherwise she might slip up, might forget that she was supposed to be a boy, that she was supposed to be lying. He might notice that though her face was that of a male, her body was not. The baggy clothes hid it well, but in these close quarters, she had to be careful.

No matter how many times he taunted her, Rhen had come to be a friend, and she would not mess that up, not yet.

"This is one of my favorite spots on the ship," he said, eyes still closed in relaxation, "though many wouldn't say the same. It's considered a punishment to be put up here, because of all the movement, but I've always found it very peaceful, very liberating."

Feeling her stomach unsettle slowly, Jinji might have agreed with the others, but there was something oddly comforting in her mood and oddly settled too.

"This was where I came to escape the castle and my father and mostly my responsibilities. Even if I was only on the dock, still stuck in Rayfort, I seemed miles away on top of this ship."

He opened his eyes slowly. The wind rustled his red hair, forcing it to spill over his forehead. Jinji wondered if her own short hair was doing the same, without her braid to keep it still and steady. Just the other night she had borrowed Rhen's knife to cut it short again, not ready to stop her mourning period—not even close.

"Do you have a place like that?"

Jinji closed her eyes tight, fighting back the water gathering there.

The clearing.

The meadow.

It used to be her spot, but all she saw now was Leoa, tying her braid, pulling over her joining dress. Both of them giggling, completely ignorant to the cries of their people, to the children and the women, to the warriors, to her parents. Even to Maniuk, singled out by the shadow for his strength and his skill—used and discarded.

All she heard now was the blood-curdling scream that cracked her spirit in half, the pounding of her footsteps, the soft thud of a body as it fell to the ground.

"No," was all she said. No, she didn't have a safe place like that, not anymore.

"It will get better," Rhen said. Jinji wouldn't look at him, but instead focused on the far away horizon. "I know it doesn't seem like it, but it will."

He took a deep breath, cracked his knuckles. Jinji almost heard the words waiting on his lips, could feel them press against his tongue wanting to come out. The air was static, electric from his pounding heart, his pulsing nerves.

And then it all stopped.

Silence.

"I had a younger brother once," Rhen confessed, his words heavy with an emotion that was mirrored by Jinji's wounded soul. "He was barely a year old when he was murdered by the man my father trusted most in the world. And I could have stopped it, if I had only understood what—" His voice shook, wavered on an edge. "I found papers that held evidence the murder was going to take place, but I was too young to understand what they meant, too naïve to know what I had found. And for that, my brother paid the price." He turned, met her stare with eyes a deep dark green, like the forest at twilight. "I know what it means to lose someone, but I also know that though the pain will never fully fade, eventually you will be able to endure it."

Jinji didn't know what to say, so she said nothing at all. Silence was the better option. Silence let the words sink in, let their truth ring, let her realize that Rhen had allowed her a peek at a place within himself that he didn't show to everyone—that he did not even show to most people.

Jinji opened her mouth, aching to tell her own story, but her throat closed up, stealing the sound from her voice.

She trusted him, after all he had done for her, Jinji trusted Rhen. But trusting someone was one thing, and opening herself up to him, making herself vulnerable to be hurt again, that was something else entirely. Rhen might have been willing, but it was only because he didn't know that in the end, he would just be wounded—by her lie if he ever found out the truth or by her leaving without a word of goodbye.

And Jinji couldn't handle any more pain.

"Thank you," she said quietly, instantly regretting it. Rhen blinked once, but once was all it took for his gaze to unglaze and his features to retreat, to harden. One blink was all it took for him to shut himself off again.

She looked out over the water, the small space of the crow's nest suddenly crunching in on her, suffocating her.

In her panic, she almost missed the unusual color on the horizon, the black speck that seemed to grow larger in her vision. But her brain registered what her heart did not, and before she realized it, Jinji was leaning forward, asking, "What's that?"

Rhen followed, his features popping in shock when he locked in on the speck. "A ship," he said and grinned, standing instantly.

"Captain!" He shouted down toward the deck. Having caught several people's attention, he pointed. "A ship off the starboard side."

Captain Pygott immediately pulled a long brass tube from his vest, extending it, holding it to his eye.

"I don't see any colors," He yelled back up toward them. Jinji watched Rhen's grin spread wider. His fingers tapped his leg energetically.

"Let's take a closer look, shall we?"

The captain nodded.

Rhen swung his leg over the railing, moving to leave the crow's nest and Jinji behind. All notions of sadness had fled his gaze, replaced by pure adrenaline. Jinji began to stand but Rhen shook his head.

"Stay here, Jin. It'll be safer, just in case."

"In case of what?" She asked.

He grinned.

"Attack."

And with that, he was gone, slipping down the ropes faster than her eyes could follow, landing with a thud on the deck as he charged Captain Pygott, demanding a look through his metal device.

Jinji looked out toward the ship again, and the spirits flung into her view, filling her head with a somewhat crazy idea. She looked down at her hands—were they up for the task?

It would be a larger illusion than any she had woven before.

But, she paused, looking down to the deck once more. Jinji owed it to him to try. She owed it to all of them.

Her secret way of thanking Rhen for the moment of peace, for the first moment of true companionship she had felt in a while, for the memory.

Jinji cupped her hands in her lap, thinking of the mother spirits, of jinjiajanu, preparing herself for the weave.

And without her realizing, Jinji's fingers began to glow.

8

RHEN
~OPEN OCEAN~

Thank the gods for unflagged ships, Rhen thought as he stared through the telescope, searching for some sign of coloring on those distant masts.

Why had he told the boy so much? The words had just spilled out, uncontrollable. He hadn't spoken of little Whyllysle in years, to anyone, his family let alone his friends.

But even after burying it in the back of his mind, the memory came to life just as clearly as if it had happened yesterday.

Rhen, seven years old, searching through the old spymaster's papers as he usually did, barely able to read them but able to read them just enough. The year before, when he had been locked away in his room for misbehavior, Rhen had discovered the secret passage behind his bed, the one that led directly to the master's office. He was just able to sneak through, just small enough to fit under his bed, and a year later, he was still snooping around.

But this had been different, now he had a younger brother to take care of—one he would treat far better than his own older brothers had treated him. And part of taking care of him was making sure Rhen knew everything that was going on.

Hours and hours of looking through parchments and Rhen had never found a thing—until one night, when he found his brother's name scribbled in the margins of a sealed letter. *Whyllysle*. Immediately, Rhen had stolen the paper, folded it, and tucked it into his shirt before scurrying back to his room. He read as much as he could, picking out words like *queen* and *king* and most importantly, *poison*. But he didn't really understand, and he definitely didn't know what to do. Show it to his father and risk being punished? Or pretend he had never found it in the first place?

What Rhen didn't realize at the time was that there were no options. He had been too late either way.

Not even an hour later, word spread like wildfire through the castle—the youngest prince was dead. The king, like a madman, demanded information. And Rhen, not knowing what he held, gave the parchment to his father, waiting for the blow to his head for stealing another person's things.

Instead of a blow, the king disappeared. A day later, the spymaster was hung for treason and the entire castle dropped into a deep despair.

And this was the part Rhen had never told anyone, the part he had almost spilled but was able to keep secret. Eventually, Rhen did understand what the papers had held—they had named the fourth heir to the throne a babe born out of infidelity, the queen's bastard, not the blood of Whyl. For that, an innocent child paid the price. The spymaster, rather than admit what he had found, poisoned the boy in his sleep, hoping the king would never understand, hoping that it would turn into an unsolved mystery allowed to linger.

Clearly, he had been wrong.

King Whylfrick was a proud man—he never said a word to his sons and never to the queen that Rhen could tell. It was a secret between the two of them; one he wasn't sure his father even realized they shared.

But sometimes when he caught his father's gaze, Rhen was sure the king knew. Deep down in his green eyes, so like his son's, there was a speck of resentment, a glimmer of unspoken rage, and Rhen could think of no other cause.

Which was why he remained silent—was why Rhen would never tell a soul—not even a small boy who had no one in the world he could tell.

And maybe that, Rhen realized, was why he had allowed himself one moment of vulnerability with Jin. The boy had no one—no political motivations, no idea of what it meant for a prince to be indebted to him. For the first time, Rhen had someone other than his two brothers he could be honest with, could show his real self to.

But that wasn't quite true, no matter how much he hoped it was.

Rhen thought of the snoring comment. A lighthearted story, a good laugh—but also so much more, a little tale that could wreck a reputation.

Jin's innocence was his appeal and his danger—he could break Rhen's hard work without even realizing it.

He could destroy it all.

"See anything, Prince Whylrhen?"

Rhen dropped the telescope—he had stopped scanning the waters a few minutes ago.

"No flags."

A child-like glow burned in the captain's eyes.

"Attack?" He asked.

"Your call, old friend," Rhen replied, nodding his head. Rhen might be leading this expedition, but he trusted the captain. What very few knew, no one outside of this ship, was that the two of them had made an arrangement. When Rhen officially earned his knighthood, he commissioned Pygott as the first member of his spy network—his own personal captain.

That was the reason Pygott had left the crown. Not for the queen, a ridiculous rumor. But because Rhen had always been like a son to him, the son he and his wife could never have, and he could not say no.

But at times like this, looking at the fast approaching ship, Rhen understood what the captain had given up.

He loved a good fight.

And he was about to get one.

"Archers!" The captain yelled. Immediately, the crew stopped in place. Even the air seemed to still.

Then chaos—organized, as these men all knew their places.

Six of the crew ran to the bow of the ship, opening a chest that held their weapons, searching for nicks in the wood and stretching out horsehairs that had been hardened by the salt air.

Six more men ran down below deck, readying the anchored crossbows—three two-man machines that fired a spiked anchor into the hull of another ship, latching it to the *Old Maid* to enable boarding.

And Rhen, along with the remaining crew, readied for hand-to-hand combat, field battle on the water.

He pulled his sword from the scabbard strapped to his hip, swinging it in a wide arc over his head, stretching his shoulders and loosening up. His body felt light without the heavy armor of a knight, armor that was too arduous for travel. He would just have to be good enough to not get hurt.

"Prince." One of the sailors approached, holding a shield. It was wooden, the length of half of his body and unpainted. Deep holes already punctured the surface, blows from arrows in previous fights, but it would do well enough.

"Thank you, Geoff," Rhen said, pulling his arm through the strap on the back, his bicep straining under the weight. The man's eyes lit up, surprised and thankful for the recognition. Rhen nodded once more, releasing him, and Geoff circled back to the captain brandishing more weapons.

It was odd, Rhen realized as he stood there, so odd to be waiting on foot without Ember's strong body to hold him aloft. But it was better this way, better she was safe with Cal in the castle stables than at risk on the water. Even if he would pay for it when they reunited in Rayfort, Rhen smiled, picturing the moment. Leaving Ember was never easy, even when it was for her own good, but trying to get back in her good graces would be pure torture.

He looked back to the horizon where the ship was quickly becoming more visible. The center mast held no flag, no identifying marker as were the rules of sea travel. Each ship must have the flag of its kingdom and the flag of its city or occupation. Looking up, Rhen took note of the flags on this ship—the brilliant red flag of Whylkin decorated with a deep black rearing stallion, the great horse of Whyl the Conqueror that was said to be twice as large as any that had been born since. Below it, the flag of a merchant, a blue canvas split diagonally down the center with a white stripe and the image of a ship's wheel.

Below that, Rhen caught sight of Jin standing with his hands outstretched, pointing to the sea, silhouetted by the sun. His fingers seemed to almost glow against the clouds—impossible. *But*, Rhen squinted, *can that truly be just the sun?*

He stepped forward.

Why was the boy holding his hands like that? They moved in circles, in some sort of dance, fingers twisting in and out of one another.

"Prince Whylrhen," Captain Pygott said from behind Rhen.

He didn't want to look away.

Something was happening—something the boy had been hiding.

Some might think it crazy, but Rhen lived and breathed magic—was it even possible the boy did too?

Or—Rhen paused, taking a moment to slow his racing mind—he could be praying, practicing some Arpapajo ritual that he, a newworlder, knew nothing about…

Rhen turned, facing the captain and forgetting about Jin—there were more pressing matters.

"We engage on your command," the old man said, bowing his head. Rhen balled his hands into fists, looking back out toward the ship now twice the size it had been moments before.

"As soon as it is within distance," Rhen said, "make the call."

The captain nodded, moving back to the stern, standing at his proper place behind the helm. And Rhen turned, standing with the other soldiers, just waiting and watching as the enemy neared. All of them fidgeted, anxious and excited, too much electricity for their bodies to contain.

His feet held firm, but even Rhen couldn't stop the ticking of his fingers on the hilt of his sword, over and over, in a subconscious pattern he had been using since his time as a squire.

When the ship was so close that Rhen could begin to make out the men on board, Captain Pygott raised his voice.

"Ready!"

Rhen flexed the muscles in his hands, tightening and loosening his hold on both sword and shield.

"Aim!"

He held his breath.

But before the word *fire* could leave the captain's lips, a flight of arrows from the other ship flew over the water, fast approaching. Rhen lifted his shield, waiting for the thunk of metal on wood, but instead he heard the pattering of splashes.

He looked up, catching sight of the amazed gazes beside him.

The other ship had missed—their arrows sailing at least thirty feet to the right of the ship.

"Fire!" Pygott yelled and the archers stood from behind the protective wood at the bow of the ship to launch their own set of arrows.

A hit.

Five arrows landed directly on target.

And with that, the battle had begun. Without needing orders, the archers continued to launch wave after wave, sending blankets of arrows onto the opposing ship. The enemy continued to misfire, landing set after set of arrows into the sea, almost as though they believed the *Old Maid* was fifty feet to the right of where it actually stood. Either the wind was being unusually favorable, or…

Rhen shot a quick glance up at Jin, whose hands still danced before his face, a face that spoke of intense concentration.

He scrunched his brows, smelling a secret, sour taste on the wind. But now was not the time.

Screams ripped through the air. The opposing ship was in turmoil, and it was still early in the fight. The *Old Maid* remained untouched, unscathed.

"Petore," the captain called. A man beside Rhen turned around. "Send word downstairs to prepare the crossbows!"

He dashed away.

Rhen focused ahead. The other ship was not two-lengths away, the men aboard were in complete madness. Even at such a length, Rhen could see soldiers running from side to side, looking every which way, confused and terrified, shocked each time a new volley of arrows landed on top of them.

One length away.

Suddenly, a shout went up, ringing in Rhen's ears as the remaining soldiers on the enemy deck turned on their heels. Like one, they moved in a wave across their ship, to their starboard side, looking at the *Old Maid* with shock and horror written across their faces.

Rhen heard the harsh, guttural sound of Ourthuri words being screamed, too soft to make out but loud enough to cause Rhen to lift his sword.

He had been right.

It was the Ourthuri driving unmanned ships.

It was the Ourthuri preparing for war.

In one moment, Rhen felt totally vindicated, totally satisfied in all of the lies he had been spouting over the years, all of the secrets he had found and kept.

For once, his hunch had paid off. For once, his spying had done the trick.

And then the ship was right beside them.

"Steady!" The captain called. But the men all knew what to wait for.

In an excruciatingly long pause, both ships seemed to stop, as though time had ceased to exist, halting on a note of pure anticipation.

Wind pushed against flapping sails, but nothing else moved.

Almost afraid to avert his eyes, Rhen continued to look ahead, meeting the terrified stare of an Ourthuri soldier as the enemy ship pulled perfectly parallel to theirs. The man's eyes were almost black in the daylight. His skin was hardened, tough like leather, dark brown with the hint of green.

Whipping chains blasted through the air, ripping through the silence. The crash of splintering wood followed, and it could only mean one thing—the anchors had been loosed. Brown chips exploded into the sky, raining down on both decks, splashing into the water, smacking into the sails.

A second later, the chink of a crank hit Rhen's ear, and the Ourthuri ship began to move against the tide, unnaturally closer to the *Old Maid*. Ten clicks later and *boom*, wood slammed into wood.

The anchored crossbows had done their job, securing the bond between the ships.

Knowing what came next, Rhen raised his sword and yelled, a deep and throaty sound, rippling with the anger that boiled under his skin.

Those Ourthuri wanted to hurt his people. And thinking of Jin, Rhen knew they had already succeeded. But they would not succeed again. Rhen had a nephew to protect, a new babe in the palace, a new future of the kingdom.

He would not let his family or his people down.

Without blinking, he charged, running to the edge of the ship and stomping over the wooden planks that had just been laid like bridges across the gap.

Slicing his sword through the air, the crash of metal clanking metal reverberated from mast to mast.

A man possessed, Rhen moved on pure instinct, lifting his shield to catch a blow from one soldier just to turn on his heal and cut another with his sword. Years of playing at battle had prepared him well, and the training from old knights resurfaced, letting his muscles move on pure memory.

Silver danced across his vision—silver and red.

Rhen pulled his sword from the chest of the man before him, blood spurting from the wound, already turning to face the next foe.

Geoff stood behind him, engaged with a lesser swordsman. He would be fine.

Spinning, Rhen searched through the curtain of moving arms and shields for anyone in need of help.

There.

Captain Pygott had abandoned ship, running across the boards to join in the fray, and had been caught against a man twice his size. Rhen charged, kicking the chest of a man who tried to face him, pushing him out of the way. He held his shield to the left, over his head, to guard against any flying daggers, and moved swiftly parrying enemy blades with his broadsword.

In one move, he pushed the captain out of harm's way and swung his right arm high overhead, catching the Ourthuri's curved sword in its path. A deafening clang roared in his ear, his bicep straining against the strength of his foe, his elbow twisting painfully toward the ground.

Rhen stepped back out of the way and dropped his shield, gripping the sword with both hands. He would need his full strength for this.

The Ourthuri twisted the curved blade before his face, spinning it in a circle, trying to intimidate Rhen. But then his eyes flicked to the gold hilt of Rhen's sword, his lids lifting high up into his brow before narrowing to a slit.

I guess he knows I'm a prince, Rhen thought. Gold encased swords were rare in both kingdoms. Ones decorated with precious stones? Even rarer.

Good, Rhen thought, angling the sword just slightly so the reflection hit the other man's eye.

And then he charged, aiming low and for the man's leg, an unexpected spot. But his opponent saw it coming, slapping Rhen's sword away, returning with a strike at Rhen's neck.

Rhen dodged, jumping back and out of arm's length before surging forward once more. Up then down, circling left and swinging right. He feigned one way, moving his sword to the other.

They were evenly matched.

And Rhen's strength was running low.

A whistle tickled his ear, and too late to do anything but duck, Rhen fell to the floor, smacking his nose against the wood. Blood pooled from the wound, forming a puddle on the boards below his face.

He jumped up, preparing for a sword that never came. The Ourthuri stood before him, arrow lodged in his chest, looking just as surprised as Rhen before sinking to the ground.

What the…?

Rhen curved his neck, searching for the archer. No man from Whylkin would shoot so close to his prince, no one. But what Ourthuri would have taken the same chance?

Not ten feet away, an Ourthuri stood, aiming an arrow into the fight. He let go. The bow whipped. The arrow soared.

Rhen followed as it flew through the crowd and watched, disbelieving, as it landed squarely in the chest of another surprised Ourthuri warrior.

Yet one more arrow raced through Rhen's vision.

A third Ourthuri fell.

"Keep one alive," Rhen screamed, suddenly understanding what was going on. Ordered suicide, the man had been ordered to do this, ordered to maintain secrecy at any cost. And there was only one person who could demand such a thing, one person who held so much authority—a king.

A fourth arrow.

And then Rhen was on the man, his sword slicing through soft flesh. The bow clanked to the ground, precious nerves in the man's wrist had been severed.

But there was no scream.

Instead, as Rhen took one small second to look at the man's already paling face, there was only a small smile, bubbling over with foam.

The man fell next to his bow, body shaking wildly on the wood.

Poison.

The entire deck was still, silent except for the rivers of blood spilling and splashing into the ocean.

The enemy had been destroyed.

"Idiot," Rhen cursed softly. *Leave one alive, always leave someone alive to question.* "Search the ship," he said louder, a command.

"In all of my years," Captain Pygott said softly, approaching Rhen with a grim expression, "I have never seen something like that. A fight to the last man, yes, but never such a surrender. There are stories, of course. But there are always stories. To witness such a thing in the flesh," he shook his head, "even I am left speechless." He paused, and then raised his hand to Rhen's shoulder. "What have you uncovered here?"

"You mean what did I fail to uncover?" Rhen shrugged out of the captain's grip, balling his hands into fists, fighting the urge to punch at the floor.

"Whylrhen—"

"Prepare the ship, we continue on to the Golden Isles," Rhen interrupted, not meeting the concerned blue eyes that stared him down.

Only when the captain left did Rhen move, running his vision over the bodies crumpled on the floor. He shuffled to the closest man, kneeling to get a look at his arm.

Three ebony stripes were tattooed around his wrists and a triangle of dots decorated his hand.

Rhen recognized the mark. A soldier.

He flipped the fingers over, searching for another mark on the palm, something else to identify him, but there was nothing.

Just a common soldier.

Rhen walked around the other bodies, doing the same, but they were identical.

Until he reached the archer, the body Rhen had saved for last. Each wrist wore the standard soldier marks, but when he flipped it over, the same dotted triangle had been painted on the inside of his palm.

He was from the inner ranks, the warriors specially chosen to protect the king. But if he was meant to protect the Ourthuri king, what was he doing so far from home?

"Prince Whylrhen," someone gasped from behind.

Rhen stood, facing the voice. It was Geoff. And behind him, chained and shackled together, stood four very skinny Ourthuri. Rhen grinned, heart feeling light as excitement bubbled in his brain.

Perhaps all hope wasn't lost. Not yet.

"Help them aboard the *Old Maid*," Rhen ordered and moved to the makeshift bridge between the ships. "We'll question them from safer grounds."

He crossed over, hearing the creak of straining wood.

As soon as everyone had touched safely down on the clean, and now cluttered, deck of the *Old Maid*, the chains released from the crossbows below deck, detaching from the ship and dropping into the sea. Immediately, the other ship caught the tide, slipping slowly away.

It was only a matter of time before it sank, but Rhen hoped to be miles closer to the Golden Isles before that happened. And much closer to answers too.

If only he could get these prisoners to talk.

He looked at the rusted chains around their hands, the red welts on their wrists, the bones pushing against thin skin.

Treating them like anything but prisoners might just do the trick.

"Do any of you understand what I am saying?" He asked, looking down at their wrists. All four were painted with three thick bands of simple black lines. Farmers, peasants, the lowest class. The Kingdom of Ourthuro was composed of a hundred islands, each with its own somewhat individualized language—

that Rhen knew half of those tongues was something he preferred to keep secret for as long as possible. But as it was, only a member of the upper classes would understand his Whylkin speech.

Movement brought Rhen back as one of the men stepped forward. He was tall and lean, shaped completely different from Rhen. His hair hung in straggles over his face, black and wiry, malnourished, and his eyes held the calculating tick of intelligence.

"I understand," he said in a deep, cautious voice, accented harshly, choppy so two words came out sounding more like four. As he moved in front of his companions, Rhen saw burns on his hands, bumpy scars in place of tattoos, and it could only mean one thing—the man was a criminal, he had been degraded, his old marks burned away and replaced with those of an unmarked—a slave.

Perfect, Rhen thought. *Just the sort of man who might talk.*

"Why were you imprisoned on this ship?"

"I tried to marry above my station," he said softly, shuffling his feet.

"Your companions?"

"They sold their labor in return for food for their families."

"And what labor was that?" Rhen asked, leaning in closer, moving his hand subconsciously to the hilt of his sword. The man's gaze flicked down, but he returned Rhen's gaze, unafraid.

"We were told very little, but I believe we were being taken to Whylkin to steal supplies—wood, livestock, food."

Rhen leaned back, brows scrunched together as he ran a hand through his wild hair. "Why? The Golden Isles are richer than our lands have ever been."

"Richer in metal, yes, but not in other things like fertile soil and hunting game."

Rhen exhaled heavily—this was news to him.

"With so much gold, why not buy it? Why risk so much for something you could purchase justly?"

The man shrugged. "My king is a greedy man."

"All kings are," Rhen said under his breath, wondering what his father would do with this information. Try to push trade prices up between the kingdoms, or try to weaken Ourthuro until they would pay anything for the supplies they needed. But could that really be it? Why the suicide? Why the poison? "Did you hear anything else? Any conversations between the men aboard?"

He shook his head.

Rhen sighed. It would not help to push these men, not yet at least. He could tell they were tired with their backs hunched in, swaying on feet that looked barely able to hold them upright.

"Captain," Rhen said. Pygott turned to face his prince. "Please help get these men unchained and fed. Show them below deck and give them anything they require." Rhen raised his voice, to be heard by the rest of the ship. "These men are our guests, not our prisoners, and I expect no harm to come to them. We are giving them safe passage home."

The crew nodded. The Ourthuri bowed in thanks, but Rhen couldn't help but see the fear in their eyes, fear that only sparked at the mention of their home.

They were hiding something.

And they're not the only ones, Rhen thought as Jin walked back into view, finally descended from his safe haven in the crow's nest. He stood apart from the crowd, behind the rest of the crew, staring in disbelief at his own hands.

He looked up, meeting Rhen's gaze, and his arms instantly slackened, dead by his sides. Even from the distance, Rhen could see the challenge in Jin's eyes. A challenge he intended to take.

But not yet.

Everyone on the ship needed a moment to rest, a moment of peace.

He looked to the horizon.

One week left on the open ocean, one week left to Ourthuro. Plenty of time.

He turned back to Jin and winked. The boy jerked and dashed to the bow of the ship, not once looking back.

You can run, but you can't hide. Not on this ship.

9

JINJI
~DUELING SEA~

Jinji's fingers buzzed, still alive with the spirits even though many days had passed since the fight. She had never woven an illusion so large, so intricate. Mirages of Janu had always come naturally. She pictured his face so often that it was imprinted on her brain, easily sprouting to life when called.

But this had been something different.

Something more powerful.

She had created an illusion that could only be seen from one side. Jinji hadn't even been certain it had worked, not until the enemy arrows flew and landed uselessly to the right of the ship—dead center on the illusion of the *Old Maid* that she had woven. And still, she prayed in the back of her mind that no one in the crew realized what she was doing, that no one could see the false picture.

The second her feet landed back on deck, Jinji had her answer. Rhen's eyes pierced hers, pricking her heart, and instantly she knew that he knew. There was enough curiosity, confusion, and determination in his gaze to put her at ease for a moment— he knew she had done something, but he had no idea what that something was.

Whatever relief she felt disappeared quickly. Since that instant, Rhen had made it his personal mission to uncover all of her secrets.

And the longer they remained on the ship, the more and more difficult it was becoming to evade him.

But the outsiders, the men who had been stolen away from the other ship, had saved her—a miracle distraction keeping Rhen at bay. He coveted their answers even more than hers, and those answers were more urgent. They had a time limit—one that seemed fast approaching judging from the words of Captain Pygott.

He expected to sight land early today, and to arrive in the Ourthuri capital tomorrow evening.

One day, Jinji thought, *one last day of living constantly on edge.*

She listened, waiting for the sound of a snore that did not come, and squeezed her eyes tightly shut before taking a deep breath and relaxing them.

Keep closed, she ordered.

Try not to move.

And then she felt his gaze land on her, scanning her face. A shadow penetrated her lashes, hot breath kissed her cheek, and a tingle shivered up her neck.

"Jin," Rhen whispered.

She ignored him, counting to ten in her head.

"Jin, are you awake?"

He poked her shoulder gently. Jinji moved, rolling over, groaning in protest as though still caught in a dream.

A loud, frustrated sigh flowed into her ears.

"I'll get to you later," he said gruffly, and then Jinji heard bootsteps on wood, the creak of a door. She counted to fifteen, knowing Rhen could not remain quiet for such a lengthy stretch of time.

Still silence.

Jinji stretched her arms overhead, sitting up slowly in the hammock and opening her eyes, wincing at the bright sun filtering through the window. Another cloudless day. Another unbroken stretch of blue.

The novelty of the sea had most definitely worn off.

Jinji needed the forest.

She yearned for it.

She looked down at her hands, almost surprised to see them look just as normal as ever. Her skin its usual brown, but underneath it, the spirits were dancing, tingling, urging her to weave more, to keep building her power.

Curious, Jinji closed her eyes, picturing trees and grass, sunlight filtering through leaves, the gentle patter of a stream, and the flutter of a butterfly hovering over the bright red of a flower.

Her eyes widened instantly, and she stepped down off the hammock into her forest. The clearing, almost the same as she remembered it, minus the laughing face of Leoa. She walked forward, just a few steps, and there was the patch of yellow, perfectly shaped for her body, the spot where she had sat for hours and hours just to think, just to be. Jinji sunk to the floor slowly, waiting for the comforting cushion of her home, her sacred place, but the ground below her butt was still hard wood. Unyielding. Unnatural. Not the soft patch of dirt she wished it was.

The illusion fell, shattered, taking Jinji's mood with it.

Time to face the day, she sighed.

By the corner, under her hammock, were the fresh clothes Rhen had promised the night before. Newworlder clothes. Her first.

Yesterday, pestered by the stink of Janu's skins, skins that were never meant for the sea, Jinji asked for something new to wear. But now, faced with the reality, she didn't feel ready. Not ready to remove that last tie to her home. But what had once been soft, comfortable fur was now harsh and scratchy, itching her skin, causing a rash.

Biting her lip, Jinji pulled Janu's shirt overhead, holding it before her.

Eyes watering, she removed the pelts around her legs and balled them all into one lump, stuffing it under the hammock.

Naked was not enough to describe how she felt, shivering there, staring at the bleached out skins. Exposed. Alone. Abandoned. Judged.

What would her mother say if she saw her only daughter dressed like one of them? What would her father do if he knew she had killed like one of them? What would Maniuk think if he realized she was sharing this room with one of them? Would Leoa still laugh with her, brush her hair, or would she look from a distance with scorn?

Jinji couldn't breathe.

Her throat closed in, held by invisible hands, the very spirits of her tribe calling her to join them, to be at her rightful spot.

Better dead than unrecognizable.

Diving forward, Jinji cried out, gripping the skins in her hands. Stumbling backward, she reached for the clasp on the window and tossed Janu's clothes outside.

Her neck loosened. She gulped in one strained breath.

Then panic.

Shoving her head out of the hole, she searched for the skins, finding them just in time to watch them sink below the surface—gone.

Her hands shook.

Her lip quivered.

She took a deep, uneven breath.

Then another.

One more.

Her mother, her father, Maniuk, Leoa, even Janu—they could say nothing. They were gone. They had left her alone.

Her mind settled, her heartbeat slowed, her thoughts cleared.

They loved her—they would not have judged what it took for her to survive.

Turning slowly, Jinji unfolded the clothes Rhen had left. The pants, a deep soft black leather, slipped easily over her legs, loose and clearly meant for a larger person. But better that than have them stick to her thighs or her bottom, round like a woman and not flat like a man.

The shirt hung loosely too, stretching inches past her fingers. She tucked the fine linens into the hem of the pants as she had seen Rhen do, rolled the sleeves up above her elbows. The neckline gaped open, slipping low on her chest. Jinji looked down, spotting the small but most definitely feminine curve of her breast, wincing.

But there was one more folded cloth. She put her arms through the sleeveless holes and awkwardly buttoned the front. A vest Rhen had called it. Still mildly loose, but, Jinji looked down, it kept her womanly assets very well guarded.

She felt for the spirits surrounding her face, as she did every morning, welcoming their familiar presence. The illusion over her features still held, made only stronger with time. Running her fingers gently through her hair, Jinji felt the short strands spike up, hardened by the salty air.

She missed the weight of her curls, the silky way they spilled down her back, drifting over her shoulders, made shiny by the sun.

But she was not prepared to completely abandon her tribe—her hair would never flow freely again.

Jinji stood straight, facing the door. If she only had one day left onboard, she would try to make the most of it. She had been hiding out below deck for too long, and fresh air would likely do her good, even if it meant an inevitable run-in with Rhen.

Well, she shrugged, she had held her own so far.

Minutes later, Jinji emerged to the curious stares of a few men onboard, including the Ourthuri. It was her clothes, Jinji assured herself, just her clothes. Rhen looked over momentarily, but didn't let his gaze stick. He was talking to the tall man, the one with burns on his wrists. Judging by the puff to his chest, it was not going well.

No matter, Jinji walked to the front of the ship, ready to look out past the waves for the first sight of these Golden Isles she had heard so much about.

The horizon was flat, dark blue fading into an almost white sky. She could see no mountains, no shorelines, and after a while, even the line faded away as her eyes glazed over, full of dreams and not reality.

"Land ho!"

Jinji snapped back to attention, her head twisting to the noise. She had no notion of how much time had passed, but her body felt stiff and stuck. Rhen was nowhere in sight. But one of the crew was in the crow's nest, pointing straight ahead.

Looking out to sea, Jinji scanned the blue water but could find nothing. And then there, right in front of her eyes, was a golden shimmer, a slight spark like a flame in the distance, almost like the first glance of the rising sun. Could it possibly be?

"Have you ever seen the Golden Isles?" A voice asked, deep and unfamiliar. She spun, tearing her eyes away from the view.

It was an Ourthuri. Eyes scanning, her pupils took in the rippled and raw flesh at his wrists. Parts of the skin seemed almost the same color as her own hand. Other parts seemed a color no human flesh should hold.

He was tall, her neck hurt to look up at him, but narrow.

"I have not," Jinji answered, looking back out toward the bright bump in an otherwise smooth horizon, leaning her forearms on the ship in a relaxed pose.

"I thought so," he nodded to himself, turned to copy her body language, languidly placing his own arms to the rail.

"Why?"

"You do not look like the others, and until today, you did not dress like them. You were not made for the sea like these men."

"No," she responded quietly, sadly, thinking of the trees and the grass.

"At first I thought perhaps you were Ourthuri, but you do not look or sound like us either. And you just said you have never been to the isles."

"I am Arpapajo," Jinji told him, ignoring the cloud of confusion that drifted over his features. "My name is Jin."

"I am called nothing now." He stood taller, bringing his hands behind his back, out of eyesight, a pose both strong and suffered. "But I was once Mikzahooq."

"Where did your name go? I don't understand," Jinji said. How could his name just be stolen away? Erased? Her people were gone, her life shattered, but her name was one thing no one could steal.

"Then you are definitely not from the isles."

That seemed like a very good thing, Jinji suspected, shivering as she caught sight of his mangled hands once more. The isles did not seem like a very forgiving place, though now, growing in her eyes, sparkling like the gems on Rhen's clothes, she did not see why a place so beautiful should be anything but good.

Though, she thought with a smirk, *looks can be deceiving. Everyone aboard thinks I'm a man.*

"Why do they shine like that?"

"Those islands are not made of plants and dirt like Whylkin, but of metal and rock. They leap from the ocean, harsh and jagged, as though knifing their way through the waters. The edges are steep cliffs, full of silver and gold and copper, and when the sun hits them, well, you can see." He shrugged, eyes glued to the sight even though he had likely seen it a thousand times. There was something wary in his expression, but nostalgic too.

Minding his words, Jinji turned to look over her shoulder. It was true, she hadn't even realized it, but the sun had crossed overhead, starting the slow descent back down to the earth. The deeper it sunk, the more brilliant the islands before them became.

"And that is why you were chopping down my trees?" She asked, flashing back to the first time she and Rhen had met, a memory she wasn't fond of reliving. But remove the men, the deaths, the pain, and she could still envision her trees, mutilated and chopped to pieces. Stacks and stacks of them, more than any man should use in a lifetime. A waste.

"Not me." He grinned, stepping back playfully as if whipped from her tongue. "But yes, I believe that is what I was meant to do when our ship arrived. Steal trees and animals that cannot grow or survive on islands made of gold."

"But why steal?" It was not a term she was used to, but neither was *gold*, or *ship* or anything that had seemingly transitioned into daily vocabulary for her. *Money. War. Steal.* All things the Arpapajo had no use for, but the rest of the world seemed all too eager to discuss.

"That is for kings to know." He shook his head. "Not me."

"Why not?"

He laughed, a deep baritone that vibrated through her chest, catching her off guard. "You ask a lot of questions. You always seem so quiet. I didn't realize what I was in for."

Jinji bit down on her cheeks to keep from smiling and to keep the blood from rushing to her cheeks. "So much of this world is new to me."

"And I thought your friend put you up to it. He is also a man with a lot of questions. Too many."

At his mention, Rhen popped into Jinji's peripheral vision, his eyes boring into the side of her head. She felt them there, staring at her. A tingle spread down her neck, stretching across her back and to her fingertips, an awareness. She shifted slightly, so his body was no longer in view, but that did nothing to calm the nerves cascading down her limbs.

Had time run out?

She coughed and swallowed, gripping the banister tightly, trying to focus on the islands still coming into view. A second had poked through the horizon, to the left of the first, close behind it.

A thought popped into her head as she silently stared ahead. Maybe she asked so many questions to avoid giving many answers. Maybe she could use that against Rhen.

Maybe.

Her gaze flicked to the Ourthuri, his deep brown eyes were studying her, trying to read her reaction. They were almost black, she realized, but there was no sign of the shadow there.

"You do not seem happy to be going home," she said quietly. A crease surfaced in his olive skin, just above his brow. He released a long breath, looking through Jinji and not at her.

"I have no home."

A feeling she knew well. But surely the Ourthuri were still alive, unlike her people. She couldn't help but wonder what could be so bad that this man was an outcast to his family, his land? But she held her tongue. There was a haunt hovering over him that she did not want to awaken.

"So what will you do?" What did other people who had no home do? Did they travel the world looking for answers that might never come? Or was that just her?

"I will die," he said simply, matter-of-factly, as if there were no other outcome. His eyes sharpened, retreating from his glassy vision, returning from his memories. "It is not as frightening once you've accepted it," he added quietly, voice wavering.

Before she could ask the question burning her lips, he nodded his head, a quiet goodbye. And then he was gone, walking away and back to the group of three men who also looked out of place on this ship.

Who is going to kill you?

She wanted to ask it, almost spoke it loudly into the wind to make him turn around. Somehow, it felt important to get the answer, to push for one.

Jinji lifted her foot and prepared to go after him when a hand clamped over hers, trapping her fingers against the ship.

"Nice chat?"

Rhen.

And he felt like fire. His skin burned, flames against her palm, as though the spirits had awakened upon contact.

Jinji yelped, pulled back, but Rhen would not release his grip.

"I think you've been avoiding me Jin, and I would like to know why."

She met his eyes briefly and they flashed blue. A ghost passed over his face, momentarily changing it, lifting his cheekbones, darkening his skin, brightening his eyes to the color of the ocean instead of the grass.

Jinji blinked.

The mirage was gone. But she couldn't get it out of her head.

Somehow, she recognized the face—a face she was certain she had never seen before. But deep down beneath her memories, a primal instinct flinched with awareness.

Fire spirits brightened her vision, circling his features, surging down Rhen's body. Her fingers tingled, begging her to craft the illusion of the face again, to study it, to remember it.

Jinji shook her head, pushing the spirits out. They clung to her eyes, refusing to disappear, sparking her fingers until they stung.

All Jinji could think to do was shut her eyes tight, cramming her lids into her cheeks, blacking out the world, breathing, until she felt Rhen's fingers release her hand, felt the fire in his touch evaporate.

She opened.

Everything was normal.

Except Rhen.

His curiosity had been piqued even more. Eyes narrowed, lips pursed, he studied her, tried to read her.

"Jin?" He asked slowly.

"Yes?" She responded, pretending ignorance.

"I think you know."

"I'm not feeling well," she said, and looked back out over the rail, leaning her hands against the wood for the strength to hold herself upright. A quake rumbled her insides.

"Really?"

She nodded, actually feeling her face turn green. Something in their touch had affected her, had rolled her stomach into knots, had made her body turn against itself.

"Will you still not tell me about the fight?" He asked, leaning in, lowering his voice. "I know you did something, Jin, I told you before. Whatever it is, you can trust me."

Jinji just shook her head, feeling bile rise in her throat.

"I cannot help you unless you tell me the truth. You might be surprised at how I react. At the," he paused, sighing and running a hand through his hair, "at the assistance I can provide."

Jinji opened her mouth to reply, but instead of words, vomit spewed from her lips. She recoiled, dropping her head over the side of the ship, coughing as the shakes wracked her body. Her stomach rolled, forcing everything out, until only vile air remained, and still she dry heaved, sapping the energy from her now aching limbs.

He put a hand on her back, trying to soothe her until it was done.

But her vision had gone blurry. When she looked at Rhen for help, all she saw were flames, rising from his body, smoking into the wind, flaring in her eyes.

Jinji dropped to the ground.

"Captain!" She heard Rhen shout, but already her vision was going spotty.

"The sea has finally claimed its victim," a voice said. Blue splashed in her vision as an old, gray faced leaned over her. "It was only a matter of time, Whylrhen, until the sickness came on. No one survives his first trip without being tested at least once, not on the open ocean."

"So it's just sea sickness?"

"A bad case, but yes."

"What can we do?"

"He'll be fine by the time we reach port. And you and I must talk before then. Geoff! Take the lad below decks."

The voices deepened, words catching each other, stringing together until one was no different from the other, and it all blurred into the sound of her own moaning.

Someone picked her up, but she did not feel it.

No, she was floating, apart, drifting through time.

Pictures began to dance in her vision.

Strange images, shadows flying, dancing. Spirits chasing after them.

The caress of a hand across her stomach, up her arm, down the back of her spine. Chills. Pressure on her lips. Pleasure.

And then pain, a knife stabbing her back, crying out. Dropping to the ground, helpless, knowing death was near, knowing she could not stop it.

A room. Large white columns, arching into a vaulted ceiling, rock. Other people. No faces, no names. Children, men, women. All looking at her. All falling before her. Red spilling out onto the floor.

Holding a hand, squeezing it, praying, knowing her other half was slipping away, was leaving her, was gone.

And then flying, soaring over land and sea. Wind whipping her scaled body, large yet graceful, different yet familiar. Wings fanned out on either side catching the breeze, drifting higher, sinking lower, floating over rock and river. Free.

Jinji rolled in her sleep. Her eyes flicked back and forth beneath closed lids as she moaned and thrashed. She pushed sheets onto the floor only to reach down and wrap them around her body once more.

A fight had risen within her; some foreign body had awoken and was trying to take over. All she could do was resist.

Resist and hope it would end soon.

10

RHEN

~DA'ASTIKU~

They had arrived.

Da'astiku. The capital city of the Kingdom of Ourthuro. Home to the king's palace.

"Raise the royal flag," Rhen told Captain Pygott. They had been waiting for the perfect time to call out his princely presence, and this was it.

Looking ahead, the ship was just close enough for Rhen to make out the great pulleys of Da'astiku, the Mountain City. Unlike the cities of Whylkin—flat on the plains, settled beside a bay, or nestled in a river bend—Ourthuro cities were built on the top of island mountains, none more so than this one.

Rising above, gleaming like the sun itself, was the golden palace, visible from all parts of the city as it sat on the highest mountain peak in the center of everything. From that level, metal bridges connected mountaintop to mountaintop, cascading down the side of the cliffs from plateau to plateau. The homes shrunk in size and fine materials the lower you went. The Ourthuri were a people of metals—gold for the king, silver roofs for the highest classes, and nothing but dull iron for those in the lowest. Everything about their society denoted class—the lower on the mountain, the cruder the metal, the simpler the tattoo.

All the way at the base of the city were the docks, holding ships of every shape and size. And rising from the floating docks were the giant pulleys. Huge platforms that hung from metal chains, lifting to bring supplies from the ships to the different layers of the cityscape. They were operated from large wheels beside the palace manned by the unmarked, who strained themselves almost to death, pulling and pulling all day long in an endless cycle—their punishment.

It was no wonder, Rhen sighed, that no king in the history of Whylkin had been able to win a battle against this city. Even Whyl the Conqueror had been stopped, his last attempt at expanding his empire.

"Still a sight to behold," Captain Pygott said beside him. Rhen just nodded. He had been here before, but still his throat was trapped in awe. "Poor Jin, too sick to see it. The boy is missing the best part of the journey."

Poor Jin was right. Rhen had returned to his cabin late last night, too dark to make out the boy's features, but the sound of painful gasps had made him wince. Still this morning, when Rhen had briefly glanced over before getting dressed, the boy was curled in the hammock—hands covering his face, knees balled right up to his chin. So small Rhen could barely make him out in the dull morning light. But the groans had stopped. Perhaps that was something.

"Surely he'll wake today," Rhen said, "at least in time to catch a quick sight before we leave for Rayfort."

"Ay, I hope so." The captain paused, rubbing gloved hands together. "Have you thought on what I advised last night?"

Rhen nodded. "I know what you're saying, but I must go alone. Nothing can be perceived as a threat, not so close to their home territory. If what I suspect is true, even arriving unannounced will make King Razzaq wary. I am going on behalf of my father to return the four men we found on an abandoned ship floating in the middle of the sea, nothing more."

"Will he kill them?"

"The prisoners?" The captain nodded. "King Razzaq is a notoriously harsh man." Rhen looked to the side where the four Ourthuri sat, hands chained behind their backs and ankles locked to one another to keep them from running once the boat docked. Their faces were stoic, unreadable and hard like their mountain homes. Storm clouds brewed in all eight eyes. "But I hope we have not brought them to their deathbeds."

"And you will not stay the night?"

"No." Rhen shook his head once. "I will use the news of my nephew's birth as an escape if I must. I will engage in conversation, stay for the meal he will offer, and try to uncover as much as I can from the sights around me. But too much foul play happens under the cover of darkness, I won't risk it."

"That is something at least." Pygott sighed, worry weighing his bones down into a slouch that wasn't normally there.

Rhen slapped his back.

"Getting soft old man?" A teasing glint lit his eyes. A grin picked up the left corner of his lip.

Captain Pygott raised his brows, blue irises going crystal clear. "Still young enough to whip you into shape."

"A futile effort I'm sure."

"That's what they tell me." He shrugged, lips fighting to keep from laughing. "In serious though, the queen will kill me if you leave an Ourthuri bastard behind. Bad enough I'm assisting another reckless adventure. Try to keep on the mission, for my head?"

Rhen cracked, breaking his calm composure. A second later, the captain did too.

A horn sounded across the water, announcing their arrival at the port. Both Rhen and Captain Pygott turned. Somehow, the city had snuck up while they weren't looking, towering over their heads, sparkling to an almost blinding degree.

"Better change your clothes, Whylrhen, it's time to become a prince once more. There are royal silks in my chamber left over from our last journey."

Rhen looked down at his chest, bare, as he liked to be on a ship, so the sun sank right into his skin, searing him like fire. It was the only way he felt connected to the flames, the only way that wasn't in the least magical or noticeable.

Sighing, he nodded and made his way below decks. Steering clear of his room, trying to give Jin the peace he needed, Rhen walked to the captain's rooms, pulling open the closet until he saw the bright red silks of Whylkin. Throwing a white undershirt over his head, he shrugged into the royal jacket, embroidered with diamonds and secured with pearl buttons. He found a pair of thick black leather breeches, dyed from the best hides in the kingdom. Next came his boots, tall to his knees and lined with secret pockets for the few small daggers he would bring as a precaution. Belting his scabbard around his waist, Rhen secured his golden sword. This palace was the only place in the world where it would be unimpressive, but still, Rhen felt more secure with his weapon at his hip, especially without Ember by his side.

Taking a deep breath, Rhen prepared himself.

He had never been alone with King Razzaq. And it was still not the safest plan to venture into the Mountain City without guards at his side, but the sailors on this ship were not guards. It would be more suspicious to bring them, more alarming, more aggressive.

Rhen thought of Awenine, his brother Whyltarin, and their newborn baby boy. The future of his kingdom. Was the baby's hair shocking red like his father's? Or brown like his uncle's? Amber eyes like his grandfather or emerald like the queen's?

Would he act like Whyllysle did as a newborn? Chubby and full of laughter? Never silent and commanding the attention of an entire room? Would he grow to a toddler who ran around the castle playing with wooden swords and talking of legendary battles?

No matter what, Rhen's nephew would not share the same fate as his younger brother. Rhen had come so far to keep that child safe, to keep his family safe, and though the path was uncertain, he could not stop now. Not when answers might be within reach.

Besides, attacking a Son of Whyl would be seen as an act of outright war. Surely, King Razzaq would not take it to that point, not after being so careful to keep his tracks hidden thus far.

The ship shuddered, wood screeching in protest.

The anchor dropped.

The ship was docked.

Rhen cracked his knuckles, balling his hands into fists, squeezing tightly, getting all of the anxiety out of his muscles, before relaxing and straightening his spine.

It was time.

He emerged to the craze of the docks—men shouting, ropes whipping, carts rolling, goods shifting from platform to platform. Almost like Roninhythe, but this dock was made of metal, not wood. And its people spoke a guttural language mostly foreign to Rhen's ears.

As he expected, farther down the metal walkway a servant in the bright gold robes of Ourthuro was sprinting toward the ship, jingling as his metal jewels clanked together. Rhen moved beside

Captain Pygott, waiting for the man to scurry within hearing distance as the crew lowered a bridge to the dock.

"Son of Whyl," the man bowed as he reached the edge of their bridge. His clothes were long and free flowing, a slight band of gold secured around his waist, suggesting armor but more decorative. His wrists bore three straight black tattoos surrounded by delicate swirling patterns that wove a few inches above his wrist, denoting his membership to the palace house. Silver and gold dripped from his ears, circled his neck, and even jingled around his ankles. Definitely a messenger—a show of the king's power. "Our king bids you welcome to his city."

"On behalf of the Kingdom of Whylkin, I, Prince Whylrhen, Son of Whylfrick, thank your king for his kindness." Rhen put his hand over his heart, nodding his head in greeting. "I hope our unexpected arrival has not caused any trouble, for King Razzaq is nothing but a friend to my house and my people."

Beside him, Captain Pygott released a light breath, holding in laughter for only Rhen to hear.

"Dear Prince Whylrhen, quite the opposite. My king bade me bring our finest carriage to carry you to the palace. He is most glad to see you and wishes to hear of your father, King Whylfrick." He spread his arm wide, indicating an enclosed gilded box near the end of the dock.

"I send my thanks to your king for his overwhelming kindness and will gladly visit with him. I must also request that my four guests gain passage with me." Rhen turned behind him, motioning for the four Ourthuri on the ship to step forward. Clinking from the chains, they moved to the rail. The servant gasped, eyes widening, before recovering his stoic pose.

"Of course. A guest of Whylkin is a guest of Ourthuro." He licked his lips, fingers twitching, before adding, "Please, follow me."

Rhen turned, picking up the end of the chain to lead the prisoners with him. Before stepping onto the bridge, he looked at the captain, whose blue eyes were dark with worry.

"If I have not returned by nightfall, you will know my plan has gone awry. If that happens, you must notify the king immediately—of everything we have found." He reached with his free hand, gripping the older man's shoulder. "Can you do this for me?"

"Of course, my prince." The captain nodded, clasping Rhen's arm quickly. "Of course."

Rhen nodded, squeezed his fingers in farewell, and stepped onto the ridged incline, bringing both him and the prisoners securely onto Ourthuri territory.

A few more steps and he was in the carriage. The prisoners were chained to the back, to be pulled like cattle behind him. Rhen didn't like it, but he was in no place to demand a change. This was not his kingdom—these were no longer his rules.

The servant sat beside the driver, leaving Rhen alone. The carriage rocked back and forth as the horses began the long journey up the steep incline of the Mountain City, and even the plush cushion beneath his bum was not enough to provide comfort.

Rhen pushed the curtain to the side, opening the view by a few inches—just enough to gaze out at a city still as foreign to him as its people.

The commoners stopped as he rolled by, careful not to move, not to breathe, and especially not to dare look into the window. Their clothes were loose, without shape, aside from the occasional metal belt around the waist. Homes were rectangular—small boxes piled atop one another. The bridges were firm. Even as Rhen looked below at the far fall down steep cliffs, he was not worried—the Ourthuri were known for their craftsmanship, for their unbelievable skill, which unfortunately put the blacksmiths of Whylkin to shame.

No, the more Rhen watched, the more he marveled at the sight.

As they continued to climb, houses gained more shape. Copper window frames, dome-like silver roofs. But no glass, he realized. All of the houses were open, welcoming in the wind, blocking it only with thin gauzy curtains that seemed more for privacy than anything else.

Jewelry clanked around people's ankles, their necks, draped from their earlobes—both sexes alike. As they entered the silver district, headdresses of woven metal dripped down women's foreheads, covering their faces like veils. The one consistency, whether rich or poor, was the open sleeves. Every person was bare from shoulder to fingertip, his or her tattoo the only decoration of need. And the higher Rhen climbed, the more intricate, deluxe, and lengthy those tattoos became.

Suddenly, gold surged into Rhen's view, tickling his irises from the brightness. After a moment, he realized they had crossed a golden bridge, carrying them higher into the topmost platform of the city—the palace.

As they rolled through a towering golden archway, the spindles of the great pulleys took up Rhen's entire view. Giant golden wheels stretching at least one hundred feet across were circling slowly. The steps of a thousand men stomping in unison thundered in Rhen's ears, deafening in their roar as the unmarked moved to bring the platforms higher and higher up, pushing golden spires in circles all day and night.

This was King Razzaq's show of power. His mode of intimidation.

And damn it if Rhen couldn't hold back a gulp, his throat suddenly dry and his palms increasingly sweaty.

At a time like this, it was hard to believe that his people outnumbered the Ourthuri ten to one. That his army was greater, his ships stronger, his land heartier.

The carriage stopped.

The servant scurried down from beside the driver to open the door, and Rhen emerged into the bright sun of the palace courtyard, fighting the urge to put a hand over his eyes.

The scene did not disappoint. Brilliant golden spires, domes, and pillars sunk in and out of the earth to create the palace. It was not as tall as the castle at Rayfort, built from gleaming white stone slabs, but it was just as grand. Stretching wider and longer, far more open in its corridors, as though the king had nothing to fear, was not worried about protection.

There were no walls. No slits for arrows. No fortified enclosures.

This was a king secure in his power.

And Rhen wished for nothing more than to run through the front corridor and plunge his golden sword right through King Razzaq's chest—just to prove him wrong—but he held steady, muscles hard as the rock beneath his feet.

Wordlessly, Rhen followed the servant, regaining his hold on the prisoners as they walked across the courtyard, through several rows of thick columns and into a grand atrium.

Not one door, Rhen shook his head, amazed at the hubris on display here.

Halfway through the giant room, the servant fell to his knees, arms plastered flat against the floor. Behind him, Rhen felt his prisoners struggle to do the same.

For his part, Rhen inclined his head in greeting at the man sitting yards away in his golden throne. A headdress almost as large as King Razzaq's face sat atop his brow, dripping in jewels and golden chain links. But more than anything, Rhen took in the black tattoos curving and swirling all the way up his arms, ringing the base of his wrists up through his shoulders. Floral designs, island mountains, faces, animals, stones—everything Rhen could imagine was painted with intricate detail on the king's arms. A permanent display of his place above his people.

To each side, a series of guards stood, arms decorated with varying levels of lines and dots. Over their flowing robes were metal plates of armor. In each hand, a metal weapon.

Rhen looked at the iron chain in his hand, feeling how out of place it was. Even chains were made of gold here.

"Prince Whylrhen, welcome to Da'astiku. What brings you to Ourthuro?"

Rhen tugged the men behind him forward, watching the king's reaction. His black-brown eyes remained impassive. His larger build didn't jerk or bend. His darkened olive skin didn't pale.

Someone must have sent word, Rhen concluded, but no matter. He would press forward.

"King Razzaq," he inclined his head, "My king thanks you for your kindness in welcoming his son to your grand home. I am overwhelmed by the bountiful city I have seen thus far. A true masterpiece."

"We thank you," the king nodded ever so slightly, the muscles on his thick neck coiling.

"I have traveled far to return these four men to your person. We found a ship floating aimlessly through our waters, adorned with the flag of your great kingdom, and took it upon ourselves to search for survivors. Locked below deck, we found these four men alone in the dark. In a show of no bad will between our two kingdoms, peaceful now for over a hundred years, I, a Son of Whyl, came to deliver them unharmed."

"Step forward," the king commanded, eyes narrowing on the four men. His pupils shifted to their wrists, checking each for a station, pausing on the unmarked man the longest.

Raising his hand, the king flicked two fingers toward the group.

Before Rhen could move, four spears soared through the air, followed by the thud of four bodies falling to the ground.

He gasped, fighting the jerk of his limbs, trying not to show any weakness.

It didn't matter.

A cry echoed through the hall, piercing his ears, surprising everyone—everyone aside from the unaffected King Razzaq. Even the guards jumped slightly.

Rhen furrowed his brows, searching for the source of the noise through the walls of thick columns, but there were too many places for someone to hide.

Blood pooled by his feet, brilliant red and glistening from the reflections of the sun. Unable to stop himself, Rhen looked down, into the eyes of the unmarked man. They held no shock. No surprise. Almost as if he knew this would be his fate.

But why not mention it? Why not fight to survive?

Rhen's gaze returned to the king, who studied him with a slight smile on his lips. What did the man know? What plan was circling in that calculated gaze?

"We thank you, Son of Whyl, for returning these men, but as you can see it was unnecessary. Traitors have no place in Da'astiku."

"Had I known their fate, I would not have dishonored this palace with their presence."

King Razzaq waved his hand aimlessly through the air, shaking his head. "It is no matter." He paused, leaning forward ever so slightly. "Tell me, Prince Whylrhen, how is your king? We hear Whylkin has a new son to welcome."

"The kingdom rejoices, and with it, its king." Rhen held his hands behind his back, widening his stance and gaining a more relaxed pose despite the tightness in his lungs. The air felt heavy, electric somehow. His eyes flicked around, looking at the spaces between the columns, trying to find a stone out of place. But each curve blended into the next, deeper and deeper, until his mind hurt from the illusion.

Something within Rhen did not feel right.

An unease burrowed between his shoulders, coiling into a painful knot.

"Our own son is not old enough to birth children, but we can only imagine the joy of solidifying the future of the kingdom with another strong heir. We are surprised you were able to leave such celebrations. Did you not miss it?"

"King Razzaq," Rhen said, forcing his voice to carry louder as his nerves grew. Why had he come alone? He was a prince, not a spy. A prince, no matter what he wanted. That position demanded protection. "You have touched my heart with your concern. I did in fact miss it, but I did what any good son would and followed my father's commands. The prisoners were delivered unharmed." Rhen looked at the blood seeping under his shoe, his chest burning with injustice. "And now I must bid farewell and return to my kingdom."

"Will you not stay for one meal? Surely the longs days of travel were tiresome."

Rhen raked the room with his eyes, noticing that a few more guards had moved around the columns, holding their curved swords before their faces, alert.

His own fingers itched for the smooth hilt of his weapon.

"I am afraid, great King, that I cannot."

Rhen swallowed his spit, wetting his scratchy throat. Steps drummed in his ear, loud in the silence of the hall. A guard walked past him, bowing on bended knee at the base of the throne before handing the king a golden box.

Rhen stepped back, creating red footprints on the tiles below his feet.

Something was very wrong here.

"We are very surprised by your urgency, dear Prince."

"My captain waits for me."

He took another step back, making no pretense to hide the hand reaching for his sword.

The king smiled wider, fully opening the golden box in his lap. His arm muscles flexed, rippling along his tattoo, as he clutched at an item out of Rhen's view.

Slowly, he lifted.

White strings circled his fingers.

White curls.

Moving quickly, King Razzaq jerked. His arm pulsed fully aloft, throwing the object at Rhen.

It rolled, over and over, with a red river flowing in its wake.

Only when it stopped at his feet, did Rhen see the blue eyes looking up at him—the eyes of the father he always wished he had.

"Your captain waits for nothing."

The words like knives pierced Rhen, sinking under his skin and cutting him apart. His hands shook. His eyes widened, water pooling at their bases. But his pupils were like iron, nailing King Razzaq to his throne.

In one swift movement, Rhen pulled his sword from its scabbard, charging. A furious yell spilled from his lips, echoing through the hall, bouncing from column to column with no wall to stop it.

He bounded the steps, eyes on the throat of his enemy—a throat gyrating from laughter. A throat that would look much better cut in half.

Hands gripped his ankles, and Rhen fell, forehead slamming against the step in front of him. Drops of blood slipped from his brow, blocking his vision. Black dots invaded his sight.

But it would not stop him.

Swinging blindly, his sword dug into something. A cry hit his ear. Rhen rolled to the side, narrowly missing the blade that clanged to the ground next to him. Wiping the blood from his eyes, he kicked out, slamming his foot into a guard. His sword followed, partially severing the man's arm.

Rhen jumped to his feet.

There were too many of them. Everywhere Rhen looked, gold plated men were running toward him, eyeing him, pausing just out of reach.

Circling.

Like an animal, Rhen was trapped.

"My father will destroy you," Rhen seethed, sword still held up for protection.

"We don't believe so," King Razzaq chuckled. Then deeper, "Disarm him."

As one, the ten men surrounding Rhen jumped forward, careful not to scrape his body. Five swords crashed down on his blade. Rhen lost his grip, letting his weapon clang uselessly against the floor. It reverberated throughout the atrium in an echo that faded along with Rhen's hopes. Along with his dreams. Until his heart felt empty.

There was no fight left.

A boot shoved into his back. Hands gripped his arms, pushing him to the ground, securing him.

Rhen couldn't move. He could hardly breathe against the pain searing his joints as the guards continued tugging his limbs. Try as he might to squirm away, there was no freedom.

A hand gripped his hair, forcing his face up, forcing his eyes to the king, who dismounted the throne and stepped down off his dais.

Leaning in close, so that Rhen could smell the fish on his breath, King Razzaq whispered, "See, dear boy, unlike your father, I have friends outside of my palace—friends who informed me that the youngest Son of Whyl had run away from the castle again, without a word to anyone. Your father has no idea where you are. But I know just what you've been up to."

"Your friends have been misinformed," Rhen spat, louder so the guards could hear. Sweat dripped from his lip as his body strained. "Before I set sail, I left a note for my father, sealed with my personal royal emblem. My king knows exactly where I am."

King Razzaq stood, eyes widening slightly as he clasped his hands behind his back, trying to read Rhen's expression.

Time to push it further, praying Cal had indeed sent the note.

"If I am not home for the Naming, my father will know exactly what happened to me. And he will come. No amount of gold in the world would stop him."

The king's eyes narrowed. After a moment, he flicked his gaze to one of the guards behind Rhen and nodded to the right.

Louder, so the room could hear, King Razzaq pronounced Rhen's fate. "You will die, Prince Whylrhen, just like the others you came with. And I will return your lifeless, drowned body to the king myself—a sign of no bad will between two peaceful kingdoms, of course."

He winked.

Something heavy slammed into the base of Rhen's skull. Pain exploded down his neck, his head whipped forward, and all breath was stolen from his body.

He could not move.

His limbs would not respond as throbbing prickles continued to stupefy his nerves. Useless.

The hands gripping his arms tightened, walked forward slowly, and dragged him behind.

And all Rhen could think was, *Just like the others.*

Captain Pygott was dead. The ship was compromised. The crew…

Jin.

Poor boy, forced to live just to die.

Black spots closed in on Rhen, color drained from his eyes, and the world melted away until everything was gone.

Everything except the pounding of his heart.

Captain, Jin, I'm sorry.

And then all thought ceased to exist.

11

JINJI
~DA'ASTIKU~

Consciousness came slowly.

In her head, Jinji was still flying, still soaring over trees and grass. Images flashed behind her pupils. Memories flickering and fading. Faces. Words. Places she wasn't sure she wanted to remember or forget.

Her eyes slid open, then shut tight against the sun.

But one flash was enough.

Her mind opened, and everything she had seen for the past few hours tumbled back down into the unknown, cascading out of her thoughts, locked away once more.

In their place, a daze.

Total confusion.

Where am I? What happened?

Jinji sat up, hand holding her aching head as her stomach growled for attention. Her vision gradually came into focus.

A bed. Wooden slabs. A small circular window. Maps. A hammock below her. Blankets around her.

The ship. Rhen's ship.

How much time had passed, she wondered, looking around the room for some sign. She remembered talking with the Ourthuri, remembered touching Rhen's hand—she could still feel the fire that had burst under her skin, awakening the spirits.

But everything else had vanished.

The door behind her slammed open, jolting her muscles to life.

Jinji's mind pricked at the sound of heavy breathing. The echo of clashing swords rang in her ears. The thud of boots was suddenly louder than it had been a moment ago.

"Jin, you must run." Someone panted.

She spun.

Captain Pygott stood with blood falling down his cheek—his blue eyes glowing from pain and fear. Jinji knew whom the fear was for.

They must have arrived at the Ourthuri city. Rhen must have gone to the king.

The captain gasped, stepping forward, and held her chin in a viselike grip.

"Who are you?" He questioned.

Instantly Jinji understood. She felt for the spirits, felt for their now familiar presence around her face, but nothing was there.

The illusion had fallen.

She was a girl once more.

"I…" She opened, but no words came out. "This is my true face." She said simply. What else could she say?

"A woman?" He stepped back, mouth hanging agape.

Quickly, Jinji called to the spirits, wrapping the knots around her features once more, hiding herself back behind the mask of her long gone brother's face.

"Just as easily a boy," she said quietly.

Shouts reverberated down the steps. More voices seeped below decks.

Captain Pygott shook his head. "There is no time. You must run, Jin. Rhen is inside the city, in the golden palace, you must find him and you must save him. Before any of the Ourthuri knows you are here."

"But how? What happened?"

The captain put a finger over her lips, nodding slightly, sadly. A crash sounded above him, the crack of wood splintering.

"They are about to find us, you must go before they do. I don't know what happened, why the Ourthuri are attacking, but I know the prince is in danger. Please, on my life, you must help him."

Jinji bit her lips, eyes narrowing to hold in the water about to leak. She nodded, subtle but enough. Yes, she would try her best to save Rhen, to save her friend. She owed him that much for everything he had done for her.

Captain Pygott reached behind him, closing the wooden door at his back, latching it shut.

"It won't hold for long. To the window."

They moved as one, opening the thick glass until the wind whipped Jinji's short hairs. She stuck her head out, noting the ocean a long way below her body.

She would have to jump.

Panic stabbed her heart. Her fingers twitched.

The captain reached out, holding them.

"Can I see your face one more time?" He asked, softly. She could not deny the plea of a dying man. For she knew in her heart that this was his last stand, his goodbye to the world.

Pulling the spirit threads, Jinji let the illusion fall. His eyes widened once more, running over the contours of her cheeks, her plump lips, her curvier nose, her feline eyes.

Reaching up, he cupped her cheek, sighing.

"What a story this will make," he said.

Then *boom*.

Something heavy thudded into the doors behind them. The wood splintered but did not break.

No need for words, the captain cupped his hands. Jinji stepped into his palms, taking once last look into his deep blue eyes—swirling with the stories he would never get the chance to tell.

Another *boom*.

And Jinji was gone. Captain Pygott stood, thrusting her body through the window, and Jinji flew, just like in her dreams, until she hit the water with a smack that stung her skin.

A scream caught in her throat, stifled by the sea.

A prick stabbed her heart, and she knew he was gone.

But there was a chance Rhen still lived.

Pushing her feet, Jinji broke to the surface, taking a deep gulp of air before melting back into the waves.

Hiding.

Looking for a place to run.

A dark shadow caught her eye through the blue—immobile—and she swam, praying for the cover of wood. Another ship or the dock, anything to keep her out of sight from the attacking Ourthuri above her.

Breaking the surface of the water, Jinji looked up into rows and rows of metal slabs. She was under the dock, the waves rocking her. She dipped under the water again. It was calmer. Safer.

Her eyes stung from the salt, but she forced them open, following the shadow of the dock until the ground closed in on her and rocks filled her vision. Every time she tried to surface, a new wave rolled in, pulling her to the side and underwater. Finally, feeling the strength in her limbs start to fade, Jinji swam to one of the columns and hugged her body close to it, inching higher and higher until her grip was strong enough to fight the waves.

Above the roar of the ocean, she made out voices, but they were foreign words that meant nothing to her. Through the slits in the dock, she saw boots moving this way and that way, coming from nowhere and disappearing just as quickly.

How would she get away unnoticed? Surely, even in a scene as crazy as this, the men who invaded the ship would be wary of a stranger emerging from the ocean.

And then, farther to the side, Jinji saw a sight that made her eyes bulge from her head, practically popping free of her skull. The ground, as if by magic, lifted from the sea, swinging and swaying, rising higher and higher into the air. The movement was slow, methodological. Chains, she suddenly realized, spotting the coils attached to the four corners of the platform. Chains were lifting the land.

Hidden by the dock, the platform lifted out of view, but it didn't matter. Behind it, Jinji saw another mound of boxes piled high. It was another platform, waiting to fly.

Suddenly, she had a plan.

Crazy? Yes.

But also her only hope.

Jinji dove back under the water, pulling the elements around her body so it looked blue, just like the ocean. She was a ghost under the surface of the sea, an invisible outline that only the spirits could spot.

And she swam.

And swam.

Pumping her legs, pushing her arms to the side, repeating the motion and fighting the current. Every so often, she popped her head above the water for a mere moment, locating the boxes and moving forward again.

When she was close, Jinji stopped and surveyed the scene. No one had spotted her, hidden as she was in her illusion. Men took turns holding one box, passing it on, placing it on the platform. A long line of constantly moving parts, until one leader positioned at the very front of the platform shouted something. He wore different clothes—a long cloth draped from his shoulders to the floor, the color of the glowing moon.

Jinji didn't understand what he said, but all of the other men stopped and stepped backward. The leader was lifting a large red flag above his head, looking up, and she realized it was a signal.

Pushing forward, Jinji swam around to the back of the platform and placed her palms on the cold metal. No one on land could see her. Looking behind, she realized she was in full view of some ships.

But there was no other option.

Heaving herself out of the water, Jinji landed with a thud on the platform. In one swift move, she was on her side, curled into a ball with the illusion of a box woven around her, hiding the fact that she was human to any wandering eye.

She waited, breathing heavily.

One.

Two.

Three.

No alarm sounded.

Instead, the earth below her shifted, and suddenly she was flying.

The ground below her swayed, pushed and pulled by the wind, but she felt more and more secure the higher she climbed, knowing every inch brought her closer to Rhen and farther from the soldiers below.

Keeping her eyes closed, Jinji practiced breathing, praying to the spirits to keep her safe, to help her find Rhen, to get them both out of there alive. Somehow, she knew she could do it. The spirits would not abandon her, not after pushing her so far into the unknown. It was just another test. Another stop on her journey.

The platform screeched to a stop.

Metal clashed against metal.

Jinji opened her eyes, finding that the sun had disappeared and her nose rested inches from a solid wall.

Her muscles tensed, alert. Feet thudded behind her, and she heard voices. Somehow, during the climb, she had neglected to realize that getting onto the platform was only half the battle.

Getting off unseen would be impossible.

Getting off unnoticed, unsuspected, might be just within limits.

Thinking quickly, she pictured the only Ourthuri man she had ever really come into contact with—the man on the ship, with burns along his wrists and a haunt to his eyes. She pictured his face, his tall lean build, his olive complexion. Dancing with her, the spirits coiled together, binding to her skin.

The men at the docks who had been piling boxes onto the platform had been like him, unmarked and burned. She prayed that those tasked with removing the items would be the same.

Copying their garb, Jinji pictured Mikzahooq, the Ourthuri who had been so kind to her, and silently thanked him for letting her borrow his face.

Opening her eyes, Jinji brought her hand before her, sighing with relief at the sight of callused fingers. The skin around her wrists bubbled an ugly red, mixed with flecks of black ink that could not be completely washed away. Letting her eyes travel farther down, Jinji saw her chest was bare with hard and flat muscles. Cloth was tied around her waist, and she didn't care to look any farther.

Taking a deep breath, Jinji crouched on all fours before gripping one of the boxes closest to her and standing fully erect.

It took a moment for her eyes to adjust, and when they did, she fought to hide a smile.

Her gamble had worked.

Men circled the platform, dressed like her and unmarked like she currently was. Their eyes carried the same haunted glaze that Mikzahooq's had. They didn't make eye contact with each other or with anything, like their souls had been erased along with their tattoos.

Gripping the box tightly, Jinji tried to blank her stare as she followed another man off the platform and into an open room. Guards dressed in flowing golden robes held swords before their eyes, but none of them looked twice at her. So Jinji continued following the line of unmarked men as they silently trekked across the room and into a sunlit corridor.

She couldn't help but peek from underneath hooded brows at the shimmering gold all around her.

It must be the palace. No other place could be so grand and so commanding.

Her blood began to buzz with energy, sizzling into her limbs.

Rhen was close. She could feel it.

But Jinji had no idea where to go. Columns lined her vision, opening into different rooms and different atriums, acting like walls. The unmarked in front of her continued stepping at an unchanging pace, weaving intentionally and with purpose through the maze before them.

Veering to the left, the men turned into a closed corridor with solid gold walls and openings that let the breeze fly in unchecked.

A hand gripped Jinji's arm, squeezing her skin tight, and yanked.

Dropping the box, Jinji tumbled sideways, pulled by an unseen force. She pressed her lips to keep from shouting, wincing as the boom of the box echoed down the long hall.

Pushed by invisible arms, Jinji crashed into a wall.

A soft thud sounded behind her.

Spinning, Jinji caught the sight of a door slamming closed—it was the first door she had seen in this city. As it sealed shut, it melded into the wall, almost indiscernible, and Jinji was left in a small boxy room with no way out.

A body slammed into her, knocking her tight against the wall as the cool steel of a knife settled against her throat.

It was a woman.

Her face was hidden underneath of veil of golden links, dangling from a delicate jeweled crown that rested on her head. But even through the small metal pieces, Jinji saw hardened wet eyes, read the anger and hurt pouring out from them.

And then something truly magical happened. The spirits awakened in Jinji's eyes, circling the woman before her in a shroud of blue so bright that it almost hurt. Water rippled along the girl's skin, clinging to the decorations on her tattooed arms, flowing down her long dress, and splashing around her face.

Jinji's heart stopped.

Aside from Rhen, she had never seen the spirits cling to a human before. And now it was happening again. But not with fire, with water. The girl was a walking ocean, her anger like waves crashing into Jinji's skin.

But instead of fear, Jinji felt comforted. The spirits had sent this woman to her. Somehow, she was meant to help.

The Ourthuri was speaking, shouting, pushing the knife deeper into Jinji's skin.

Slowly, with as much confidence as she could gather, Jinji said, "I do not understand."

The woman paused, tilted her head, and forced the knife closer as her gaze narrowed.

"You are not Ourthuri?" She asked, her voice deep and full of pain.

"No."

The knife pressed closer as the girl leaned in. Jinji didn't try to fight back.

"How do you wear that face?"

Jinji gasped. The girl recognized her, recognized the illusion—the man, Mikzahooq. Closing her eyes tight, she bit her lip, before breathing deeply.

Please, Jinji asked the spirits, *please let this work*.

The illusion fell away.

Jinji stood before her attacker unmasked.

The girl stepped back in shock, her mouth dropping along with the knife she held.

"I traveled with Prince Whylrhen," Jinji spoke quickly, "who came to the palace today to return four Ourthuri men that we found on a ship. One man, Mikzahooq, was very kind to me, and I borrowed the image of his body to sneak here to save the prince, who I believe your king is going to kill. I can sense the spirits around you. I can sense that you have magic too, and that it does not frighten you. I promise I did not come here with the intention to hurt anyone, only to save the prince who has become a dear friend to me."

While Jinji spoke, the girl lifted a hand to her mouth. Tears dropped below her veil, falling swiftly to the ground. She nodded slowly.

"He was kind? Mikza?" She asked, voice wavering and warming as she said the name. The man had meant something to her, Jinji realized. They had been close.

"Yes." Jinji nodded. "He told me about these islands, so foreign from my own home, and comforted me. We were trying to help him, to bring him back to his family, but…"

The girl took an unsteady breath. "But what?"

Jinji shrugged, not sure how much to say. "I do not believe he was very excited to return. I sensed that there was something here he missed, something that had been ripped from his side, leaving a gaping wound in his heart. But there was something he feared as well—or someone, maybe."

The girl's expression hardened. Her lips pushed into a flat line and her pupils dilated. She wiped the tears from her cheeks, standing straighter and squaring her shoulders.

"I know who he feared. It is the same man we all fear, but cannot escape."

"Who?"

The girl looked up, met Jinji's eyes.

"King Razzaq…my father," she said, ice cold, and picked her knife up off the ground. "I will help you save your prince, but only if you can promise me one thing."

"What?" Jinji asked, relaxing, letting a little ray of hope leak into her senses. Perhaps all wasn't lost. Had the spirits saved her once again?

"Protection," the girl said quietly, and lifted her hand to remove the crown covering her features. Her umber eyes were large, unusual, and beautiful against her pale, brown skin with the slightest leafy hue. Her lids were painted golden, but even that brightness couldn't hide the heartbreak shadowing her young face.

They were the same age. And Jinji felt an instant connection with this girl, another person not ready for the pain the world had thrown at her.

"I cannot stay here with that man anymore. No matter what it takes, I am finding a way out, and when I do, I will need protection and a safe place to live where he cannot touch me. If your prince can help hide me, then I will help save his life."

"My prince has a special liking for saving people," Jinji said, unable to cover the smile that spread across her face. "He will help you. I swear it."

"Then use your magic to change your clothes to match mine and follow me."

The girl spun without looking back and walked to the door, opening it and jumping into the hall.

Quickly, Jinji closed her eyes, picturing the spirits as they wove around her. In her mind, she imagined wearing a dress of golden silks that hung from one side, leaving her shoulders almost bare. She pictured black tattoos sprouting on her arms, the image of flowers and curving swirls. And finally, she saw a golden belt cinching her waist and a golden headdress cascading over her face.

When her eyes opened, Jinji instantly knew the spirits had listened as metal hung before her, partially blocking her vision.

Without wasting any more time, she followed the Ourthuri princess into the hall, praying that her instincts to trust this girl were right.

They moved swiftly through the palace. Jinji, always the shorter one, struggled to keep up until the princess stopped, throwing an arm to the side, and catching Jinji around the waist to keep her from moving.

She put a finger in front of her lips, signaling silence, and stepped slowly around two wide columns, until a giant pool of water came into view, a brilliant turquoise nestled in gold. At the far end, Jinji saw Rhen crumpled on the floor—unconscious and surrounded by men holding swords.

Her throat dried. She couldn't swallow. Couldn't breathe. Her chest contracted.

Then Rhen shifted, his arm twitched.

Jinji relaxed—he was alive. It was the only sign she needed to press forward. The princess tugged Jinji back until the two of them were hidden behind a wide column.

"They are going to drown him," the princess whispered, "to make it look like an accident, as though he died in a shipwreck."

"How can we save him?"

162

The princess smirked underneath her veil, raising one eyebrow. "I create a scene, something my king will love, and while I do, you grab the body. Can you only change your image or can you mask other things as well?"

Jinji paused. She had never talked so openly about her gift, her connection to the spirits. It felt odd. Yet at the same time liberating. "I can mask other things as well," she said, matching the princess's grin.

"Then do it, and meet me back here."

The princess stepped out from their hiding spot and walked confidently forward. Soon enough, Jinji heard raised voices, a commotion, and she stepped from the column. The guards were talking with the princess, looking away from her and away from Rhen.

Lifting her hands before her, Jinji prayed to the spirits. Her emotions warmed when the mother spirit, jinjiajanu, jumped into her vision, encircling her in what felt like a loving hug.

Instantly, the elements heeded her call, weaving together in an invisible wall along the edge of the pool, enveloping Rhen in the scene so he was on the side with Jinji, hidden from the rest of the world. Any guard that looked over would see Rhen immobile beside the pool—the scene would remain unchanged as long as they kept their distance. But in reality, Jinji had just crafted an illusion of the hall.

Holding her breath, she ran forward, not wasting time.

The illusion worked.

Not one of the guards sounded an alarm. No one saw her. No one realized she was currently cradling Rhen's head in her lap, brushing the hairs from his forehead, wincing at the cut that dug deep into his skin.

He didn't stir. But it was better that way.

He could never see her like this. Could never see her for what she truly was—a girl.

To Rhen, she would always be Jin. But staring at his closed eyes, Jinji couldn't help but wish for an instant that they would open and uncover her secret.

A shout sounded behind her.

Jinji's head whipped around.

More guards were coming. Whatever time she had was gone.

Standing, Jinji pulled on Rhen's hands, hoping she wasn't causing any more pain as she dragged his body across the cold, hard floor.

Her arms ached. Her shoulders felt as though they would detach from her body at any second. Every muscle burned, screaming at her in protest.

Rhen was heavy. Really, really heavy.

And all Jinji could do was keep pulling, hoping that they got out of sight in time.

12

RHEN
~DA'ASTIKU~

A goddess.

Every time Rhen closed his eyes, he saw her. A vision in gold. His head was nestled in her lap and she looked down over him, hidden behind a veil of shimmering metal, but there was affection in that gaze. Rhen could still feel her fingers brush over his cheeks, push his hair to the side, run over his lower lip. His skin tingled, alive at the touch.

In the dream, she leaned down, pressing a long, soft kiss to his lips.

Then his eyes opened and he was back here, shoved in a crate underneath some sort of moving contraption, unsure of where he was or who was holding him there.

But something was certain: King Razzaq had not killed him, despite the ringing pain in his head that said otherwise.

Rhen sighed, trying to shift his sore muscles, but his wide body was cramped in the small space. There was nothing to do but wait.

He closed his eyes again, welcoming the vision of the nameless woman. Who was she? Was she even real?

The bouncing stopped.

Rhen's eyes tore open, flicking through the darkness. He balled his hands into fists, trying to reach for his sword but he could not access his hip—he couldn't even tell if his weapon was still there.

Rhen took a deep breath, darting his vision in circles, waiting for the crack of daylight. His body tensed, all muscles contracting in preparation to strike.

Suddenly, he was drenched in whiteness. The sun enveloped his gaze, blinding him.

Rhen blinked rapidly, waiting for hands to grab him.

A black silhouette haunted his vision, slowly coming into focus.

"You're awake," a voice said—a somewhat high-pitched voice that Rhen recognized.

"Jin!" A goofy smile wrapped around his face as the boy's features filtered into view—the short hair, the small grin. He still wore Rhen's clothes, far too loose and far too Whylkin for this city.

Rhen sat up. "How…what…?"

Jin lightly tapped his arm.

"I will explain in a moment," he said and offered his hand. Rhen ignored it, standing slowly on his own.

When his feet touched land, Rhen realized they stood in an alleyway, a metal enclosure open to the sky. Everything was gray, dull—not at all like the golden palace.

He spun. Behind him was a small box strapped to the back of a golden carriage—a royal carriage. Rhen stepped to the side, just in time to view a head covered in gold, hidden behind a draped veil.

He gasped—breath stopping—and stepped closer.

But the woman wasn't looking at him—she was looking past him at Jin.

"Good luck," she said, her voice soft and full of emotion. And then she leaned back, hidden behind a heavy curtain. Two knocks and the cart started rolling away.

Rhen fought the urge to chase after her, stuck in his spot by one thought—she was Ourthuri. And by the look of it, royal.

His mother would kill him if he fell for a foreigner.

Would kill him.

His eyes closed and the vision returned. Heat flooded his veins at the sight of her, almost as though his body remembered something his brain did not.

Rhen shook his head.

Another time. When he could process the information. When there weren't a million other questions filtering through his mind.

"Jin," he said, awed, "how in the world?"

"It is a long story." The boy sighed and handed Rhen a plain brown robe, keeping one for himself. "Put this on."

In a daze, Rhen nodded and pulled the garment over his head. His hip was weaponless, he realized, disheartened.

Jin pulled a second robe over his head—it pooled on the ground by his feet, far too long for the small boy.

"In short, I managed to escape the ship, break into the palace, and convince a princess to help smuggle you from the castle." The boy took a deep breath, as if he couldn't even believe his words. "Oh, and in return I promised her safe haven when she runs away from her father."

Rhen choked.

"And the long version?"

Jin shook his head. "We must find a place to hide. Do you know anyone in the city? The princess said she could take us no farther than the lower districts."

"What was her name?" Rhen asked, still lagging behind Jin's words.

The boy's eyes narrowed and his head titled slightly to the side. "Leenaka…" He said slowly.

Leenaka.

Odd. Foreign.

He let the sound roll over his tongue.

Lee. Naka.

Leenaka.

He could get used to that. Now he just needed to see the face hidden behind the veil.

"Rhen?"

"Yes?" He said, jerking up. Then he remembered. "Wait, when she runs away?"

"Rhen, the king will soon be looking for you. He wants to kill you. We must find a place to hide. Now."

Rhen looked around, pushing his distracting thoughts to the side. They were hidden in this alley for now, but the boy was right—more than he realized maybe. Rhen lifted his hand, running his fingers over the ridges of the cut on his forehead. King Razzaq wanted him dead—but now he needed him dead, needed to stop this story from making its way to King Whylfrick.

The robes would help, but even still, Rhen would be noticeable. Jin's darkened skin and black hair hid him a little. But Rhen, with his reddish white skin and cherry-auburn hair, would stand out from the crowd.

Sons of Whyl weren't made to blend in.

"Come on." He motioned for Jin to follow. "I know just the place." *And surprisingly it's not a brothel*, Rhen thought, proud of himself.

It was a ship. One had luckily been sitting in the harbor earlier that day. And Rhen prayed it was still there.

He walked closer to the busy street, checking once to make sure Jin was ready before stepping into the crowd. Carts rolled, pulled by neighing horses or the owners themselves. People walked. Children ran. Merchants shouted.

Rhen looked around, trying to spot a marker and catch his bearings in this strange city. When he looked left, his gaze traveled up an incline. When he looked right, it slanted down.

Right, Rhen decided and stepped forward. Down meant farther from the palace and from the king. Down meant closer to the docks and to freedom.

An instant after they started moving with the crowd, bells sounded from above. At first, it was just a dull twinkling, distant and musical. But with every passing step, the sound grew, almost as if the notes were raining down from the palace, pelting Rhen in the head the farther he ran. By the time they reached a bend in the street, the ringing had grown to a furious roar—menacing and omnipresent. There was nowhere to hide, to escape.

Spotting a street vendor, Rhen pulled Jin to the side and casually grabbed two scarves from the cart when the man was busy and not looking. The material was coarse and scratchy, but it would do.

When they disappeared from eyesight, Rhen lifted the rectangle over his head, draping it like a hood down over his forehead.

"Jin," he whispered, looking over his shoulder, "put this on."

The boy took the cloth and copied Rhen's style, but still, the two of them were being stared at. The hood hid a little bit of Rhen's skin and hair, but it could not cover everything—especially his size, which was almost double that of the men around him. But more so than anything, people stared at their covered arms, hidden beneath the robes. No visible tattoos. A sure sign that they were not from the Golden Isles.

They needed to get to the docks and fast.

Reaching back, Rhen tugged on Jin's robe, urging him to move faster.

An iron bridge slipped into sight on the horizon, leading down to another plateau of the multilevel city. Guards in deep conversation blocked either side. In the archway, a bell shook back and forth, joining in the cacophony.

And suddenly Rhen realized what it was—an alarm. The city was being locked down, which could only mean one thing—the king had just learned of Rhen's escape.

Letting his thoughts wander for a minute, Rhen prayed for the mysterious princess's safety. But—he glanced at the soldiers as they weaved into the busy streets with weapons held high—his own safety was clearly the more pressing issue.

The bridge was close.

But a gate was being cranked across it, sealing the opening shut.

How would they make it through unnoticed?

A commotion filtered into Rhen's ears—shouting and yelling. He shifted his gaze to the left, smiling when he saw a man sitting atop a wagon. A man who was fighting with two Ourthuri soldiers and gaining more attention by the minute.

He couldn't understand much over the din of the crowd, but it sounded like the man was a merchant trying to return to his ship with the goods.

Which meant one thing—the next platform had to lead to the docks.

Reaching out his arm, Rhen halted and stopped Jin behind him. He shifted to the right edge of the street, across from the fight about to break out, and kept creeping slowly closer to the bridge.

More soldiers stopped patrolling, instead turning to the noise of the argument. A few walked out of the guardhouse beside the bridge, joining their comrades against the sailor. The rest of them moved past Rhen, who was bending his knees to shorten his stature.

When he was a hand's length away from the now half-closed and abandoned gate, he stopped.

It was a miracle.

The gods were smiling on him today.

All of the guards had left their station, distracted by the sailor, who now waved a dinged weapon in the air. All of the townspeople watched, hunger for justice in their eyes. The guards stood in a straight line, trying to intimidate even though their numbers were few.

They were one breath away from a riot.

"On my count," Rhen muttered, and Jin nodded in understanding.

Rhen held out one finger.

Two fingers.

And then he moved, holding his breath as his foot stepped across the entrance of the bridge.

No shouts.

No clanking swords.

No arrows.

He looked down. The metal below his feet was a marvel. Sturdy and unlike anything he had seen before. Bridges were supposed to be made of stone, and even then surpassing a deep river was near impossible. But—he eyed the edge and looked down to the ocean deep below his feet, nestled between the rocks—this seemed held up by magic.

Rhen glanced at Jin, comforted by the boy's wide, staring eyes. He was not the only one impressed by the scene.

Farther over his shoulder, the sailor was sitting back down. The crowd started to disperse.

"Run!" Rhen gasped as a guard started to spin.

The two of them took off, not waiting to see if they were being followed.

Their feet touched on solid rock once more, and Rhen shoved people to the side as he made his way through the winding roads, down and down, praying that the streets would soon level.

Through a boxy building, he saw the sparkle of blue.

"We're almost there," he shouted back, too excited to contain his enthusiasm. One more wide bend, and the ocean burst fully into view. The deep sapphire sent a wave of warmth into Rhen's chest that crashed against his heart, exploding down his limbs in a giddy burst. He felt like a child running from the castle guards, hiding from his father. It was a game.

A game he had won.

Pure adrenaline kept his legs pumping.

The cloth fell from his head, slipping over his ears and free from his throat. But it didn't matter. The docks were alive with men of Whylkin and Ourthuro—skin of every shade mingled and mixed, making Rhen and Jin just two more in a crowd of foreigners visiting the capital city.

A laugh escaped his lips—freedom spilling through his system like a drug.

But he wasn't safe yet.

Not yet.

Finally, when Rhen reached the edge of the docks, he stopped and scanned the ships for the flag of his kingdom.

There.

At the end of the row.

A spot of red in a cloudless cobalt sky.

The air shifted, bringing the design fully into view. Rhen grinned—he would recognize that rearing black stallion anywhere. In fact, it might be embroidered on his breastplate underneath the Ourthuri robe that now felt heavy in the salty air.

Without wasting time, Rhen strode confidently forward, walking over the boards until he reached the base of the ship where a bridge already sat extended.

"Hello!" He called, but didn't wait for a response. Turning to look back toward land, he saw the golden garb of King Razzaq's guard shimmering in the distance.

It was against protocol to board unannounced.

But, Rhen smirked, breaking rules was one perk of being royal.

He mounted the bridge and walked slowly on board.

"Where is your captain?" Rhen asked, louder so his voice carried. This time, he was noticed—and not kindly.

"Who's asking?" A sailor stepped forward, his skin wrinkled and hard from the days at sea, his nose upturned in disgust. Hostility prickled the air around him, almost tangible.

Rhen looked over his shoulder. High on deck where he stood, the docks below were mostly out of view. He prayed no Ourthuri would see him now, as in one swoop of his arm, the foreign robe was whisked from his body and dropped into a pool on the floor. In its place rested the royal garb he had donned to see the king.

Sure, it was ripped and bloodied, but that just made the whole scene more intimidating.

"I am your prince," Rhen said, dripping with authority. He was in no mood for games. Now that he had stopped moving, the weary ache of loss taunted his bones. The threat of death was still heavy.

The man's eyes widened, shocked, and he immediately dropped to his knees in respect, dipping his body far lower to the ground than was necessary. "My Lord," he blurted.

Rhen rolled his eyes—now was not the time for overdone displays of loyalty. He walked closer to the man and leaned down to lay a palm on his tense shoulder. "It is no matter. Anyone would have made the same mistake. Your captain, please?"

The man stood—a speck of gratitude in his crinkled eyes—and nodded. "Right this way, my Lord."

As they walked down the length of the ship, crew members paused, staring with open mouths as Rhen walked by. Many men would go a lifetime with nothing more than a glimpse of their prince, but to have him aboard their ship—a merchant ship, not a war ship—that was something unheard of.

They reached an open door and trotted down a few steep steps until they were completely below decks. Rhen's guide knocked on a closed door. A gruff "come in" sounded through the wood.

The captain sat behind a desk, hunched over maps and charts with a bulbous glass pressed against his eye. His hat hung from a hook on the wall, black with one white plume. He was bald. His features were sharp, angular despite his age—an age where skin usually began to sag. He looked like a man who did not like to be bothered. A loose, open white shirt hung over his frame. And the only jewel Rhen saw was a ruby circled in gold that hung from one ear.

After a minute, he looked up from his work, dropping the quill that had left small black stains on his fingers.

"What…" He trailed off when his eyes came in focus, settling on Rhen and studying him for a moment, confused. "My Lord." He stood to present Rhen with a deep bow. "I am Captain Jelaric, and I am honored to have you on board the *Skipping Stone*."

"I fear that will pass." Rhen sighed. "I am Prince Whylrhen, son of Whylfrick, and this," he motioned to Jin behind him, "is my traveling companion, Jin of the Arpapajo people. We arrived this morning on the *Old Maid*, a retired war ship led by Captain Pygott. While I was visiting with King Razzaq, my men and I were ambushed. Now Jin and I are the only two who remain. I must get back to Rayfort immediately. My father must hear of King Razzaq's treachery as soon as possible, and I am afraid that you are in possession of the only Whylkin ship currently in the harbor."

The more Rhen spoke, the lower the captain's shoulders fell. His pupils clouded over, filled with worry, and he looked down quickly at the papers below him before returning to Rhen.

"Da'astiku is being locked down by the king," Rhen continued, pressing on despite the slight twinge of guilt, "but I cannot be found. You must hide both of us and provide safe travel back to my home. Trust you will be handsomely rewarded for all of the trouble this will cause."

The captain looked down at the papers on his desk, blinked once, and pushed them aside until only one remained. Rhen recognized the hills, the outline of the White Stone Sea, the circle allotting his home city.

"It would be an honor to help a Son of Whyl," the man said. His deep voice hinted at no ill will, just pure loyalty—a true subject. Looking past Rhen, he asked, "Have they raised the black flag?"

"Ay," the sailor who had led Rhen below decks said, nodding. Jin remained quiet, surveying the conversation.

Captain Jelaric sighed and ran a hand through imaginary hair.

"The black flag?" Rhen asked. Definitely didn't sound very good.

"When the Ourthuri raise the black flag, it means their harbor is on lock down—no ships in and no ships out. Normally, they believe the king has been cheated and run inspections to make sure no goods came into the city unannounced—no black market deals. But now, it likely means they are looking for…" He motioned forward, shrugged, "well, you, my Lord."

"What will they do?" Rhen asked, brows furrowed. He refused to escape one trap just to be led into another.

"My guess, Prince Whylrhen, is that they will be here any minute. If, as you say, we are the only Whylkin ship, they will want to come below decks, make sure you are not on board and then usher us out as quickly as possible." The captain grabbed his hat from the wall, squeezing it snuggly onto his head. He wore a red sash around his waist.

Unexpectedly, the captain's entire body stopped, stuck with indecision mirrored in his halted breath. There were options being weighed in his head, different paths with different possible outcomes, until finally he looked at Rhen with an open, honest plea.

He leaned forward, knuckles resting on the wood of his desk, and whispered, "Luckily, this is not just a trading ship."

Rhen squinted, looking harder at the red ruby dangling from his ear, the lack of jewels, the multiple maps highlighting very unusual routes across the open ocean.

He grinned.

"You're a smuggler," he said.

A twinkle lit the captain's eye—he had made the right choice in trusting his prince, a prince infamous for his own wayward ways.

"I assure you, my Prince, that I follow the laws of our lands very precisely. But there are times…" His lips twitched. "Times like the current, when certain circumstances require a somewhat open interpretation of the rules."

"I couldn't agree more," Rhen said, his voice full of mirth.

"Then follow me, Son of Whyl, and I will return you to our great King Whylfrick as fast as the *Skipping Stone* is able."

13

JINJI
~DA'ASTIKU~

Jinji blinked.

But when her eyes opened, it was all the same.

Darkness. Complete and total darkness.

When the captain said he could hide them, she had had her doubts. But when he moved his desk a few inches to the side, revealing a trap door to a secret compartment, she relaxed.

Now, shrouded in black with nothing but the echo of her breath against Rhen's, Jinji's hands were starting to clam. Her heart was starting to race. And her breath was starting to quicken.

Closing her eyes did nothing to halt the fear, because even then all she saw was shadow. Unlike in dreams, where opening her eyes was all it took, here there was no escape.

The hairs on the back of her neck stood, feeling the imaginary creep of invisible hands. The shadow was here. The nightmare.

She could feel it around her, ensnaring her just at her moment of escape.

And the only image that kept flashing in her mind was of Maniuk. Of his eyes—his clouded over, white eyes the moment before he took his own life.

A shiver jetted down her back. Jinji bit her lip to keep from yelping.

No, she thought, *there is nothing.* But try as she might to reason, to use logic, the darkness had invaded more than just her vision. It was haunting her, taunting her.

"Jin?" Rhen's voice floated into her ear, a cool breeze. "Are you okay?"

She nodded. Then remembered he could not see.

"Yes." She forced the word out as quietly as possible, hoping the slight crack would not give her away.

"Jin, can I ask…" Pause. She waited. "Can I ask what happened?"

"We are supposed to be quiet," she whispered back, but hoped he would not listen. The words were helping ease her mind, were helping distract her from the darkness.

"I know," he said. A hint of pain laced into the tone, just enough to make him sound like a child, to sound vulnerable. "I just…" He sighed. "Did Captain Pygott suffer? Can you tell me that much?"

Jinji winced. That was not the question she expected, but her mind flashed to the soft blue eyes that had wished her farewell, the strong arms that had pushed her to freedom. "No," she said, a pang of loss tightened her heart. "No, it was over quickly. He raced down to your cabin to wake me and helped me escape just as the Ourthuri were breaking down the door. I believe they acted very swiftly, as they did with everyone else."

A deep, shaky breath was her only response. In and out. In and out. Then a sniffle. Another breath. A deep swallow—the gulp was loud enough to hear.

Jinji sat still, experiencing Rhen's pain with him, wishing she could help. But she knew better than most that there was very little anyone could do to mend a broken heart.

Her fingers twitched, itching to reach across the small enclosure and wrap around his, but she remained still. Hand-holding was the comfort of a woman, of a—of something she wasn't.

Men preferred their pain in solace and in silence. At least that was her experience. Her father had always grieved at night, when he thought the rest of the world was fast asleep and safely in the realm of their dreams, a place where they would not hear his cries.

But Jinji heard.

She always heard. Her heart ached alongside his, burning with the memory of her brother Janu, but she never reacted. Never stood from her sleeping pad to provide comfort. Because her father, like Rhen, needed to feel strong. Untouchable.

Even still, her arm moved over an inch.

Another inch.

Heat radiated from Rhen's skin, warming Jinji as her hand shifted closer.

Stop, she commanded, but her wayward fingers disobeyed, pressing even closer, until she was sure their hairs were touching, tickling.

A creak sounded from above.

The thud of footsteps.

Jinji balled her fingers into a fist, hugging her arms close to her chest. Her ears were alert, listening for any and all sound.

Boots pounded closer. Multiple sets.

Muffled voices dropped through the floorboards.

The Ourthuri were right above them, pacing, searching, shouting in anger.

Yet, somehow, Jinji felt calm. Deep in her heart, she knew the spirits would not have brought her so far just to fail her now—she had to trust in them. And in Rhen, in his decision. The two were all she had left.

Gradually, the sounds grew softer.

They faded away.

Until silence and darkness circled Jinji and Rhen once more.

This time, Rhen did not break the quiet. So Jinji sat, imagining daylight, using all of her strength to keep her hands still—to keep them from weaving the illusion of light just so she could escape the shadows.

After a while, the ground below her shifted. The gentle sway of water roughened. The bounces became choppy. They flew higher, landed harder.

It could only mean one thing—they had set sail.

They were free.

A grin took over Jinji's face.

Boots sounded above them, but no fear flooded her system. The desk scraped against the wood above her head, roaring in her ear. And the trap door opened, gloriously invading Jinji's vision with the sun.

Rhen climbed out first while Jinji continued taking deep breaths of the fresh air coming in through the open window.

A hand reached down, gripping hers, and Jinji was airborne as the shadows fell away behind her.

"We passed the inspection, Prince Whylrhen," Captain Jelaric said, his voice light with amusement.

Rhen smirked. "I had no doubt. What other nooks do you have tucked away on this ship?"

The captain winked, bowing deeply. "I'm afraid that is a secret that cannot be shared."

"Even with your prince?"

"Especially with my prince, my Lord."

Rhen nodded in understanding. "Have no fear, the king will not hear of your extra pursuits because of me, not after this."

"Many thanks, Prince Whylrhen. I suggest you stay below decks until Da'astiku fades from sight. My chambers will be yours for the rest of the journey until we reach Rayfort. Do make yourself comfortable."

"Will you have food brought? My stomach grows hungrier by the second," Rhen said, his belly rumbling in agreement.

"Right away, my Lord." The captain bowed and backed away, not turning until he reached the door. It closed quickly with a resounding bang.

Immediately, Rhen sighed heavily and ran a hand through his curling hair. He turned to Jinji, eyebrows slightly raised. "This is going to be a long trip."

"It must be shorter than our last one?" Jinji questioned, picturing the maps Rhen had drawn for her in the dirt.

"I'm not talking about that, Jin. Traveling through the Straits, we'll reach Rayfort in little over a week. But it will be excruciating."

"Why?" She asked, honestly curious.

He looked at her, smiling a half smile, shaking his head slightly.

"You're so entertaining because you don't even know, the politics never even cross your mind. Did you hear the 'my Lords' dripping from their tongues? It's exhausting. And Captain Jelaric, he knows. I heard it in his voice. Make myself comfortable? He meant stay out of sight or his men will trip over themselves to bow every time I step on deck."

"I guess I do not do that," Jinji mumbled.

Rhen's grin widened. "No, quite the opposite in fact. The first time you met me, I thought you might kill me. The idea of you bowing has never entered my mind."

"But these are things I should learn, now that…"

She trailed off. Now that, what? Now that her family was gone? Her people? Her way of life?

Now that she was going to meet the king?

Jinji bit her lip, sinking into the captain's vacated chair.

What would she do when they reached the King's City? The spirits were guiding her, but to what and where? Despite her earlier fears, the shadow was not here. It had disappeared. And the last she had heard of it was from the two sailors in Whylkin, whispering about mysterious deaths. She was no closer to answers.

Rhen stepped into view. His black boots were covered in grime—scraped and roughed.

Jinji's eyes traveled up his legs, up his broad chest, right into his concerned gaze.

I could tell him.

It wasn't the first time the thought had crossed her mind.

She could tell him about the nightmare, about the shadow, about the massacre. She could tell him all of that without telling him she was a woman. And maybe, just maybe, he would be able to help.

But would he believe her? Fire spirits might cling to his figure, but that didn't mean he knew they were there. It didn't mean he would believe in magic, would believe in something as preposterous as spiritual possession.

Yet, in Da'astiku, the princess had believed Jinji enough to abandon reason and help her rescue a stranger. Her figure had been draped in blue strands of elemental water, and she had seemed well acquainted with the idea of magic, completely unafraid of Jinji's illusions. That had to mean something.

Even if Rhen had given no hint of—

A knock sounded at the door.

"Come in," Rhen said.

The door swung open to the top of a man's head.

"My Lord," he said, speaking to the ground. "I brought food." The tray was nearly to the floor he was bent so low.

"Just put it down here, please." Rhen pointed to the desk. The man scurried forward, keeping his eyes downcast.

It was a wonder he didn't fall flat on his face.

But in almost no time, the tray was prepared and he was backing out of the room.

"See?" Rhen scowled at the closed door before reaching to grab a piece of ripe fruit. He stepped back, jumping onto the tall bed in the corner of the room, sprawling out until he was comfortable. Still frowning at the door, he took a large, crunchy bite.

"Can I…" Jinji paused, fiddling with her fingers before finally grabbing a slice of bread from the tray.

"What?" Rhen raised an eyebrow.

"Can I ask what happened to you in the palace? And to the other men?" Her mind filtered back to Mikzahooq as he stared out at the horizon, unabashedly proclaiming his own death. He had known exactly what his king would do.

"I'm still not sure." Rhen shook his head while he munched. "The second we got to that city, our fate was sealed. King Razzaq had no plans to ever let any of us escape. But I don't understand why or how. He must have spies within my kingdom. He's been planning something for a long time, something he was afraid I would mess up.

"War?"

"It has to be." Rhen stood and began to walk slowly across the room, just to turn and walk back to the bed, then back across the room, pacing. "I thought it was just the ships," he said slowly, working through his mind, "but it has to be more. He was stealing resources he could easily afford. Ourthuro is flooded with gold, so why resort to thievery? Unless the entire point was to see how much he could take before we noticed? Unless it was a test to see how easily he might invade? Killing your people, that was the first stage, the first unnoticed move against my father. He is planning to attack, of that I am certain—the only question is when."

"When do you think?" Jinji asked, ignoring the mention of her tribe. She couldn't—wouldn't—tell Rhen the truth until she knew he had magic inside of him, until she knew he would believe her.

He stopped moving in the middle of the room, jaw dropping open as he slowly spun to face her. His pupils dilated. His nostrils flared wide. Jinji noticed his hands begin to shake until they were balled into tight, trembling fists.

"The Naming," he said, deep and growling. Rhen took a long breath. "It's so obvious. At the ceremony, my nephew will be given a name of Whyl. It symbolizes the future of the kingdom. Every lord and lady will be there. Every knight. The outer cities will be defenseless. It's what he's been waiting for all this time, a moment when we're all distracted."

Rhen's feet seemed to step of their own accord. His mind was elsewhere. Jinji saw the vacant absence in his eyes, the mounting dread. He reminded Jinji of a caged animal. His movements became quicker, jerkier. The wooden walls of the small room were like bars, containing him.

She sat in wonder, wishing there was something she could do to help. But there was something behind his expression that stopped her—some memory playing in his head. Her thoughts filtered back to the afternoon not too long ago, when she was sitting with Rhen on the crow's nest—her first sea adventure. He had spoken of a younger brother, a brother who had been killed. A murder he had tried to stop but couldn't.

And suddenly it became clear—his hunched shoulders, flexed muscles. He just cared so much. About his family, his people. He cared. Why else would he have taken in a lost little boy? Why else?

Jinji opened her mouth, not sure of what would come out, but it was only air.

"The Naming," Rhen spoke right before her, stealing the words from her throat, "it is likely in two weeks, maybe less." He gripped his skull, sinking back against a wall. "I'll be too late. We'll be there after all of the guests have arrived. They won't have time to send word, to prepare their homes. We'll all be too late."

"Rhen," she said softly, "I'm sure everyone is prepared. It cannot be as bad as you say."

He nodded, trying to convince himself. "You're right. They would have left a second in command; the men must be prepared for an attack when the lord of the city is gone. The people would not be helpless."

"Of course not," she quickly agreed, "and you will talk to your father as soon as we arrive. There will be time."

"There will be time," he repeated, "everything will be fine."

He walked back to the desk, grabbing another piece of fruit before crashing onto the bed again.

"I need to think on lighter things, Jin, or I will go crazy trapped on this ship for a week."

"What sorts of things?" She leaned back in her chair, relaxing just slightly now that he seemed more composed.

"Tell me about the princess," he sighed.

Her body went rigid.

Jinji began to cough, doubling over in her seat and clutching her stomach.

"Why?" She squeaked.

"Because I cannot stop picturing the face hidden behind that veil of hers…or the body under that golden dress."

"She was in a carriage." Jinji rolled her eyes. She was very sure that Rhen had seen plenty of women—what was hidden under any dress was no mystery. She shivered, remembering the tavern. Some women left little to question even fully clothed.

"No, I saw her before. She was holding me."

Jinji jerked, widening her eyes as she stared at Rhen, but he was looking dreamily at a painting of storm clouds on the wall.

"Holding you?" Her voice was airy. Shallow.

"I have this memory." He paused, smiled. "A golden-veiled woman cradled my head in her lap, ran her fingers over my cheeks, and then it ends. It had to have been the princess, right?"

It was me! She almost yelled.

Instead, Jinji clapped her hands over her mouth, stuffing the proclamation back down her neck, swallowing it down her dry throat.

All she could do was nod.

"I knew it," he said, leaning forward. "This sounds odd, but I felt like maybe I knew her, somehow. Her eyes looked familiar, golden-speckled and warm."

Jinji immediately studied the floorboard beneath her feet.

"I think her eyes were blue," she mumbled.

Rhen shrugged. "Maybe."

"I spent more time with her, they were definitely blue."

"That's why you must tell me about her, distract me." He sighed. "How did you even meet? How did you get her to help rescue me?"

Jinji pursed her lips, unsure of what to say without giving her powers of illusion away—a secret she would not share, ever.

At her silence, Rhen looked up, frowning.

"Come to think of it, how did you even get into the palace?"

"I..." Jinji took a deep breath, swallowing the saliva now pooling in her mouth. "I snuck onto one of the flying platforms."

"The flying plat...oh, the giant pulleys." His eyebrows lifted. "The gods, Jin! How?"

"Well, Captain Pygott, he threw me from the ship and I swam under the docks, trying to remain hidden. I saw the platforms and knew it would be my only chance, so when no one was looking I swam over and climbed into one of the boxes."

Jinji tensed. She hated talking this much. Her limbs felt squirmy as her chest squeezed with pressure.

"Genius." He shook his head in awe. "What next?"

"Um," she paused, eyes flickering around the room. "I stayed hidden in the box, I felt someone carry me and then set me down. After a while, I got out of the box and realized I was in the palace."

Rhen's eyes started to narrow.

"How did you meet the princess?"

"Well, I was running through the halls trying to find you when I came upon her crying. She was sad, someone she loved had just been killed." Jinji was hoping that thought would distract him.

It didn't.

He leaned closer, eyes pinning her to her seat.

"And you didn't run into anyone? No guards?"

"No," she shook her head. "No, the guards were all with you. The princess hid me in a servant's robe. She knew her father had taken you to the garden, and she convinced one of the guards, her friend, to help. When no one was looking, we pulled you away from the pool. He carried you to the carriage, hid you in her traveling box."

Jinji was rambling. She felt words tumble unbidden from her lips. Felt them fall to the ground, crashing every time. Each sound made her wince.

Outright disbelief shone in Rhen's eyes.

"So you just walked into the palace, befriended the princess, and walked out?" The sarcasm was not lost on her.

"I was very lucky," she said, playing innocent. "You were very lucky, too."

Rhen sat back as she said it. She could see him weigh the words—almost believe them—but his gaze sharpened.

"We never did get a chance to talk about the battle against the Ourthuri, the one aboard the *Old Maid*."

"Hmm?"

She squeezed her palms together, turning away from Rhen, observing the items on the captain's desk. Papers. A feather. A dark black liquid.

There were scrawls all over the pages, symbols she could not read or understand. But they meant something. There were charts with the images Rhen had once described to her—maps. She looked closer. One of those depicted her home. Did it mean anything that she could not say which?

"Jin, what are you hiding?"

There was a light next to her, a flame flickering inside a warm glass bulb. The oil was low. The cloth holding the flame looked short.

"I really do not know what you mean, Rhen."

"I think you do, or you would not be so panicked right now."

Jinji leveled her gaze, meeting his eye.

"What are you hiding?" She asked.

As soon as the words were spoken, the spirits sprung to life in her eyes—the fire spirits. They circled his figure, dancing around him like a living flame. Only this time, they extended beyond him, stretching out from his arm, connecting him to the light. The fire arched in his direction, calling for him.

With no plan, no thought but a need to know the truth, to know if Rhen was like her and held magic in his bones, Jinji acted.

She did not want to be questioned any more.

She did not want to have questions any more.

She just wanted to know, for the first time in a long time, that maybe she wasn't completely alone.

Reaching her hand to the side, she gripped the glass and threw the light onto the floor between them. It crashed, breaking into a thousand pieces, sparking as oil slipped over the floor.

"Jin!" Rhen shouted, jumping back.

The flames grew, spreading with the spill then sinking into the wood.

Jinji looked away, looked at Rhen. He was mesmerized by the fire.

Do it, she thought. She didn't know what it was, but there was something the spirits were trying to show her.

Something about Rhen they needed her to know.

The flames grew, burning against dry wood, creating a wall between the two of them. Smoke began to filter through the window.

Jinji choked as the char grew.

Rhen had to act now.

The crew would notice any minute, would see the black billowing into the sky.

He looked at her, green eyes prickling something in her soul. The muscles in his neck were coiled tight, pulling away from the fire as the rest of his body sunk closer.

And then he stopped fighting.

His hands sunk into the depths of the flames and with a deep sigh of pleasure, the fire started melting into his skin.

A different person might have screamed, backed away, run in fear.

But Jinji smiled. Her heart sang. And something so deep inside of her that she didn't even know was there thrummed with the rightness of that moment.

Then the fire vanished, leaving a black stain on the wood at their feet.

"Rhen," Jinji said, but he was already gone, running from the room as fast as his feet could take him.

14

RHEN
~DUELING SEA~

Rhen was sulking. He knew it. But he just couldn't stop.

More than a full day had passed since the fire, and his mind was still consumed with what had happened. He had never shown anyone his gift—not even his own family. His mother, Rhen knew, suspected something. But she never pressed, never asked, and in truth, avoided learning more.

But Jin—the boy was different.

Rhen just couldn't get that look out of his mind, that look on Jin's face that was positive Rhen would somehow be able to stop the fire he had created. It was so confident, so demanding—and more than anything, so unafraid.

And Rhen, instead of facing it like a man, had run away like a little girl—a princess not even in corset strings. Now too much time had passed, he didn't know what to say or how to start the conversation.

Rhen shook his head and stared out at the horizon, letting the wind whip his hair.

The men on deck were avoiding him, not even looking at him. If they did happen to meet his eyes, they immediately bowed their heads out of respect. Even the captain was treading lightly, speaking in hushed tones to his men and only talking to Rhen with polite pleasantries.

This was how a prince was supposed to be treated, he tried to remind himself, with respect—especially on board a ship that was built for less than lawful activities. He was not surprised at how polite and disingenuous everyone was acting.

But it hurt, nonetheless. Because all it did was remind Rhen how different things had been with Captain Pygott, a man who had felt more like a father to him than the king at times. More caring certainly. And his men had understood that all Rhen wanted was to feel included.

On the *Old Maid*, Rhen was nothing more than an extra set of hands. On the *Skipping Stone*, he was a burden.

Over his shoulder, Captain Jelaric stood relaxed behind the wheel, laughing with his first mate.

Things were better this way, but that didn't mean Rhen had to like it.

Hence, the sulking.

Okay, fine, the sulking might have had a little something to do with Jin, too. Rhen missed the boy. Despite the secrets he knew Jin was keeping, they had become true friends. They trusted each other. And more than anything, they understood each other. Unlike Cal, who seemed to battle Rhen at every turn, Jin got him. It was easier to talk to him.

Well, usually.

"Land ho!"

Rhen lifted his head, looking up from his twiddling thumbs to focus on the horizon. A flat stretch of brown and green land was sandwiched between two limitless blues.

Whylkin.

Home.

Warmth flooded his chest. He was almost back in Rayfort. Almost back to Ember. Almost back to his brothers.

He searched for the seam, the break in the shoreline. A little to the left, he saw it. The land faded away and for a brief instant, sky and sea were connected once more.

The Straits.

They were a place of myth, of legend.

They were something Jin should see.

Finally, Rhen had the conversation starter he was looking for.

Before he could change his mind, Rhen spun and raced for the steps. He paused for just a moment outside the door, taking one deep breath, and then plunged in headfirst.

Jin sat with his arms crossed, staring through the circular window on the far side of the room. He didn't hear Rhen enter, too lost in his thoughts. His shoulders were hunched over, even his eyebrows looked heavy.

Rhen cleared his throat.

Jin sprung to life, turning in fright but relaxing the instant his eyes fell on Rhen. Half a second later, the boy's lids widened. His body tensed. And before Rhen could even open his mouth to speak, Jin was out of the chair.

"I must speak to you. Please don't leave."

Rhen stepped farther into the room, closing the door behind him. "I came to talk too." He pulled the large wooden chair from behind the captain's desk, dragging it behind him until it rested across from Jin. He didn't realize he was sweating until a cool breeze fluttered against his warm cheeks, prickling his skin.

"I'm sorry," Rhen said, still not looking at Jin, instead focusing on the white puff of a cloud outside.

"Please, I must tell you something," the boy said, so softly that Rhen almost couldn't hear. There was a vulnerability in that tone, something he had never heard from Jin before. Not in that way. He had heard the boy talk with sadness, with longing, but never with such openness.

That was enough to make Rhen meet his muddy eyes, tight with worry.

"You were right, I have been hiding something from you," Jin said. Rhen leaned forward, placing his weight on his forearms, invested in what would come next. Jin did the opposite—he pulled his knees into his chest, curling into a tight little ball.

"I knew." The boy dipped his head into his knees, breathing deeply before looking up once more. "I dropped that lamp because I knew you would do something. I didn't know what, but I knew the fire wouldn't hurt you."

This was it. What Rhen had been waiting for—Jin's secret. He licked his lips with anticipation. "How?"

"I could see it," Jin said, hesitantly releasing one word at a time.

Rhen tilted his head, confused. "See it?"

The boy nodded. "I can see them—the elemental spirits— earth, air, water, and fire. They're in everything, everywhere. And the fire spirits cling to you, they latch onto your skin, they fuse to you. I had never seen anything like it before I met you. So I knew, I knew the fire wouldn't, couldn't hurt you. Because you are fire, Rhen."

I am fire, Rhen thought as lightness sparked in his chest. He was fire. He had never thought of it that way, but something about the wording was perfect. Was right.

"And is that all? You just see them?"

Jin hugged his legs tighter, biting his lip, nostrils flaring as he looked at the ground.

Rhen held his breath.

There was more.

Everything in Jin's body language told him the boy was hiding something.

Suddenly, Jin looked up, a grin slowly spreading across his face, as though he had just discovered something, just realized something. His eyes glowed gold with excitement.

They looked almost familiar...

"That's not it," Jin said, sitting tall. "I can't control it, but sometimes, the spirits help me, like they're guiding me. I felt it the day we met, after you saved me. I felt the trees slide out of my way as I ran to save you. I felt it during the attack. The winds blew harder against our enemies, sending their weapons off track. And I felt it a few days ago when I went to the palace—as though the spirits led me to the princess and to you."

Rhen didn't know what to say, how to respond. He was too shocked. The spirits didn't choose people, did they? Rhen had certainly never felt chosen.

In his silence, Jin shrunk a little. His excitement wilted.

"I would have told you," Jin said meekly, "but I didn't think you would believe me. And that's why I threw the light. I wanted to make sure I wasn't crazy—that the fire did speak to you."

"It does," Rhen said. Jin perked up. "For as long as I can remember, fire has called to me, cajoled me. But that's all. I can't create it. I can't move it. All I can do is reach into the flames and pull them under my skin."

"That's enough." Jin smiled. It was contagious.

"Enough for what?"

"Enough for us to believe each other."

"What else do you need me to believe?"

196

"The shadow," Jin said, low and ominous. Before Rhen could ask, words spilled from the boy's mouth, confessing the truth about what had happened to his people.

A massacre.

Total destruction by one of their own.

It was never the Ourthuri, but Rhen decided that didn't matter, not now, not when Jin was reliving the most devastating memory of his entire life. It changed nothing. King Razzaq would still need to be dealt with. And Jin would still need a friend and caretaker.

But this shadow was something unheard of. Bodily possession? Mind control? The longer Jin spoke, the more Rhen wanted to believe him. His words dripped with agony, with truthfulness. He said he saw a bleak emptiness in place of eyes, darkness in place of a soul.

When Jin was done talking, tears rolled down his cheeks. His eyes were red, puffy. His breathing was deep, as though speaking had been more strenuous than even a battle.

Rhen reached out and squeezed his upper arm, trying to infuse comfort.

"I will help you," he said, emphasizing his honesty with one more tight squeeze of his hand. "We will defeat this shadow, together."

Jin nodded, smiling weakly.

Rhen returned it more reassuringly. The boy sounded mad, crazed. Rhen didn't believe in this spiritual beast, but he believed that Jin thought it was real. And that was enough for now.

"Come." Rhen nodded toward the door. "There is something I want to show you."

"What?"

"You have to see it." He grinned slyly, satisfied when he saw Jin's brows knit together and his eyes twinkle with interest.

They both needed this.

They both needed some fun.

When they emerged on deck, Rhen felt the crew staring. A prince and an Arpapajo—this was the stuff of excellent gossip. But he didn't mind, because not being alone somehow made all the difference.

Looking at the horizon, Rhen saw the land had enlarged, taking up a deeper portion of the sky. He could make out jagged cliff faces, the tops of pointed pines, flat grassy hilltops, even the smallest bit of gold ore shimmering against the sun. The western shore of Whylkin was not for the faint of heart. The waters roared in from the chaos of the dueling sea, where warm southwestern currents met with cold northern tides and crashed against the coast in an endless battle, cutting the land into steep walls of rock. Quite different compared to the calm beachy shores of the southeastern lands.

But Rhen preferred the wildness—the mysticism, the magic mirrored in his own soul.

There was a little bit of time before the ship would enter the Straits, a river running through the center of a deep ravine—just enough time to reach the perfect viewpoint.

Knowing Jin followed, Rhen stepped to the edge of the ship, reaching for the ropes knotted into a climbable structure. They were going back to the crow's nest.

Gripping firmly with one hand, he pulled, loving how his muscles burned to life. Every nerve singed with the mix of pain and pleasure, of exertion.

The crew began to stare more openly the higher Rhen climbed, looking on in awe at a royal son so comfortable on the water—a royal son who could scale the ropes just as naturally as one of them.

When he reached the top, his chest was heaving, but his face was plastered with a smile. *The gods!* It felt good to be in the fresh air, the open water. He had to savor these moments, because in no time he would be stuck behind the palace walls, under the all too close watch of his father.

"Rhen," Jin gasped.

He spun, smirking at the small boy a few feet below him, hugging more than climbing the ropes.

"Give me your hand," he said, reaching down. When Jin held on tight, Rhen pulled him up, still mildly surprised at how weightless he felt. At the same age, Rhen was probably twice or three times his size.

But I was training to be a knight, he reminded himself. Jin had trained for nothing more than hunting game in the woods. And arrows were a lot lighter than broadswords.

The boy would grow with time.

"Hold onto the edge if you need to, but try to stay standing," Rhen said, turning easily on his feet as they swayed with the boat.

The Straits were closer.

"Have you ever heard of the Great Flood?"

No answer came.

Rhen turned to find Jin struggling to stand. He reached his hand out to steady the boy, but Jin shied away, gripping the edge of the wood even harder, until his tanned hands turned almost white.

Stubborn.

"Legend says that thousands of years ago, humans weren't always alone in this world. Other creatures lived among us. Some believe they were giant beasts able to tear trees clean from the ground. Others say they were more cunning creatures—small and terrible that would wreak unseen havoc. And still others claim they were monsters that fed on the blood of children, enslaving us under their reign of doom."

Rhen paused to look at Jin, who, he begrudgingly admitted, didn't seem the least bit scared or frightened—not the reaction Rhen had been hoping for. These were the sorts of stories that only felt satisfying when the listener was cowering in fear—not mildly aloof and turning slightly green.

No matter, Rhen loved to tell it anyway. He imagined Captain Pygott—blue eyes gleaming against less-wrinkled skin, voice hushed and restrained. The captain hadn't been the first to tell him of the Great Flood, but he had been the best.

"We'll never know the truth," Rhen continued, "but we do know one thing—the earth was on our side. These creatures were unnatural, were destroying the world around them. They had no regard for the natural order. Their powers tested the fates, reversed the paths laid down for us by the gods, and because of that, the humans were granted a weapon—nature itself would rise to do our bidding, would help us defeat them.

"So, on the eve of a great war, the humans gathered. Different races, different peoples from all over the world joined together in one place to pray to the spirits, to the earth, to save us. And we were heard."

At that, Jin did begin to pay attention. His body stiffened. Rhen bit his cheek to fight off a grin.

"The spirits listened?" The boy asked, wonder coloring his words.

"They did." Rhen nodded. "As our enemies marched their warriors closer and closer, nature fought against them. Wind crushed buildings to the ground. The earth rumbled beneath their feet, breaking into cracks that swallowed entire villages whole. Fire rained from the skies, burning these creatures alive. But still, they kept on marching, kept on coming. The humans would die, would be enslaved by the all powerful creatures that were stronger than the world itself."

"How did we escape? What did we do?"

"We didn't do anything. The gods did, the spirits did. They sent a wave of water taller than the highest mountain over the land. It drowned the entire world, covering the earth in an endless sea, killing all but the most devout humans who had gathered here, at the base of the realm of the gods, the mountains we now call the Gates. It was the Great Flood. And when the waters receded, all that remained were the lands of Whylkin and the handful of islands we now call the Kingdom of Ourthuro. Everything and everyone else was buried, lost to the world for all time."

Rhen let the silence stretch and hang, filling the tiny space between them. The shoreline had closed in; the sky was slowly disappearing as the cliffs took over. The Straits waited before them, an open mouth poised to swallow the ship.

"That's a good story," Jin whispered.

Raising an eyebrow, Rhen looked at the boy, then back to the sea. They were so close. So close. He waited, one more moment, before responding, "It isn't just a story, Jin. Look."

Rhen pointed to the front of the ship, to the blue waters extending beyond the bow, and past them to the start of the Straits.

The ship was still a little far away, but Rhen knew where to look. Already, he could see the white and black dots scattering along the inner walls of the Straits. The closer they got, the more obvious it became to his well-trained eyes.

Jin's brows were still furrowed. His neck was extended, stretching as close as possible to the scene. Rhen watched as the boy pursed his lips, as wrinkles spread along his forehead.

A shadow fell over them.

Jin gasped, head wrenching up to the sky. A yelp escaped his lips, as though he expected something to drop from the clouds.

Rhen smirked. It was just the cliffs, stretching high overhead and blocking out the sun. They were just about to cross over into the mouth of the river.

Which could only mean one thing…his story was working. It wasn't right for someone to be anything but scared during his first trip through the Straits—it was a rite of passage, one step in becoming a man. Plus, his brothers had done the same to him. It was only fair that Rhen got to inflict the pain on someone else.

"Rhen!" Jin gasped. And Rhen knew he had finally seen it—the thing that legends were made of, the unanswerable mystery. "Are those…?"

"Yes."

He crossed his arms over his chest, looking at the scene that still made his throat hitch in terror, and gulped deeply.

Bones.

Skulls.

Armor.

All of it, stuck between layers of hardened, immobile rock.

Most of it just looked like thin strips of white or black sandwiched between brownish-gray stone. But every so often, two empty eyes would peer out, hollow and haunting. The glint of a now dull blade might catch the sun. Or the chink of rusted armor. The longer one looked, the more there was to see. A hand pushing out through rock. A spine bending almost in a circle. A helmet, cracked clean in half with the bone missing, taken by time.

"Buried by the flood, by nature itself," Rhen said.

An entire battlefield lay stuck in these walls, frozen in time yet completely forgotten.

Rhen snuck a quick look at Jin, who was still enraptured.

He took a small step back, the biggest the tiny space would allow, hoping Jin might forget he was there.

He waited.

Waited.

Slowed his breathing.

Knelt down.

Hid.

Then in one quick motion, he sprang forward, wrapping his hands around Jin's shoulders and throat while yelling as loud as he could into the boy's ear.

Perfect.

Instantly, a screech, as high-pitched as any Rhen had heard from a woman, broke free of Jin's lips. And kept going. And kept going.

Until Rhen, enveloped in a fit of laughter, fell to floor of the small crow's nest—his body too uncontrolled to hold him upright.

The screech finally came to a halt.

Below them, Rhen heard muffled coughs—coughs that sounded distinctly un-cough like.

He rolled onto his back. He felt the boy's eyes on him, heard his heavy breathing.

Then suddenly, Jin was on the floor too, next to Rhen, bursts of joy escaping his lips.

"Jin," Rhen forced out between deep breaths, "you, you sounded…that…a girl…so high."

The words were incoherent, but he knew Jin would understand.

They stayed like that, comfortable, until all sound except deep breathing died away. Then Jin stiffened, sitting up, pulling his thighs flat against his chest.

Rhen stayed where he was, watching clouds float by overhead, perfectly content to let his feet dangle in the breeze.

"Rhen?"

"Hmm?"

He shifted his gaze to Jin, whose head rested on his knee, pensively studying the cliff face to the side of the ship.

"Do you think…" He paused. "Do you think the flood was real?"

Rhen shrugged. "I don't know, Jin, it's just a legend."

"Do you think…" He paused again. "Is it possible that a human caused it? Someone like you or me?"

Rhen sat up, listening.

"What if before, people could use these gifts, could actually make things happen?"

"How so?"

"What if before, instead of just pulling the fire under your skin, you could create it? What if someone could do the same thing with water?"

"That's not natural," Rhen said the first words that came to mind. But part of him was intrigued—the part of him that as a boy had tried to do that very thing.

"I think it would be the most natural thing in the world," Jin said, soft and fragile.

"Well, if you feel a sudden urge to drown the kingdom, let me know, okay?" He grinned.

Jin rolled his eyes, but a smile tugged at his lips.

"We're in this together, you and me," Rhen said, nudging the boy with his knee. "We'll defeat the Ourthuri. Dissipate your shadow. And with whatever time is left over, we'll figure out what the spirits mean to do with us. Agreed?"

He offered his hand.

Jin looked at it, and then slowly stretched his own forward.

A pact.

Clouds gathered in the boy's eyes, but Rhen chose to ignore them. Instead standing, stretching his arms high overhead, and letting a yawn open his mouth.

"I think I need some food," he said sleepily, before jumping easily down onto the ropes, starting his descent.

The day was too beautiful for doubts.

15

JINJI
~WHITE STONE SEA~

Jinji was leaving.

She would wait until Rhen was reunited with his family, until he was distracted, but as soon as that happened, she was gone.

She had to be.

It had all started with a dream—so small, so insignificant, yet everything.

Jinji sat in the golden palace. Rhen's head rested on her lap. A gold dress flowed over her limbs, her eyes were hooded with the veil, and she ran her fingers lovingly over his cheeks.

"Rhen," she whispered, dipping her lips down so they skimmed the soft skin below his ear. "Wake up."

Hair fell over her shoulder, hair that was black and long and luscious— hair that was not cut in mourning, that showed no respect for her heritage, for her family.

A hand gently cupped her cheek. It was coarse and callused, yet comforting.

"Jinji," a deep voice said. She pulled back, meeting sparkling green eyes—the color of the forest just before twilight.

Rhen.

And he looked at her like she was his world.

Slowly, she pulled the metal mask off her head, but his expression bore no surprise. He knew who she was. He had known the entire time.

His fingers slipped behind her neck, running through her heavy locks, massaging the skin around her shoulders before pulling her down.

Down.

Closer.

Until their breath mingled, hot and electric.

And then his lips were on her skin, setting it ablaze. His fingers like lava as they traced a path down her back, over thin fabrics, to her hip, and still lower.

Jinji gasped.

She had never been touched like this before. Never been held like this.

Her skin prickled, hot to the touch. Her fingers stretched into his hair, gripping the short strands, forcing his face closer.

But then they both stopped moving, halted in time.

Suddenly, his lips turned cold. His hands fell away.

Jinji sat up. But it was not Rhen below her anymore.

It was Maniuk—face frozen in betrayal.

She blinked.

The face changed to that of her father—eyes downcast with disappointment.

Tears blurred her vision, so she rubbed them away.

Now her mother—mouth open in disgust.

"No!" She yelled and stood, backing away.

The body shifted, flipped over—rotting fingers gripped the ground, pulling the carcass closer. The figure stood.

And it was Janu.

"Have you forgotten?" He asked. The skin around his lips flaked away. "Have you forgotten what you are?"

His hands rose up and gripped her cheeks. His skin melted off, dripping to her feet until finally it was her own face that remained.

"Remember," she said, "remember."

And then she had awoken, panting in the darkness, her heart racing as fast as it had ever felt. But it wasn't the shadow—it was her own guilt haunting her.

The dream played on repeat in her sleep, sometimes changing location, but always the same. Rhen or her family. Rhen or her vengeance.

She could not have both.

Traveling with Rhen had brought her no closer to answers. It had been a distraction—perhaps a needed one, a way to free herself from the loss, to open herself up to the outside world, now far less scary than it had been only weeks before. But there was no forgetting her people or her mission.

The spirits were guiding her, but toward what? It was time to take fate into her own hands. And if Rhen could not help her defeat the shadow, she needed to leave him behind and find someone who could.

No matter how much her heart tightened at that thought.

"Are you practicing? Like that?"

Jinji turned. She had forgotten about the sword resting in her lap, the one Rhen was trying his best to teach her how to use. Her mind had been elsewhere, but now she was aware.

The world filtered back into focus.

"No." She shrugged, removing it and letting it drop onto the ground beside her. She was at the bow of the ship, sitting with legs crossed as she gazed out at the waters before her.

They had left the deep canals, the cliffs, and the river behind long ago. Now they were in the White Stone Sea as Rhen had called it, affection evident in his voice. This was his territory, his home. And it was as beautiful as anything she had ever laid eyes on.

The sea was turquoise—brighter and more vibrant than any waters she had ever seen before. Rhen said it was the sand.

There was a mountain range in the middle of the sea, huge peaks that stretched endlessly into the clouds. The locals called them the Gates—the entrance to the spirit world. No humans had ever been able to climb them and live to tell the tale, though Rhen assured her that some had tried. But the stones, he said, were pure white. The mountains looked like snow and ice from afar, but they were rock. A smooth, polished stone unlike anywhere else in their world.

The sand was made from that rock—the waters beat against the mountains, knocking pieces off and breaking them down into rubble. The pure ivory that decorated the sea floor turned the water the most unbelievable hue, a liquid gemstone.

"We should be arriving in Rayfort today, a few hours at the most," Rhen said from above. He stood next to her, resting his forearms on the wooden rail, eyes focused on the search for his home. "I recognize the shoreline."

Jinji stayed seated, keeping her distance. "What will happen when we get there?"

"I imagine my family will be both relieved and annoyed at my appearance. The Naming should be happening soon, they've likely been postponing it until I return. The ceremony cannot be completed without the entire royal house present. My brother and I must hand over our right to the throne to the new Son of Whyl, removing our claim to keep the future succession untainted."

"And what will happen to me?"

"During the Naming? Nothing. Only the noble—well, let's just say it is a closed ceremony. But afterward, I will show you my home. We can train you to be a knight, you can grow up to serve your kingdom and your king." Rhen shrugged, as though that was the normal—the only—path for her to take.

Was that why he had wanted to teach her swordplay? Why he had demanded?

Jinji pulled her legs into her chest.

She had been right. Rayfort was the end. After that, she and Rhen would have to part ways, to follow different fates.

Part of her had hoped that things would change after she had forced him to dance with the fire. And it had. They had drifted closer—too close.

Despite being just Jin to Rhen, she felt like he knew her better than anyone else ever had—anyone except Janu. She understood Rhen. He trusted her, likely against his best instincts. And she had faith in him.

But it was that very connection, deep and only strengthening by the day, that made Jinji uneasy. No one could ever take the place of her people in her heart. She wouldn't allow it, not when their legacy depended on her—she owed them at least that.

"Do you think we will find any answers in your home? Any word of the shadow I mentioned?"

It was a stretch, a faint hope, but she had to ask the question.

He tore his eyes away from the land laid out before them, looking down at her in sympathy.

"I don't know, Jin. I don't even know what to look for."

Her heart sunk, dropping an inch deeper into her chest.

"In Roninhythe," her mouth stumbled over the long word, still not comfortable on her tongue, "I heard sailors talking. They said two of their own had died, one with a slit throat just like…like Maniuk," she forced the name out, taking a deep breath. "And two children were found dead by the wall. The lord said they fell, but one of them had a slit throat too. It can't be coincidence, it—"

"I heard the same, Jin," Rhen said, reaching down to pat her shoulder, "my friend, son of the Lord of Roninhythe, he told me something similar. But what would the shadow want with all of those people? The Arpapajo, children, soldiers, sailors? They have nothing in common. It is more the act of a thief than a ghost."

"I—"

"And even if it is this shadow, what do you mean to do, Jin? How can you catch something that does not exist, that jumps from body to body, that ensnares the mind? How could you even fight it?"

"I don't know," she said softly, chin sinking down into her chest.

Rhen knelt.

"I know it hurts, but your family is gone, Jin. It would be better for you to move on and live your life."

And there it was. The very thing she had been dreading Rhen would say, would believe. He wanted her to forget.

Janu's face flashed before Jinji's eyes.

Had she forgotten?

Never.

Jinji turned to Rhen, eyes narrowing as her heart started to pound. "Move on?" Her nostrils flared. Her lips quivered. "Move on? As if you have any right to tell someone else to move on, Prince Whylrhen."

"Jin, I didn't mean—"

"Didn't mean what?" She stood, meeting him as close to face to face as her small size would allow. "That they are dead? That they are never coming back? And that means I should just let them go?"

"No, but—"

"Do they not deserve to be avenged? To be cared for, even in death? Someone must remember, and I am the only one left who can."

She stopped, panting, not used to talking so aggressively. Rhen looked on shocked, a little hurt.

"Jin, why are you so angry?"

She took a deep breath, trying to control the swell in her chest, but it was no use. The floodgate had opened. And Rhen was the only person around to take the hit.

"Ka'shasten. Do you know what that means?"

Rhen scrunched his forehead, dumbfounded.

"It means family, loved ones, and so much more than that. It is unexplainable, it is part of my soul, just like my people were—are."

"Kayashastian," he tried, mumbling the word.

"Ka'shasten," she repeated, her heart melting and breaking at the same time. He had tried, tried to understand her, to help her. But the failure was all the more bittersweet because of it, all the more noticeable. Differentiating. "Do you know what it feels like to be the only person in the world who understands what that means? I cannot just let it go, let them go. We are one people, something a newworlder would never understand."

"So now I'm a newworlder?"

"You always were," she said, a hard edge in her voice. "It is not my fault that you cannot see it."

"Maybe you're the one who can't see." He pointed at her, defensive. "A sword? Leather pants? A fine silk jacket? You don't look like an oldworlder to me Jin, not anymore."

She looked down at herself, the breeches sticking to her legs, the shirt billowing over her chest. Where were the animal hides? The skins bleached soft in the sun?

A lump caught in her throat. Her eyes began to sting.

Before she knew it, she was running, stomping over wooden boards. Rhen called her name, but it was lost on the wind. She kept fleeing, not wanting to face his words, or hers.

Only when the cabin was locked behind her did the tears start to fall. She bit them back, crawling onto the bed, closing her eyes tightly and imagining a different time, a different life.

She was a little girl. It was the night before Sanjiju—their most beloved ceremony. The next morning the tribe would wake at sunrise to celebrate the spirits in prayer and dance. For the first time, she and Janu would partake in the fast. Already her stomach was rumbling. But there was an excitement in the air that only came once a year, when the winter was shed and a new spring was arriving, a time for renewal.

Jinji could remember lying in that bed as though it were only yesterday, counting the minutes as they went by. But the next morning was not her favorite part of the memory, it was seconds later.

Jinji, she could remember Janu whispering. He tapped her arm and she flipped to face him on their shared pallet.

From the other side of the small cabin, their father shushed them both, reprimanding their disrespect. It was time to sleep. Tomorrow would be a long day. They would need energy. And everything else a parent said to a disobedient child.

Jinji covered her mouth, giggling. Janu did not try to cover his laugh. She pinched his arm, but it only made him louder.

Be quiet, she remembered whispering. *Father will move you to the longhouse and then we won't be able to play.*

He sighed heavily, but quieted himself and moved closer. The starlight filtered in through the smoke hole at the top of their home, just enough to see the glisten in each other's eyes.

Then Jinji reached out, grabbing Janu's hand and flipping it face up. Using her fingers, she tapped a beat onto his palm.

One. Two. Three. Very fast with her pointer. Then one slow with her pinky. Then two fast with her thumb. Then three slow, each a different finger.

Janu watched, straining to see her fingers in the dark. When she was done, he flipped her palm, trying to copy. But at the end, he only tapped slowly twice. She shook her head, grinning, and made a new beat.

They played for an hour before falling fast asleep mid-tap, fingers holding onto each other in the dark—almost as though the spirits knew that it would be their last Sanjiju together, that they would need that extra time. By the next year, Jinji would be dancing for him, and not with him, during the ceremony.

Jinji sighed, rolling over as her head returned to the present day, to the ship—to her loneliness. Her heart had slowed, as had her tears. But she was still curled in a little ball, clutching her knees.

Someone was outside the door. She heard the unmistakable creak of footsteps, pacing back and forth. The doorknob jiggled. A curse filtered through the wood. And then…

"Jin? Did you lock the door?"

She didn't respond. She just closed her eyes, taking a deep breath.

"Look, I'm sorry. I didn't mean, of course you shouldn't forget your family and your people. I would never suggest that. And I shouldn't have said that about you being a newworlder—because believe me when I say you most definitely are not."

A thud hit the door, likely his back as he shifted his weight.

Jinji remained silent. She owed him an apology as well—she knew it. There was no reason for her to yell at him, no reason at all, except that she was starting to say goodbye. And it would be easier to say goodbye to someone she hated. Not a friend. Especially not the only one she had left in this world.

"I'll help you find this shadow, I will. As soon as the Naming is complete and I've warned my father on the Ourthuri treachery, I'll devote all of my time to the search. And we'll figure out how to destroy it together."

He paused, waiting.

Jinji pictured him, leaning against the door, fists firm over his head, his expression pleading.

"Why?" She didn't mean to say it out loud, but it happened. And words were like that. Once said, you could never take them back—no matter how much you wished you could.

"Because," he said, thinking, "you saw the part of me that I keep hidden from the rest of the world, and it didn't scare you. We're brothers, Jin. Somehow, someway, a Son of Whyl and an Arpapajo became brothers."

She took a deep breath, ignoring the sudden heat warming her chest, and sat up. *At least he doesn't know I'm a girl*, she thought, smiling to herself before standing.

Midway up, she frowned, quickly inversing her features.

This changed nothing. She was still leaving. All it did was ensure that Rhen would hate her all the more once she left.

"Now will you come open the door? I feel like an idiot talking to myself."

Jinji rolled her eyes.

As she neared the door, her heart began to flutter, sending chills down her arms. She twisted the lock. Her heart skipped a beat, waiting, watching the entrance.

It opened.

Rhen took up the entire frame, and he was looking at her expectantly.

Jinji stifled the urge to run into his arms, to throw her hands around his neck, to seek the comfort she so earnestly desired. Instead, she planted her feet, silently waiting like she always did.

"Well?" He asked. His left cheek twitched, his lip rose and a crooked lazy smile gathered on his face.

Jinji shrugged in response, not trusting her body to listen to her.

"Don't you want to see my home?"

"We've arrived?" She asked, perking up.

"It speaks!" he teased, reaching out to tousle the short hair on top of her head. She missed his touch when it was gone, leaving her colder.

"Come, Rayfort awaits."

Jinji followed him back on deck, emerging to a scene that stole her breath.

Rhen pointed to the side, where a pile of dull gray stones sat in ruin, overgrown with moss and speckled green. "Over there is where the original castle once stood. But when Whyl the Conqueror united the lands, he rebuilt Rayfort on the peninsula and to show his strength, they mined rocks from the Gates to build the castle and its walls."

Rhen pointed again, this time to the exact spot that had originally drawn Jinji's attention—a gleaming, pristine ivory castle, like something out of a dream. Similar to Roninhythe, the castle was built from sturdy stone, rising from a surrounding wall with tall circular pillars stretching high into the air. Against the blue sky and speckled colors of the surrounding city, the castle seemed almost magical. Something within her felt pulled toward it, connected to it, almost as if it were made of jinjiajanu—of the spirits.

Jinji pulled her eyes away to take in the rest of the sprawling city—the largest she had ever seen, even greater than Da'astiku. The castle sat on a hill in the center, rising above everything else, but the sea of rooftops never seemed to end. They were in front of the castle, behind the castle, to the left, to the right. More stone, some wood—grays and reds and browns—stretching until the very edge of the sea where an outer wall stood, white stones sinking into the water.

Beside her, Rhen took a deep, satisfied breath. His shoulders relaxed, and his whole body seemed to shed the weight of worry that had been holding him down.

He's home, Jinji thought.

"The city has three layers of defense," Rhen said, excitedly moving his hands around, "the outer wall is the first layer, then there is an inner wall, if you can see the white towers cutting out from the rooftops—there and there—and finally, the castle wall. It's never been sacked and not for lack of trying. Built on the peninsula, land attacks are near impossible because the enemy can only approach from one side, and it is somewhat of an uphill battle for them. And by sea, though you might think Rayfort is easily surrounded, the Straits give an early line of fire. The only time the Ourthuri tried to attack our capital, the ships were set ablaze in the Straits using flaming arrows and oil. The enemy never even reached the White Stone Sea."

Pride shone through his voice.

"Is there no other way than through the Straits?"

Rhen shook his head. "The other rivers are too shallow for warships. They only carry small merchant vessels."

"Then how do you think the Ourthuri king plans to win this war?"

"I don't know, Jin, I really don't." He shook his head. His tone lifted. Just seeing his home had made his spirits rise higher than Jinji had seen them in days.

She looked back out at the fast approaching city. Rayfort. The guards on the outer wall were starting to come into focus. Rhen waved—his red silken coat and auburn hair unmistakable, even from that distance. A horn sounded, happy and jubilant. On the docks, everyone paused, watching their arrival. People started to gather at the edges, observing with smiles on their faces.

There was no mistaking that Rhen belonged here. He was their prince. And already Jinji could tell that these people loved him.

But would they ever love her? Could she ever love them?

Her palms began to sweat on the wood.

It didn't matter, she reasoned with a mental shrug. In a matter of days, she would be gone.

And she would never be coming back.

16

RHEN
~RAYFORT~

Home, Rhen thought with a sigh. There was just something about coming home that felt so right, so relaxing.

He stepped off the ship onto the wooden planks of the dock. Rayfort.

He had arrived, hopefully in time to make a difference.

Looking around, Rhen searched for red in the crowd. No king's guards, at least not yet. But they would come to escort him—there was no way he would escape that torture.

Although…

He walked forward, knowing Jin would follow behind. He had already thanked Captain Jelaric for his services, and once he arrived at the castle, Rhen would send a handsome reward. There was little reason to wait there like an idiot, especially when he had urgent news for his father. Perhaps he could find a horse to borrow, leave before the guards even arrived.

A scream sounded on the wind.

Another.

Thunderous steps boomed in Rhen's ears.

He grinned.

It could only mean one thing.

A furious neigh cut through the shouts. And then, careening around the corner of the walk, there was a flash of red blurred by speed.

Ember.

Warmth surged in Rhen's chest, sprinkling down his limbs, comforting and exciting. His arms opened wide and a laugh spilled from his lips as he walked forward, trying to meet her halfway.

"Easy, girl," he shouted, trying to calm her from afar, knowing it was a long shot.

She charged through the sailors, almost shoving one man into the water, until a few feet short of Rhen, she came to a dead halt.

Rhen sighed and rolled his eyes. So this was how she was going to play it.

He stepped forward, smiling with arms wide.

She stepped back, stomping her right foot hard against the wood and shaking her head with a whining neigh.

He tried again, moving forward very slowly.

She jumped onto her hind legs, rearing and throwing her front feet forward.

"Ember!" Rhen gasped.

She stomped again.

"My Lord, stay back," one of the guards came running from behind.

"Stop!" Rhen shouted at the man, knowing that Ember would have no shame kicking him with her hind leg if he got too close. He had trained her, after all. "She is my horse. I do not want anyone interfering."

The guard nodded, keeping his distance. But he still looked far too ready to pounce.

Rhen tried stepping forward again. Ember looked at him, squinting with her one eye.

He tried to reason with her. "I know you're mad, but I'm sorry. You couldn't come with me. The open ocean is no place for a horse. You barely even like walking through a deep stream."

She sneezed, slobbering all over his face.

Rhen frowned, exasperated, determined not to move another inch. They stared at each other, each more stubborn by the second, until finally Ember threw her head to the side, breaking contact, and letting Rhen win.

She dipped her nose, hanging it a little low, and stepped forward into Rhen's waiting arms. He hugged her thick neck, rubbing the red hairs flat as her breathing slowed. Reaching up with his left hand, Rhen felt along the side of her face, running his fingers down the length of her muzzle until she sighed and relaxed. Then Rhen gently scratched the diamond puff of white hairs between her eyes. She pushed her head closer, letting him know everything had been forgiven.

"Good girl," he cooed. "Now what do you say we go for a ride?"

Her ears perked.

"You remember Jin, right, Ember?" He turned, spotting Jin closer to the ship. The boy looked on with a soft smile and warm eyes, with a feeling Rhen couldn't quite place.

He shrugged, no matter, and motioned for Jin to walk over.

"Hello, Ember," Jin said, hesitant, and then reached out his hand. Rhen almost swatted it away, afraid she would bite, but instead his horse moved closer, rubbing the tip of her nose against the outstretched palm. Rhen smirked. Getting Ember's approval was no small feat, and the boy had done it twice. Jin would do fine in Rayfort. Better than fine.

Grabbing Ember's saddle, Rhen jumped into the seat. He had missed her. The only woman who had really ever held his heart.

"Come on, Jin," he said, lightly tapping Ember's rear and outstretching his hand. The boy's eyes widened. "Come on, you rode her before in Roninhythe. There is nothing to be afraid of."

Jin nodded absentmindedly.

Rhen reached farther down, gripping the boy's hand and pulling him up before another protest could be uttered. He had work to do, and there could be no more delays.

With a yelp, Jin settled in.

"Hold on." Rhen jerked on the reins. Jin gripped the top of Rhen's shoulders forcefully, rather than holding his torso, but Rhen let it go. If the boy wanted to fall on his butt, that was his problem.

"Prince Whylrhen," one of the guards yelled, but Rhen ignored him, urging Ember along and pushing his way through the crowd.

The people smiled at him, meeting his eyes before they bowed, yelling out praises and kind words on his return. Rhen smiled, waving, reaching down to touch some of their hands, tossing a few silver coins out of his purse, cracking jokes.

While his father and brothers remained in the castle, guarded and gated from the common people, Rhen had used them as the perfect escape. He was the third son, had fewer responsibilities, fewer expectations, and always worked on the reputation he had so carefully crafted since boyhood.

Instead of tending to matters of court, he visited local shops to buy goods and sat at local taverns to drink ale. And because he refused to stay hidden and locked away, the people loved him— which annoyed his siblings and father to no end.

During parades through the city, it was Whylrhen that was shouted above the others. The king believed it was purely due to gossip, to the fact that his name was on every father or elder brother's tongue…or every whore's. But Rhen knew it was more, so much more. He would never be one of them, of the common folk, but he was as close as they would ever get to royalty, and it was far closer than they had ever been before.

So he let them touch his fingers, pet his horse, try to tell their life story in a short sentence, because it made them feel special and it made him feel connected to something larger. It was only after, when he passed through the white wall in the middle of the city and entered the noble quarters, that he felt alone, emptier for remembering that it was just another show, another character.

The streets were quieter here. Men and women bowed, careful to pay him due respect. The children didn't run free and wild, but instead stood carefully beside their families as was proper. The clothes were more colorful, more voluminous, but life seemed dampened somehow.

Rhen shifted in the saddle, nodding politely to everyone as they passed by, noticing a few curious looks at Jin—the Arpapajo. Did any of these people even remember that the oldworlders still lived? Northmore Forest was, after all, a long distance away. "What do you think of my city?" He asked Jin.

"It is very…large." The boy sounded overwhelmed, his voice was meek, almost ill. "I don't know how I will ever find my way out—I mean, around."

"No matter." Rhen shrugged. "I'll show you most of it. In a few weeks, it will feel like home. I know it. Besides, the city was built that way on purpose."

"Hmm?" Jin asked, thoughts clearly elsewhere. But Rhen tried to put himself in Jin's shoes—almost any situation was rightfully overwhelming for someone who had lived most of his life in one small portion of a forest, away from the outside world.

But for Rhen, muddy cobblestone streets lined with row after row of homes was just second nature. Likely taken for granted.

"The city was built as a maze. Many streets turn unexpectedly into dead ends, or spin in circles so you might be turned completely around without realizing it. Just another method of defense. But the natives, they know where to go. And new travelers are all the more obvious to the king's guard."

A horn sounded.

Surprised, Rhen looked up, right into the blinding façade of the castle wall. The stark white burned his eyes, but it felt good in a way.

The gates slowly started to open, cracking to reveal the lush green courtyard at the base of the castle, just behind its defensive wall. The stables stood a little farther to the left, out of sight, but the horses were sometimes allowed to roam freely. Not today. Today, the place seemed pure chaos. Servants scrambled back and forth, overloaded with baskets of food and laundry, and there were too many of them. Far more than usual.

Stepping through the now open gate, Rhen saw guards from noble houses all over the kingdom dressed in all different colors.

The Naming.

And Rhen was most definitely the last one to arrive.

Perfect.

"Prince Whylrhen," he turned to see his father's courier bowed deeply, head nearly at the floor. "King Whylfrick would like to see you immediately, in the throne room."

"Of course he does," Rhen said under his breath. The whole reason he had returned was to warn his father of the imminent danger to the kingdom, but until that moment, he had forgotten that a lecture would surely come first.

There was always a lecture.

Always.

Louder, Rhen said, "Of course, Reynard, you can tell him I will be there immediately."

"Thank you, Prince Whylrhen." The man bowed his head once more before scurrying off.

Rhen helped Jin down before sliding from the saddle.

"You'll probably want to stay behind me," he whispered to Jin, before making his way to the large stone steps at the front of the keep.

When he was halfway up the stairs, the guards pulled open the entrance—two wooden doors almost fifteen feet high and decorated with intricate iron lattices. Behind him, Jin gasped. Rhen grinned.

The castle was home. He was too used to these halls to be impressed, but it filled him with a sense of pride to hear Jin's reaction. And it was well deserved. The entry glistened with polished white stones, pearlescent in the daylight. Windows made of colored glass reflected around the small atrium, bouncing the four colors of the elements into overlaying patches. Giant tapestries depicting the red flag of Whylkin with its great bucking steed hung from the ceiling. And a grand staircase curved upward to the second level where the throne room sat.

Two servants manned the space, bowing as soon as they saw Rhen enter. He nodded and moved on, tugging Jin with him. Best not to keep his father waiting.

Hurrying up the steps, Rhen stepped into the long hall that led to the throne room—white walls decorated with expansive tapestries depicting the life of Whyl the Conqueror. Every battle, every victory, every milestone—everything history wanted to remember about his ancestor was written in threads, depicted through art.

Later, he told himself, later he would explain them to Jin, would tell him the stories. But for now they rushed through, walking briskly toward the wooden door at the end of the hall, already held open for him.

When Rhen entered the throne room, his breath caught. He had forgotten how majestic this space was—an inevitable side effect of avoiding the room at all costs. But he took one spare gaze to take it all in. The atrium was gigantic, at least four stories high and two to three times as long. Thick columns extended into the vaulted ceiling, crisscross woodwork danced above his head, and more tapestries lined the walls. There were no windows except for one—but what a window it was.

Rhen let his vision extend, moving down the center of the room until the sculpted stone throne of Whylkin filled his view. The seat itself was small, and occupied by a man whom he glossed over, but the throne was another thing entirely. Carved from one piece of rock, it was at least two men high and four men wide, decorated with impressions of humans, horses, and cityscapes.

And behind the throne rested a wall of glass revealing the most beautiful view of the city of Rayfort and the clear cerulean sea beyond the peninsula. On a clear day, the peaks of the Gates might be visible, a stack of pointed clouds piercing the sky.

"Whylrhen," a stern voice commanded.

Reverting back to his four-year-old self, Rhen winced and straightened his shoulders, standing as tall as possible while he gathered the courage to meet his father's eyes. Slowly, he started walking forward, listening as his boots clicked against the stone, echoing across the room.

The entire family was there, waiting for him. His mother, Queen Katrina, wearing a long bronze dress to match her eyes. His middle brother, Whyllem, slouched and relaxed. His eldest brother Whyltarin, with arms folded across his broad chest and feet planted wide. Just behind him, Awenine sat in a flowing blue gown, her blonde hair pinned elegantly atop her head. And in her arms, wrapped in a bright red swaddle, was Rhen's perfect little nephew—as yet unnamed, but the brilliant red hair poking out from the cloth named him a Son of Whyl in a way no words ever could.

Hair just like Whyltarin.

Just like Whyllem.

But mostly, just like King Whylfrick.

With a sigh, Rhen finally looked into his father's piercing gaze and stopped five feet back from everyone else. They would give no hugs until his father allowed it, though his mother offered a warm smile. Beside her, Whyllem offered a knowing grin and elbowed Whyltarin in the ribs, breaking their eldest brother's tough exterior. The two had always been close, a pair. At only one year apart, they spent six years together before Rhen was even born, a bond that was tough for a younger brother to crack.

Trying hard to ignore them, Rhen bit his cheeks, waiting for his father to speak. But the king just watched, far too relaxed leaning back on the throne with his chin in his palm. The golden crown rested on his curling hairs. His silken robes were stark against the ivory stone around him. While his demeanor was deceptively lax, his eyes were hard and demanding.

The silence was too overwhelming. Rhen urgently felt the need to explain himself, his absence. "Father—"

"Were you not aware of Awenine's pregnancy before you mysteriously disappeared from home seven months ago?" The king's deep voice reverberated down the hall, sinking into Rhen's bones, making them shake.

"I was," he said hoarsely. Rhen swallowed, trying to moisten his dry throat.

"Were you not aware that it takes only nine months for a woman to birth a child?" Whyllem snickered, trying to cover it with a cough.

"I was."

"Then you must not have been listening when your teachers discussed the Naming, one of Whylkin's most sacred ceremonies."

Rhen frowned. "I was, but—"

"Then why in the name of Whyl has the royal family and every nobleman in the kingdom been twiddling their thumbs for days waiting for the reckless third son of King Whylfrick to return home?"

"Father, I—"

The king sat straight, leaning forward and raising his voice. "I know. Young Calen was kind enough to deliver your message. Unmarked ships. Attacks in the forest. A devious plot for our throne. More like an irresponsible son wasting my time gallivanting over to the Kingdom of Ourthuro when he was needed at home. Needed for the one thing he was born to do— gift the throne to someone who deserves it. Someone who will use his power wisely. Not to sleep his way around the kingdom and pretend to be a hero."

"Whylfrick!" His mother gasped. For a moment, he softened, hearing her voice, but then his eyes narrowed.

"What do you have to say for yourself? To your brother, the future king?"

Rhen opened his mouth, ready to let apologies spill from his lips, but then he paused. The words stopped, clogging his throat as though they refused to be said. He had apologized too many times. And this time, Rhen had been right. It was the first time in his life that he had more to offer than a lame excuse, than a lie. He finally had real information. And his father refused to pay attention, to think for a minute that Rhen could maybe be more than a disappointment.

He stepped forward, stance strong, fueled by anger.

"I've been gathering information. I've been tracking our enemies, keeping my eyes and ears open. I've been doing the one thing you've been afraid to do ever since Whyllysle died, ever since…" His eyes unwittingly flicked toward his mother, by accident, on instinct. The king's pupils expanded, turning his eyes black with fury. It was as close as they had ever come to their unspoken secret, and it was as close as Rhen was willing to get. He looked away, wishing to take it back.

King Whylfrick stood, leaping down the steps to grab Rhen by his throat. Over his shoulder, Jin sucked in a breath, but Rhen held his, refusing to yield, to show weakness.

His father pulled him close, breathing heavily while his face reddened, and shook him painfully. Rhen bit his lip, refused to blink even as his eyes stung.

He had never seen his father like this. Angry, yes. Hurtful, yes. But now he seemed beyond thought. His nostrils flared. His face twisted in a grimace. His eyes clouded over, retreating to somewhere Rhen couldn't follow. And his fingers tightened, squeezing the air from his son's body.

Protests filtered into Rhen's hearing, but they were dulled by the pounding thuds hammering his ears. His vision started to spot. But he would not, could not, fight his father. He just wanted to make him listen, to make him understand…

Without warning, Rhen dropped to the ground. His legs gave out and he fell fast. Flipping over, he coughed, heaving until he could breathe normally, without pressure on his chest.

Glittered brown swished into his vision, the folds of a voluminous dress.

Rhen looked up to find his mother hanging on his father's arm, her hand cupping his cheek, her lips whispering softly into his ear.

Slowly, the color drained from the king's face, returning it to a normal pale peach. The fog retreated. His mouth dropped open and his eyes sharpened, slipping down, down, down, until they met Rhen's.

Haunted.

That was the only way Rhen could describe the gaze.

Haunted.

Without a word, his father stormed from the room. His mother leaned down, kissed the top of his head, and chased after her husband.

A hand slipped into view. A brown hand, naturally tanned, small, familiar. Rhen grabbed it, refusing to acknowledge the pity on his friend's face. Instead, he closed his eyes, and then opened them wide, turning to his brothers with a fake smile and an unnaturally cheerful voice.

"So, can I hold him?"

Awenine stood quickly, rushed over to Rhen with concern, and offered him the child.

"My nephew," Rhen sighed, taking the small bundle into his bulky arms. He couldn't believe how tiny the infant was, barely the length of his forearm. But he looked perfect, with eyes closed tight in sleep despite the chaos that had just occurred. A knot uncurled in Rhen's chest. It was worth it. Everything. A real smile spread across his lips, untainted and true. "Have you named him? Can I get a preview?"

"The rest of the kingdom has been waiting for a week," Whyltarin said, stepping closer. "I think you can wait for a day. Father started the preparations. The Naming will be tomorrow morning at first light."

Rhen handed the child back to Awenine before turning sheepishly toward Whyltarin. "I'm sorry for the delay, Tarin." Somehow apologizing to his brother was easy.

"In truth," his eldest brother said, shrugging, "I think the lords were all too eager to eat the king's food and drink his wine. They'll likely be disappointed that it didn't take you longer."

"Some are likely disappointed I even showed at all," Rhen said, unable to hide the weight in his tone.

Tarin reached out, placing a thick hand on his shoulder, squeezing gently.

"I'm sorry for father. He acted out of line today, worse than I've ever seen. You've always been able to get under his skin, but he does love you, Rhen. Don't forget that."

"He's got a fine way of showing it."

Tarin opened his mouth, but Rhen cut him off. He had no mind to hear any excuses for the king, a man old enough to behave himself. Besides, Tarin didn't know the same king that Rhen did. His brothers would never understand—their father had been a different man—happier, prouder, more loving. What a difference half a decade could make.

"I have news, real news I meant to tell father, but I must tell you. Tarin, Whyllem." He looked farther back at his other brother. "I went to Ourthuro. King Razzaq tried to have me killed, and he almost succeeded. Captain Pygott is dead, as is his entire crew, and the only reason I survived is the boy standing next to me. His name is Jin, and," Rhen paused, flicking his eyes at the boy, "he is the last of the Arpapajo people. Everyone else was killed in an Ourthuri raid."

He knew it was a lie, but it was easier than the truth. Especially considering that Rhen didn't even know what the truth was. All he knew was that his brothers would not believe in some shadow figure, but they would hopefully believe in an attack by a known enemy.

"Rhen," Tarin sighed. Rhen knew exactly what that exasperated exhale meant.

"Tarin—" He stepped forward, grasping his oldest brother's broad shoulders. "You must believe me. I would never lie about something like this—please. I've been following information for months, truly, that is what I've been doing. And I finally uncovered a plot against us. King Razzaq is planning to attack, and I believe it will be very soon while all of the nobles are in

Rayfort, distracted. He'll start with the outer cities before working his way here, to the capital."

Tarin squinted and looked to his right, to Whyllem, to the future hand of the king—the brother he never questioned.

Rhen's heart dropped along with his hands.

He stepped back, watching his brothers engage in an unspoken conversation, until Whyllem stepped forward.

"I believe you, Rhen." He stopped, running a hand through his hair. "I don't know why King Razzaq would do this, what motive he has, especially when he knows it is a war he cannot hope to win, but I do believe you."

A weight lifted. Rhen's entire body felt light.

"As do I," Tarin added, his voice deep like their father's, commanding like a king's should be.

"Then we must act, immediately. Notify the lords, talk to father, spe—"

"Rhen," Tarin interrupted, "I believe you, but that does not mean I will shout a war cry from the castle walls. I will speak with father tonight, but the Naming is tomorrow and that must be our priority. The lords cannot be distracted with talk of battles, by fear for their homes. All focus must be on naming my son the future king of Whylkin, on securing the bloodline and the throne. Once the ceremony is complete, we will discuss our options."

"But there is no time to wait!" Rhen stepped forward, pleading. A sense of urgency crept into his blood. Somehow, Rhen knew waiting would mean disaster. He felt it in his bones.

Whyllem stepped forward, shaking his head. "Rhen, that is enough for now. Find your friend a room, clean yourself up, and meet us in the great hall for dinner."

He opened his mouth one more time, but then shut it. There was no use. It would always be two against one with them.

Instead, he nodded, trying to ignore the sinking feeling in his stomach.

"Welcome home, brother, and welcome to Rayfort, Jin," Tarin said, but he was distracted, looking over his shoulder at the baby waking up in his wife's arms. "Come, Awenine, let's prepare for supper." She kissed Rhen on the cheek, welcoming him back, before leaving the throne room.

Whyllem crept up behind Rhen, throwing an arm over his shoulder and roughing up his hair. "I'm glad you're home, little brother. Tarin's been a bore ever since he became a father. He thinks I should settle down. I wouldn't be surprised if he and the king were working out a bridal arrangement for me right now, what with so many of the noble families in town."

Rhen faked a grin and raised an eyebrow. "Well, we wouldn't want that, would we?"

"I knew I could count on you. After dinner, we'll see what sort of fun we can find—outside the wall." He winked and pulled back, releasing his hold on Rhen. "Welcome to the King's City, Jin." He nodded politely, not sparing a second glance at the boy. "Tonight," he added, emphasizing one more time for Rhen.

"Tonight," Rhen agreed. Tarin had always been the rule follower. But Whyllem, like Rhen, enjoyed pushing the limits. Unlike Rhen, he never seemed to get in trouble for it.

With a sigh, Rhen turned toward a stunned Jin. "So, that's my family." He shrugged. "Let's find a servant who will show you to a room. I'll come get you tomorrow as soon as the ceremony is over, and then your real introduction to Rayfort can begin."

The boy nodded, but Rhen noticed a sullenness sink into his gaze. His irises darkened. His brows twitched. Even his smile seemed weak and untrue. Something was bothering Jin, something he wasn't voicing.

But for once, Rhen decided he had enough to worry about already. Jin could wait a day.

The Naming? The Ourthuri? Those were immediate concerns, ones his gut was telling him he could not ignore, not even until tomorrow.

War was coming. It was imminent. And more than anything, Rhen knew there was something he was missing. Some piece of the puzzle that he hadn't seen. The most dangerous part.

And he had one night to figure it out.

One night before the world came crashing down around him.

17

JINJI
~RAYFORT~

Jinji sat up, watching the sky gradually turn lavender, feeling the minutes tick by as her mind continued to race.

She sighed, resigned.

Sleep was far off and not coming anytime soon.

Crawling out from the covers of a bed that was far too soft to be comfortable, she sank into a bench beside the window, taking in the full view of the city below her. Painted in pastels, it seemed less daunting.

All night she had been ruminating over her decision to leave. All night she had been going back and forth and more than anything, that scared her. It shouldn't be so hard to leave this place, or that man, behind.

But it was.

For the past week, Jinji had believed that leaving Rhen with his family would be natural, would be a gift. After all, he loved them enough to risk his life seeking their protection, to devote his entire being to keeping them safe. He spoke the world of his brothers. He yearned to spend time with his nephew. This was his home, and he belonged here.

But yesterday, Jinji realized nothing could be further from the truth. Even now, she shuddered, her body convulsing at the memory of Rhen's father choking him until he turned red. Of his brothers watching and not taking a single step forward. Of his mother rushing forward out of concern for the king, not her son.

None of that was natural. Or loving. Or caring. And it left a sick feeling in her stomach to think of abandoning Rhen to these people who he loved with his entire being despite their negligence.

She thought of her father kissing her goodnight—a soft brush on the forehead when he believed she was asleep. Or her mother spending painstaking hours working on the dress for her joining. And even Janu, defending her to his last breath.

That was family.

That was her family, the one she promised to avenge, not to let die in vain.

Her family—the very reason she had to leave.

Jinji hugged her knees to her chest, groaning as her argument came full circle for what seemed like the hundredth time that night.

But the night was over, and it was time to choose. The sun crept ever higher, burning the sky blue, and if she didn't leave now, Jinji wasn't sure she would ever be able to.

Closing her eyes tight, her heart wincing, Jinji quickly stood and grabbed her boots.

There was no choice. The shadow was her destiny—she had no option but to defeat it. Her soul would never feel peace until it was gone, unable to take another human life or break another human heart.

Before she could question herself yet again, Jinji opened the door.

Then stopped dead.

Rhen stood before her, hand poised to knock, a look of surprise coloring his features. His eyes were dark with drowsiness, but his skin was clean and polished, better than she had ever seen it. His hair had been neatly cut and his face perfectly shaved. His clothes glittered with jewels.

For the first time, Rhen really looked like a prince to her. Out of reach.

"Going somewhere?" He smirked, crossing his arms to lean against the doorway. Caught in the act, Jinji stood dumbstruck, unsure of what to say. "In truth," Rhen continued, completely oblivious, "I wish I could go exploring with you, but the ceremony is about to begin and I cannot be late, well, later than I already am."

Jinji smiled weakly. But her tongue was still stuck, unable to speak. A pinch suffocated her heart at the sight of him so unaware.

Rhen waited for her to speak, then shrugged. "Anyway, I was out half the night searching for anything that seemed out of the ordinary, but I found nothing. No mention of the Ourthuri and no mention of a shadow. I thought you would want to know."

"I do, thank you," Jinji said softly, her chin tucked into her neck.

He raised his brows, noticing something was off. But just as Rhen opened his mouth, a horn sounded down the halls. Face scrunching in annoyance, he cursed.

"I have to go."

"I know," Jin said, holding back the goodbye trying to force its way out.

"I'll see you afterward, tonight. I know of a tavern you'll love. It's no Staggering Vixen, but…" He trailed off with a wink.

"Go," Jinji pushed him, unsure if the catch in her throat was a cry or a laugh. Either way, it didn't matter.

Without looking back, Rhen turned down the hall. Jinji watched until he disappeared around the corner.

"Goodbye," she whispered, waiting a few more heartbeats to catch her breath.

People appeared in the hall, moving in and out of view, making their way toward the ceremony. Most spared a quick, confused glance at Jinji. But she could barely see more than the shimmer of their fine garb, the swish of a full skirt, or the click of a solid boot.

She was too busy pushing thoughts of Rhen from her mind; too busy replacing them with memories of her family.

After one last deep breath, she stepped free of the wall and made her way aimlessly down the corridor, searching for some sign of an exit.

The castle seemed empty. White and barren.

All she really had to do was follow the silence, and eventually, after many turns and many steps, Jinji came to a door that opened onto a green courtyard.

Following a trodden dirt path, she was led to an archway through the white wall into rows of endless townhouses.

And that led to utter confusion.

Just like the castle, the streets were barren. Jinji remembered Rhen mentioning that this second tier was the noble quarters—nobles who were no doubt at the ceremony. But unlike the castle, the silence didn't help.

Rhen had said this city was a maze, and Jinji believed him. After a few turns, she was completely lost. Each stone house looked the same. Each street curved around the next, removing any sense of direction. But there was no one around to ask for help. More than once, she came upon a closed wall, a dead end, and had to turn around.

Looking up, Jinji saw that the sun had already neared the center of the sky, and she was no closer to finding a way out. She had spent hours running through the streets, in circles. It was almost as though the city didn't want her to leave.

Finally, she stopped, panting.

Her silken shirt stuck to her skin, her pants felt tight for the first time and her feet ached.

Leaving was the right choice. It had to be…

A sound clicked in Jinji's ears.

She looked up and the spirits entered her vision.

It was sign. A sense of peace filtered into her heart for the first time that morning.

Following the noise, her eyes focused on the street corner to her right. At first, she didn't realize what the tapping could be, but then a long brown snout came into view, followed by a shaggy neck, and a harnessed torso, until the entire horse and its cargo emerged.

An old woman held the reins, humming while she urged the animal forward. A halo of green surrounded her figure—earth spirits, woven like vines to her limbs.

Jinji stepped out of her shady spot, holding her hands aloft.

"Please," she said, hope infused in her tone, "please, I am lost and need help getting out of the city."

"Whoa," the woman said, gently bringing the cart to a stop, pulling up almost directly beside Jinji. The woman looked her up and down, squinting and crinkling her nose. "Not in trouble, are you?" A nasal voice asked, thickly accented.

"No." Jinji dropped her hands and shook her head. "Just a lost traveler in need of assistance."

The woman leaned forward, sniffing the air. "Alright, get in." She shifted in her seat, moving slightly so Jinji could step up next to her on the bench.

The woman smelled of the earth, like dirt and grass after a fresh rain.

"I can take you as far as the market, no farther. I have to sell my vegetables, the ones the castle didn't want for their fine banquet, full of it they are."

"Thank you," Jinji mumbled, settling into her seat, feeling uncomfortable under the woman's sharp gaze.

"You've got some nice clothes," she said, touching Jinji's arm, leaving brown spots on her white shirt, "very fine indeed."

Jinji shrugged, looking away, wondering what the spirits were actually trying to tell her. But the silence paid off, because the woman kept talking.

"The name's Elga, short for Remelga, but that was my mother's name, rest her soul." She jerked on the reins and the horse trudged forward again, pulling the weight of the cart very slowly behind. But it was a direction, the right direction, and that was all that mattered to Jinji.

Elga looked ahead, watching the road, but kept chattering. "I work in the fields outside the walls, have all my life. My husband is too old to sell anymore, so I come in, do his work, little money that it is. Castle takes all the good crop, leaving barely anything left to bring to the market. But the people still buy it, and I take whatever money they can offer. They love my vegetables; best there are everyone tells me. The plants love me, that's what they say. Silly, isn't it? Thinking like that, but that's what they say."

"I don't think it's silly," Jinji said softly, almost surprising herself, but the words popped out, beyond her control.

Elga smiled and the somewhat wary tilt to her gaze disappeared. She leaned in. "That's what I tell my husband, but he says to stay quiet. To mind my tongue, little help it gives me. Talk like that is dangerous, he says, gets people hurt—killed these days."

Jinji turned sharply toward Elga, eyes widening.

"What do you mean?"

"Oh nothing, nothing, I really shouldn't." She bit her wrinkled lips, fighting the urge to speak.

"Please," Jinji said breathily. Her heart quickened. Her grip on the seat below her tightened. She was on the verge of discovering something—she could feel it.

Elga looked over, lips pursed, and then leaned closer. "Well, people have been noticing odd disappearances, deaths even, but it's real hush, hush. They say it's the king, that he's killing off people who might be, well… But not me, bless the spirits. King Whylfrick would never do nothing like that, he's a good man."

"It's not the king." Jinji frowned. Was this really happening? After so long, had she really just fallen into the answers? All this time, could the spirits have been waiting for her to get the courage to leave Rhen, to follow her own path?

Elga straightened quickly, eyeing Jinji with caution, her old brown eyes lightening with wisdom.

"Course not, that's what I said," she spoke louder, pushing the words out onto the street before her, "King Whylfrick loves his people, he would never."

"People who might be what?" Jinji asked, still stuck on Elga's previous words. What had the woman meant? Was it the ramblings of a crazy person, or was it the answer Jinji had been searching for all along?

But Elga shook her head, using her voice to urge her horse onward.

The streets had grown busier, louder. They had moved through the second wall without Jinji realizing. The people around here wore dull garments of thick wool, dark brown and black with none of the fineries Jinji had almost grown accustomed to seeing. Men stumbled around, holding cups aloft. Their faces were red, eyes glassy. It reminded Jinji of the tavern Rhen had taken her to so long ago. Madness.

Voices rose over the crowd singing songs that Jinji didn't recognize. The lyrics spoke of Whyl the Conqueror.

And that's when she realized that the people were celebrating. The nobles had the Naming Ceremony, locked behind their walls standing in formal processions, and the city had this—chaos.

Jinji focused on Elga, noticing that the woman was determinedly not opening her mouth.

"Please, people who might be what?" Jinji repeated, pleading.

But instead of answering, Elga pulled hard on the reins, muttering something under her breath—*big mouth*, *trouble*, and other words Jinji couldn't make out.

"I'm sorry, boy, but I can't say, now run along, I—I have to go back, I left something that my husband won't forgive me losing, his favorite blanket you see, and I need to get it."

"Elga," Jinji urged, reaching for the woman's arm, but she was swatted away.

"Now go," she said louder. "I said leave. Get off my cart and go!"

Men turned, hearing the shriek in the woman's voice. They narrowed their gazes on Jinji, taking a second too long to try to place her clothes and her darker skin. One man stepped forward, eyeing her with distrust, a big drink sloshing in his hand.

For the first time since Roninhythe, Jinji felt different. Her skin crawled under their lead gazes.

"Who are you boy?" One man asked, his voice deep and slurred.

"Where are you from?" Another asked.

"Where'd you get those clothes?" Still a third pressed.

More turned, eyes brightening at the sign of a commotion. The energy shifted, darkened, narrowed on her until it felt suffocating.

Elga continued to yell nonsense, even after Jinji had slipped from the cart, landing hard on the uneven cobblestones.

A hand gripped her sleeve, pinching her skin.

Without turning to see who it was, Jinji ran, wincing at the sound of cloth ripping. She looked down at the tattered shreds of her shirt, gone from the elbow down, torn free. Her arm was thin and womanly, not bulging with muscles. She kept moving, praying no one noticed. Praying to the spirits that she moved fast enough for the rest of her clothes to stay intact.

Jinji remembered what her father had told her. Old lessons died hard. And she knew without a doubt that it was much safer to be a boy in this world than it was to be a girl, especially a copper-skinned girl that no one could lay claim to—not even the man she would name her only friend.

Shouts followed in her wake, urging her forward.

Turning down a street, she risked a glance over her shoulder, cringing as an angry crowd came into view behind her. Four men in hot pursuit.

Jinji pivoted to the left, down another street, then to the right, to the left—not caring as she dove deeper into the maze of the city. As long as the cries behind her grew quieter, she knew she had traveled in the right direction.

But there was one problem, they weren't disappearing.

Jinji looked back again, but no one was there. Just ghostly voices, still yelling after her. She kept looking behind, waiting for someone to appear, to recognize her, to—

Jinji cried out as her body smacked into stone and her wrist crunched, caught between the wall and her body.

Dropping to the ground, her vision blurred. She blinked into the growing darkness, trying to dissipate it, hearing the voices raise ever louder. Seeing gray blocks of rough rock, Jinji flung an illusion in front of her, praying to the spirits that it looked enough like the wall she had run into—the one she still couldn't properly see.

Moments later, the men ran into view, huffing, surveying the dead end with the intelligence of natives, of those who had lived there for years.

As her eyesight cleared, Jinji tried to slow her breath, to quiet it. The pain in her wrist seethed out, spreading up her arm. She shifted back, wincing as her boots scudded on the dirt covered side street, stopping when her spine met resistance. Even though the illusion hid her, Jinji felt exposed. She hugged her knees closer, pulling the shirt down as far as it would go, hiding the skin that differentiated her—skin that she had never before felt the need to conceal.

Tears came unbidden, slipping down her cheeks, and her body started to shake as shock set in.

Fear. It crept down her body, strong as any she had ever felt before. Fear of a world she had never experienced alone—a world she didn't like.

The four men walked closer, confused, and then stopped. One man complained that his drink was gone. Another agreed. The third one shrugged. And the leader, taking one last look at the wall—at the illusion Jinji knew was far from perfect—spat on the mud, then turned his back to her.

It wasn't until they disappeared around a building that Jinji let herself relax, let a sigh of relief ease from her lips. But she kept the illusion up, a safety net until she regained her poise.

If that was Whylkin without Rhen, Jinji didn't know what she would do. Was that to be her fate? To be hunted, to be the outsider, the one everyone blamed with no more proof than a crazy woman's ramblings?

Was that what the spirits had planned?

She dropped her head back against the wall behind her, gazing up at the sky. The spirits didn't heed her prayer. They remained hidden, out of sight, even as Jinji demanded the comfort of seeing their ever evolving weaves. The little strands of life that made her feel unafraid, that made her feel a little less lonely, a little less abandoned.

At the exact moment the spirits relented and zipped into view, a scream filled the street.

Jinji's head jerked forward.

A boy appeared, small and cowering as he looked through an open door, into the home to Jinji's right side. Around his figure, waves of fire spun—just like Rhen, a living flame.

Jinji gasped and stood to help, but a man stepped into view, stopping her.

His eyes were white.

And they looked straight at her.

Covering her mouth to catch a gasp, Jinji's mind flashed back, back before Rayfort, before the sea, before Rhen—back to where it all began. Her small home, decimated.

Back to Maniuk—to her taikeno—with a knife at his throat as the shadow clouded his eyes, stealing his free will. Everything she had been through, every obstacle she had overcome, was for this moment, this confrontation.

The shadow was here.

In Rayfort. In this alley.

But it hadn't come for her.

The blank eyes passed over her, sparing a glance at the wall, studying it for a moment, and then returned to the little boy on the street. His small fingers were clutched over his face, praying for mercy. The word *papa* escaped his lips, over and over again, coated in confusion.

The man stepped forward.

Steel caught the sun, flashing like a beacon into Jinji's eyes. He held a knife. Lifted it. Stretched it toward the boy. A boy who made no move to save himself, whose actions were paused by incomprehension.

"Stop!" Jinji yelled.

The illusion crashed down, revealing her hiding spot. But the man did not listen.

"Stop!" She cried again and sprang forward, moving to yank his arm.

When her fingers were an inch from touching his skin, the man jumped backward and his face whipped in her direction, as if only just noticing her.

Jinji smacked the ground, creating a barrier between the shadow and the small boy it was trying to murder. She lifted her gaze, meeting those soulless white eyes with pure hatred. A snarl curled her lips. And even though she held no weapon, had no way to defeat it, she lunged.

The man dodged, escaping her touch.

With an Arpapajo war cry, Jinji ran forward once more.

The man retreated—his feet propelled backward while his hands reached toward her, as though for a hug, as though his body was at war with itself.

Jinji paused, watching the figure twitch as it fought the urge to move closer and farther away from her at the same time.

He blinked. The shadow of an iris appeared—brown—only to be quickly covered by white, dispelled.

Realization hit fast. The shadow was afraid of her, and that fear had allowed the man it possessed to fight back.

If she could only touch it, could only fight it herself…

Jinji stepped cautiously forward, arm outstretched.

Before she could move another inch, the body dropped to the ground—lifeless.

Behind her, the little boy cried out, running around Jinji's legs and crumpling onto the body of his father. The man groaned and turned over, human once more, looking at her with confusion while he hugged his crying child. Confusion turned to distrust. Distrust turned to accusation.

Jinji ran, knowing where accusation would lead.

Her mind raced even faster than her feet.

The woman Elga spoke of people dying, special people. It was clear to Jinji now what that meant. People kissed by the spirits were disappearing—people like her, like that little boy she had just saved on the street.

People like...

Jinji skidded to a halt.

A gear clicked into place. Suddenly it was all clear.

The spirits hadn't been sending her away from Rhen, they had been telling her to save him. They were trying to open her eyes, to make her see.

Their fates were tied.

All this time, Jinji had thought that the shadow was hers to fight alone. But it wasn't. It was their destiny—they needed to defeat it together.

And Rhen was in danger.

The shadow feared her, but without Jinji nearby, Rhen was vulnerable. The shadow would take him, like it had taken everyone and everything else in Jinji's life.

But this time she would beat it.

She would kill it.

Jinji looked around at the empty street, listening to the echo of celebrations filtering toward her, and wrapped an illusion around her body. To the outside world, she was nothing more than commoner, dressed in dull garb, nothing out of the ordinary.

But inside, she had never felt stronger, more true to herself.

I'm coming, she urged—for Rhen, for the shadow, for vengeance.

I'm coming.

The labyrinth of Rayfort was the only thing standing in her way.

18

RHEN
~RAYFORT~

"All hail!" Rhen said. But what he really meant was, bless the spirits the ceremony was almost over. He wasn't sure how much more standing his feet could take.

Whyllem had pulled him to the taverns last night, and using his trusted sleeping potion, Rhen spent half the night searching for any signs of an attack. But there was nothing. No signs of any Ourthuri infiltrators. No rumblings by the docks. No gossip. After a while, he had even searched for signs of Jin's mysterious shadow, but still nothing.

An evening of empty wanderings had turned into a sleepless morning, and it had all been in vain. In fact, all Rhen had managed to do was arrive late for the ceremony and further annoy his father.

Just what he needed.

Shifting his gaze to the side, Rhen looked at the babe being held aloft before the throne by King Whylfrick. Red robes of the kingdom of Whyl draped around his tiny body, cascading all the way to the floor. His curious hazel eyes were open, darting around the room. Not a single cry had escaped his lips, and it filled Rhen with a sense of pride.

Whyllean.

He had been named.

Whyllean, Rhen's nephew, the future king of Whylkin.

"All hail!" Rhen repeated with the crowd.

The baby had been dipped in the spiritual waters, blessed with the prayers of Whylkin, and told the story of his ancestors for the first time. But most importantly, Rhen and his brother Whyllem had just renounced their claim to the throne, ensuring the proper line of succession, thereby ensuring the future of the kingdom.

"All hail!" Rhen yelled for a third time.

Even as his spirits were high, fed by the energy in the throne room, a pit gnawed at his stomach. Rhen knew he had been right. The Naming. Everything centered around the ceremony. But all of the nobles in the kingdom had been sequestered in the throne room for hours and not a single thing was amiss.

He scanned the room. His father beamed. Whyltarin shone with pride. Whyllem with love. Farther into the crowd, everyone wore cheerful smiles; not a single person hinted bitterness at the ceaseless reign of Whyl.

It was perfect.

Too perfect.

And it made Rhen's skin crawl.

"All hail!" He shouted for a fourth and final time. One call for each of the spirits, as was tradition.

The king lowered Whyllean and stepped back to sit on the throne, resting the babe in his lap. He spoke the closing words, but Rhen was too busy shifting his feet and looking anxiously around the room to pay attention.

Slowly, starting from the very back of the room, the nobles entered in a procession line, waiting to kneel before their future king and swear loyalty to their kingdom. Rhen searched every face for Ourthuri skin, every wrist for powdered over tattoos and every hand for a concealed dagger, but there were no enemies hiding amongst them today.

Before he knew it, it was his turn. Rhen stepped forward, raised his right hand to his heart, and bowed deeply before his nephew.

"I swear my undying loyalty to Whyllean, Son of Prince Whyltarin, Son of King Whylfrick, and the newly named future king of Whylkin. May the Sons of Whyl forever watch over this land and protect its people from all who wish them harm. In the name of Whyl the Conqueror, who united the lands, may the spirits watch over and protect Whyllean from harm, may he know the joy of seeing his sons become kings, and their sons after that. All hail."

Bowing once more, Rhen stepped forward to place the ceremonial kiss on his nephew's brow—a right reserved for the royal family alone. Flicking his gaze up, Rhen met his father's glare. It sent a chill down his spine. He looked away, quickly grinning at the dribble of spit leaking out of the baby's lower lip. *You're almost done*, he wanted to say. Instead, with love in his heart, he knelt down.

But right as his lips were about to touch Whyllean's brow, his father pulled back on the child. Not enough for anyone to see, not enough to cause alarm, but enough for Rhen's armor to crack.

Still bent down, he looked his father in the eye. Heat singed his chest, painful and raw. The man was daring him to act out, to misbehave, to refuse to take his punishment like a Son of Whyl should. But now was not the time, and Rhen, ignoring the despair weighing heavily on his shoulders, stepped aside to let his brother Whyllem give his own blessing.

If only his father understood everything Rhen had done to keep this child safe, to keep their family safe. Turning back to the crowd, Rhen put up the mask of a jovial, carefree prince. He had become so used to playing the part, it was no wonder that everyone believed him. That no one took notice of the hurt in his eyes.

When Whyllem was done with his blessing, the king stood. He and Whyltarin were the only two who would not bow before the boy—kings and future kings bowed before no one.

A thunderous roar rose in the room, echoing against the ceiling and crashing back down. Clapping. For the first time that day, Rhen let the ghost of a true smile grace his face.

The ceremony was over. The Naming was complete.

And nothing had happened.

Everyone was safe. Everyone was alive.

Now, they would feast.

He remained with his family as they exited the throne room, his father and mother first, then Whyltarin and Awenine carrying their son, then Whyllem, and then him. Last, as always. The ache of missing Whyllysle constantly weighed on his thoughts, but it sprang to life stronger than ever in that moment.

Rhen politely nodded to the nobles as he walked past, but their attention was elsewhere. The third son, the third wheel. He was known by everyone, but as an afterthought. If only his partner had still been alive. They would both be looked over, but they would experience it together. Experiencing it alone was, at times, too much to bear.

Rhen retreated behind his façade as the procession continued, slow ceremonial steps to the banquet hall. He kept his mind on the pattern of shuffling his feet—one, two…one, two—leaving no room for self-pity.

Unbidden, Jin jumped into his thoughts. The hand that outstretched to help him up from the floor where his father had left him. The smile that greeted him after their escape from the Golden City. The priceless look of alarm when they had stepped into the Staggering Vixen. One after another, the images came uncalled, memories that began to thaw Rhen's iced over insides, to melt the hard shell he had erected to protect himself.

From the start, Rhen had known that Jin would depend on him—the last of his people thrown into an unkind, unjust, and unfamiliar world. But he had never realized that he would come to depend on the boy too—that they would maybe save each other.

Part of him wished that Jin could have been there today. Maybe the ceremony wouldn't have felt quite so lonely if he had been.

But the royals and the nobles with them, lived in a separate reality. Rhen could try to ignore it all he wanted, but on days like this, when he was forced to be Prince Whylrhen, there was no way around the rules.

Shuddering to a halt, Rhen stopped inches behind Whyllem's back. They had reached the banquet hall without his even realizing it.

The royal table sat at the far end of the room in front of the two long tables where the rest of the nobility would sit. Rhen followed his brothers there, taking his seat at the end of the row, watching absently as more nobles flowed into the room, vision glossed over by thoughts of Whyllysle and Jin.

He was too distracted to notice that only men entered.

Too distracted to wonder where the women were— the wives and daughters.

Too distracted to see weapons glinting under their jackets.

He was not, however, too distracted to hear the resounding boom of the door slamming shut.

No—at that, his heart sank and the world snapped into focus.

Rhen looked up, sure he would find olive-skinned, tattooed soldiers looking back at him. Sure that King Razzaq would be there, smug and confident, stepping from the shadows. So certain he had been right about the Ourthuri threat, Rhen never even expected the sight that awaited him.

They were men of Whylkin.

His own people.

Something Rhen, as much as he played at being a spymaster, had never seen coming. Shame filtered into his heart, curling his stomach, making his insides rot. How had he been so wrong?

They walked between the banquet tables, silently approaching, boots clicking on the stones beneath their feet. A few yards away, just before the royal table, they paused. One man stepped forward. Rhen recognized him—Lord Hamish, the Lord of Roninhythe. Brows furrowed, he scanned the group for a sign of Cal—could he have been so wrong about his friend? His loyal, trusted, friend?

But no, he looked at the dozen faces standing alert in a line, facing off against the throne. Cal was not there. These men were all his father's age, all Lords of Whylkin cities.

"What is the meaning of this?" His father stood. The echo of his chair scraping on stone filled the silence in the room. "Lord Hamish, explain yourself."

"The reign of Whyl has gone on too long," he said simply, as a matter-of-fact, emotionless. "The time has come for the old kingdoms to return. What happened to the Kingdom of Roninhythe? The Kingdom of Fayfall? The Kingdom of Lothlian?" The men behind him nodded in agreement, standing firm.

"They were conquered," the king informed, sarcasm heavy in his deep voice.

"Maybe so, but—"

"No buts," the king interrupted, anger brimming, hands slamming down on the table before him. "You were conquered, not out of spite, out of good—for everyone who now lives peacefully and prosperously in my kingdom, under my rule."

"We were conquered by the lord of a dying city who saw no other route to wealth and power." Lord Hamish's voice was sharp, dripping with the hatred of three hundred years finally surfacing. "Rewrite history how you want, Whylfrick, but we all know the truth. Rayfort had no trade, no money, and no way out of the spiral except to take our resources for themselves. And how well you've prospered selling the wood from my forests, the silks from Fayfall caves, the herds from Lothlian fields, the wines from Airedale hillsides. Every man here is lord of a city that has been dampened by the weight of Rayfort, a city that offers nothing but white rock it can't even mine."

"What we offer," the king said, stepping around the table, closing in on his rebellious lords with nothing but rage on his face, "is the same thing we've offered for hundreds of years— soldiers."

"Soldiers who are not here to protect you," Lord Hamish replied. The men around him grinned.

But at that same moment, the clash of swords rang, muffled by the door but still recognizable. A fight had broken out in the hall.

Rhen couldn't stop his lips from twitching. The royal guard was coming. They would be here any minute. The rebellion would not survive.

"You cannot beat me," King Whylfrick shouted, arrogant and strong, spurred on by the noise. He had completed his walk and now stood directly before Lord Hamish, still not a drip of fear evident on his wrinkled face.

"Wrong," Lord Hamish replied, voice cutting through the hall, low and precise, calm. "King Razzaq recognized our cause.

As we speak, his men are landing on our shores, ready to fight with us, and together we will defeat any army that dares fight in your honor. For after today, no one will fight for a Son of Whyl ever again, only for their memory, and soon even that will fade."

The Lord of Roninhythe pulled his sword free of its sheath. One by one, slow and menacing down the line, the other lords followed suit. The air was filled with the drawn out scrape of metal, a sound that only meant one thing—death.

Rhen couldn't breathe.

The word *Ourthuri* played on repeat in his mind, circling back and back around, mingling with feelings of fear and vindication that he could not suppress. All along, he had been right. No one had listened. No one had believed him enough to understand the urgency in his voice, the truth in his words. The unflagged ships were Ourthuri ships. Their soldiers were on Whylkin shores. And they were undoubtedly here for war.

But now, staring into the face of that war, Rhen wished he had been wrong. Oh, how he wished his father were laughing in his face, joking with his brothers about Rhen's new bout of failure.

That he was used to. That would be easy to take.

But watching men close in on his father—point their weapons at his unarmored, ill-prepared body—that was something that burned his eyes, dried his throat, and made his whole being tremble.

Almost as one, the sons of King Whylfrick stood and rushed to their father's side—surrounding him, protecting him. Rhen reached for his hip, pulling his brand new sword free. It wouldn't remain untainted for long.

Four against twelve.

Behind them, the baby began to wail.

Rhen wished to yell right along with his nephew, but he held steady and strong, shifting his weight between feet, waiting for the inevitable attack. He stared at the traitors, eyes narrowing, watching them examine his family with hunger in their eyes.

No one stepped forward.

No one motioned to attack.

They all surveyed each other, letting the pressure build so the room began to feel heavy, full. Tension thickened the air, pulled taut across the small space, stretching, thinning, lengthening, until finally—snap.

It broke.

With a bellowing cry, King Whylfrick surged forward, refusing to wait any longer for his enemies to make their move.

Lord Hamish blocked the blow, their swords slammed together, deafening as the ringing bounced from wall to wall across the great banquet hall.

Just like that, chaos erupted.

Rhen leapt forward, eyes on the three men before him. These were his men to fight, to take down. He took a wide swing, bringing his sword to each of their eyes, hoping just to distract the lords from his brothers, from his family—hoping to entice them into a match.

The center man immediately turned to Rhen, challenging him with a full-body charge. Holding his sword steady, Rhen deflected the blow and jumped sideways. Unprepared to be so easily outmaneuvered, his enemy flew past, pulled by his own weight—off balance and momentarily harmless.

Without a moment to lose, the second man swatted at Rhen. He was older, slightly gray haired and clearly less agile than the rest. Ducking easily out of the way, Rhen aimed his sword low, slicing the man's thigh open in a deep nerve-ripping cut.

Blood dripped to the floor and the man cried out in pain. The strength eased from his leg, going limp, until he slid diagonally to the floor, eyes wide with shock.

But Rhen had already shifted his attention to the third foe, who waited more cautiously before engaging in a fight, focusing instead on reading Rhen—moving left when he moved left, right when Rhen moved right. His eyes shifted ever so slightly, over Rhen's shoulder, signaling…

Rhen fell to the ground as a whistle filled his left ear, the sound of a sword flying harmlessly overhead. Rolling over, he kicked, nailing his first foe in the sensitive spot between his legs.

The man dropped, howling in pain.

Rhen rolled again, already anticipating the sword rushing for his head. It clanged against the stone floor. Before his enemy could right his weapon or center of gravity, Rhen kicked the man's wrist and the sword dropped to the ground.

Fear crept into the lord's eyes and he backed up.

Rhen advanced, facing the weaponless man, unsure if he was ready to kill one of his own people—even a traitor.

One thought of Whyllean was enough to destroy his hesitation.

In a quick and determined move, Rhen gripped his sword with both hands, bringing the sharp edge deep into the man's throat, wedging it beneath his skin. Life faded from the man's eyes, empty and unseeing.

Raising his boot to the man's chest, Rhen yanked his sword out of the wound, wincing as blood gurgled, spurting forth. But there was no time for that, no time for thought.

Instead, he twisted back around, facing the man who still clutched his balls in pain. As their gazes met, the man straightened, teeth bared as he raised his sword. But he was already beat. He knew it and more importantly, Rhen knew it.

Slowly, Rhen approached.

When he was within distance, Rhen raised his sword, giving the man just enough time to set up a defensive strike. As his foe parried, Rhen loosened his wrists, letting the sword twist over so he could deliver a knockout blow to the man's head with the rounded blunt end below his fingers.

He heard a sickening crunch as contact was made. Instantly, the man fell to the floor.

Spinning, Rhen searched for his brothers.

Terror clenched his gut.

Bodies were strewn all over the floor, but the only man in Whylkin red who Rhen saw standing was Whyllem—Whyllem, wounded and moving slowly, surrounded by six lords.

Pushing thoughts of Tarin and his father as far out of his mind as possible, Rhen sprinted across the hall, jumping over a perfectly made table, tossing plates to the ground, not caring as they crashed and broke into a million porcelain pieces.

Rhen's vision, tunneling narrower and narrower, shifted over his shoulder, past Whyllem to the crying women huddled together and using their bodies to shield little Whyllean from view.

"Protect the king!" Whyllem shouted at Rhen as he neared. Confused, Rhen took a second to search the room for his father, quickly scanning from wall to wall.

But his father was nowhere to be seen, hidden out of view on the ground, buried under a body or a table.

Rhen paused. He brought his gaze back around, processing the world in slow motion.

Realization dawned harshly.

Whyllean.

Whyllem meant protect Whyllean—which meant Tarin and his father were dead.

Dead.

Pain pricked his body, numbing his senses.

He had failed.

His family was dying.

"Rhen!" A woman screeched, bringing him back to reality. Back to the scene around him. Back to those still alive.

He would not lose anyone else, not today, not while there was still breath left in his body.

The spark of a flame pierced his eyes.

Rhen's memory flew back to the ship, back to Jin's swift maneuver, his trick to make Rhen speak the truth. He had been able to steady those flames, to keep them from burning the ship to ash. He had done it once…

It was crazy.

It just might work.

Dropping his sword, Rhen grabbed two lanterns from the table. Praying no weapon would pierce his unprotected belly, Rhen charged into the fray, placing his body in front of Whyllem, and more importantly, in front of their king.

"Get behind me," he yelled and threw the lanterns as forcefully as he could at the floor.

Fire flared to life at his feet, billowing up in a huge wave that soared overhead and blasted his face with heat.

The lords jumped back, surprised.

"Rhen," Whyllem yanked on his shoulder, trying to pull his brother back into safety.

Rhen shirked his hold and met his brother's eyes. "Get with the women, and stay back. For once, just trust me."

Not waiting for a response, he looked to the fire, already feeling his hands itch with longing. But he was not there to shut the fire off, to pull it into his skin.

No.

He wanted to make it rage.

Rhen glanced at the oil spreading across the floor, widening the wall of flame before him. In only minutes, it would be dried up, and the lords would be able to advance once more. He needed something else. Something beside stone. Something that would light up and stay that way.

Getting his bearings, Rhen realized he was sandwiched between the two long banquet tables, right in the center of the room. Behind him, the royal table sat undisturbed, confirming his location.

Cloth.

He realized.

Wood.

Running down the center of the table was a red silk of Whylkin, a decoration—a fire hazard. Underneath it, planks of solid wood.

The fire just needed to get there—to spread a little wider.

He stared into the orange flames, willing them to grow, to heed his command.

They shrunk.

The fire wouldn't listen. Even as his skin yearned for its touch, the fire denied him, as it had every time he had tried to control it.

A shout caught his notice. One lord had climbed onto the table, circling to fight Rhen from behind.

There was no time.

Ripping his shirt down the middle, Rhen pulled his formal jacket off and dipped it into the flames, waiting until it caught before tossing it onto the tabletop to his left.

Shrugging off his shirt, he repeated the process, only this time throwing it to his right.

Then he waited. Watching. Praying.

Suddenly a spark, a bright flash.

The fire caught.

A blaze singed the approaching lord as the silks burned hot, alighting more oil and rapidly pulsing down the table in small booms.

"Rhen, you will burn us alive," Whyllem yelled over the cackle.

But hope surged in Rhen's chest and he turned to his family, beaming with relief.

"No," he said and reached into the growing flame behind him, letting the heat seep under his skin, comfort him. His mother gasped, a memory flaring to life behind her irises. He pulled his untouched, unscalded hand free.

Whyllem's jaw dropped.

Rhen stepped closer and moved his mother, Awenine, and Whyllem so they all huddled together, covering Whyllean, cowering from the flames. They listened to his commands without protest, without pause.

Like a shark, Rhen circled them, constantly walking around their bodies, pulling any wayward flames into his flesh to prevent them from smoldering his family.

It seemed like hours that he moved, calling a flame in, releasing it, searching for the next encroaching wave.

In truth, it was only minutes.

But the fire had done its job. Rhen knew it the moment he heard the doors slam open. The lords were running, saving themselves, escaping.

Still, Rhen let the room burn until he heard voices call out for the king, the queen, Tarin. He never heard his own name, but it didn't matter. The guards were there. The people loyal to his family were there.

And the house of Whyl had survived.

When droplets of water brushed his face, Rhen knew for sure that his enemies were gone. If the guards were safe enough to concentrate on putting out the fire, his enemies must be out of reach and running.

Letting go of his concentration, Rhen dropped to his knees, throwing his hands to the side and calling for the fire to come to him.

It listened, crashing into his chest, melting into his bare skin, disappearing from the world. He pulled and pulled, demanding every last source of heat obey his will.

Lord of Fire.

That's what Rhen was—what he had always been. But now the world would know it too.

He opened his eyes and stood, meeting the amazed expressions of the royal guard, all paused with disbelief as water sloshed from the buckets in their unsteady hands.

Not waiting, Rhen spun. He had to check if his family was safe, that Whyllean remained untouched.

As he opened his mouth to ask the question, a gasp escaped his lips instead.

Rhen clutched his stomach.

He looked down at the knife hilt protruding from his skin, at the blood spilling onto his fingers, at the hand—the delicate, feminine hand—forcing the blade deeper.

Rhen's gaze traveled upward, slowly, disbelieving, until they met his mother's eyes.

His mother's empty, white eyes.

19

JINJI
~RAYFORT~

As soon as Jinji reached the castle, she knew that something was wrong. That she was too late. That the shadow had beaten her there.

While she ran up the white stone steps, countless ladies ran down—formal dresses bouncing, elegant hair falling. Screams filtered into her ears, screeching over the dull sound of her heart thumping wildly in her chest.

For every step she climbed, Jinji was pushed down three more. Her feet slipped on voluminous silk skirts, her face was pelted by wild elbows and whipping jewelry. Trying to swim upstream would be easier and far less painful. Dressed as a commoner, she was invisible to these women.

But looking into their frightened faces, Jinji had a feeling the entire world was invisible to these girls—their vision was too clouded over by fear, by the desperate need to escape.

Why?

What has happened?

Jinji's heart continued to pound. Was Rhen alive? For some reason, she felt as though she would know if he were dead, that she would feel it, a sinking pit in her stomach, the same way she had felt when Janu had disappeared.

He was alive.

He had to be.

Using her own strength, Jinji pushed the approaching ladies aside, not caring if she injured someone. Her will to enter was stronger than any of their wills to leave.

Luckily, she didn't need to push for very long. Behind her, men started to shout, to make way, to part the madness. An avenue opened up and Jinji sprinted, her short legs soon overcome by men in shimmering bronze armor and red leather overcoats.

She recognized the symbol on these men's chests. It was the same stallion that Rhen had on his ceremonial garb this morning. The symbol of Whylkin. Better to be a soldier in these halls than a commoner, that much she had learned already. So, in the midst of the chaos, Jinji wove a new illusion around her body, hoping no one saw but not really caring—there was not enough time to be worried.

After tying the spirit strands into a thousand firm knots, Jinji held her breath for a split second, waiting for one of the men to shout, or yell, or hold a knife to her throat. But nothing happened. The trick had worked, she looked exactly like a king's soldier, and now her greatest challenge would be keeping in stride with these men towering at least a foot over her head.

Together they ran.

Soon after entering the main doors of the castle, the stream of women ended, replaced by an eerie silence only heightened by the constant pound of boots on stone. By all counts, the men should sound thunderous in these vaulted halls, but they didn't. Small and powerless was more like it.

Still, Jinji preferred it to the ghostly sound that followed. A ringing. Subtle at first, but growing louder. Clangs. Vibrations. Shouts. Cries.

Somehow, something that had seemed so foreign months ago had become recognizable to her ears. The sound of battle haunted these hallways. And though it made the men around her cringe, Jinji's heart lifted ever so slightly.

War.

Just as Rhen had described, just as he had predicted. The Ourthuri had come.

It was horrific. Horrible.

But it also wasn't the shadow, which meant she still might have time to save the one person she was worried about losing.

As they rounded a corner, everything stopped.

Jinji's jaw dropped. The men around her gasped.

It was a bloodbath.

The pristine white stone walls dripped maroon, were stained pink. Bodies lined the floor, writhing, moaning—not dead but wishing to be.

Men in the same uniform Jinji now wore stood surrounded, circling, keeping men in fine clothes at bay.

And then Jinji gasped too.

These men were not Ourthuri. They were newworlders. They were just like Rhen, pale skinned and rich, dripping in sparkling fine clothes.

She looked closer, unable to tell friend from foe. Lords stood with the guards against their equals, fighting their peers.

What had happened here?

But Jinji's question would go unanswered as the men around her jumped into action, leaping over the bodies littering the floor to confront the rebellious lords now turning in dismay—having just realized they were outnumbered once the fresh round of guards appeared.

"To the king! To the king!" Men shouted around her in confusion.

"The door!" More answered.

Jinji searched, eyes widening as they landed on two towering doors at least four times her height.

Her heart sunk.

Hoping it wasn't true, she searched the crowd, through gleaming swords and lunging bodies, through swinging arms, looking for his face.

Please, she thought, *please don't be just out of reach*.

But he was.

Rhen was nowhere to be seen.

Jinji glanced back up at the door, eyes following the middle seam all the way to the ceiling. There was no way that would break down. No way to open it unless it wanted to be opened.

Still, ignoring the fight around her, Jinji ran as fast as she could and slammed her shoulder into the thick wood, not at all surprised at the pain that shot up her arm and the cry that escaped her lips.

Cutting off her senses, refusing to acknowledge her hurt, Jinji charged again, willing the wood to bend at least a little under her might. But it didn't. Hard as stone, it remained strong, immobile. Undefeatable. But still, Jinji threw her body against it, again and again, until her side went numb and she could no longer command her muscles.

Her mind urged her body forward, but her legs would not listen. Instead, they crumpled and she collapsed at the base of the door, even smaller than before, as though submitting to its greatness.

After all of this, after coming so far, this could not be the end.

Sluggishly, she knocked her head back, still refusing to give in, welcoming the headache that invaded her senses because it meant that she was still fighting.

The shadow would not beat her.

Not this time.

Her life was defined by being too slow—too slow to wake and find Janu, too slow to dress and save her village, too slow to run and save Leoa, too slow to act and save Maniuk—to tear the knife from his hands before he made one fateful final kill.

Now this.

Too slow to leave the castle, too slow to return, too slow in a world where everything happened far too fast.

Flipping over, Jinji struggled, bending her knees and raising her fists so her hands at least could still beat against the door—softly, but with all the strength she had left.

Other men appeared around her, thinking she was wounded, dying or bleeding out, but they didn't offer to help. They stood with her, beating the door, trusting their companions would protect their backs as they fought to reach their king.

With her cheek pressed against the wood, Jinji felt the rumble of their strength—felt how little it did against the door. But she also felt something else.

Heat.

Weak at first, but growing stronger, until her face began to burn.

Brows furrowed, she leaned back, watching the splintered surface as if it would reveal a hidden secret.

Looking.

Waiting.

Then *bang*, the doors catapulted inward and a blast of hot air singed her face, making Jinji fall backward in surprise. Her eyes stung, immediately watered. She blinked, trying to clear her vision. Swords rang anew in her ear, shouts.

"Fall back."

"To the king."

"Retreat."

"Find water."

Clashing, conflicting opinions shouting over one another.

Her vision returned, but still, she saw nothing but the angry orange wall before her.

Rhen was lost.

Jinji sat down, unable to move a muscle to help, not caring if the wave of fire curled out and dragged her in.

All was lost anyway. The shadow must have won.

Rhen was dead.

Staring into those flames, she knew it for a fact. Her heart froze over, a frost she knew would never thaw.

If he were alive, he would have stopped the fire. He would have smoldered it, pulled it inside of him the way she had seen on the ship.

He would have…

Jinji looked around, unsure how anyone else could be moving when the world seemed to be crashing down. Lords were retreating, some guards were following, others ran to the flames with buckets of water, trying to control something that was not meant to be contained.

Coughs spewed from her lips, forced her stomach to bend, her arms to catch her as she fell forward. Lit from the flames, shadows danced into her vision, expanding along the floor, taunting her.

Jinji closed her eyes, but still the fire flickered behind her lids, undulating, making black shadows appear and disappear from her mind.

Someone knocked into her, dousing her with a splash of cool water as he stumbled by, enough to make Jinji jump up in shock despite the protests of her muscles.

Eyes opening, she stopped.

Stopped moving.

Stopped breathing.

Stopped blinking.

Everything about her just paused.

The fire was shrinking.

Jinji stood. Her cramping muscles screamed, ripping as she stepped closer.

The flames kept lowering, sucked in by an invisible force, moving backward in a way that looked unnatural, forced. The smaller they appeared, the more her heart lifted.

No one else could do this—nothing else could.

Jinji stared, eyes widening as if it would help her see more.

A faint outlined popped into view, white behind the flames— a man.

Jinji grinned and strode forward as the fire disappeared entirely, replaced by Rhen—shirtless, covered in blood and sweat—alive. The entire room inhaled together, waiting for him to open his eyes. When he did, the green burned, sparking, as though the flames had fused with his irises.

Rhen stood, but a movement over his shoulder caught Jinji's attention. Huddled behind Rhen, were other people, shaking with disbelief. Breaking away, a woman stood—his mother. Her dress was singed with holes, her hair frazzled. Saved by her son.

Jinji smiled, waiting for the woman to turn and hug Rhen, to give him the thanks he had deserved for so long. It was enough for Jinji to know he was alive, to know he was safely within her eyesight, out of the shadow's reach—so she stopped walking forward, crossed her arms, and waited for him to share a much needed moment with his family. Maybe now they would honor him with the love and respect he deserved. Maybe now…

A glint blinded Jinji's eyes. A bright light, like metal catching the sun.

Jinji looked up. Windows lined the upper rim of the room, swords were scattered all around the floor. It was to be expected.

But then it happened again, hurting her irises, making her blink.

This metal was moving, was—

"No!"

Jinji shouted and ran forward, too slow once more. The queen looked up—her stare blank, her eyes white and emotionless.

The shadow.

Rhen turned. His back hunched. His hands flew to his stomach. Even with his back to her, Jinji saw the knife dig into his gut; she felt it sink into his stomach as though it were her own skin.

Blood dripped to the floor.

The queen pulled back. Rhen collapsed. She raised the knife to her own throat. And Jinji sprang forward, biting her lip to keep from crying out as the realization of Rhen's imminent death sunk into her bones.

The queen looked up. Looked into Jinji's eyes.

Panic.

The shadow was afraid. The queen stepped back, farther away from Jinji. The knife pulled quickly, closing in on her throat.

But before the job could be finished, Jinji was there. She slid around Rhen, careful not to harm his still body but also not stopping, not wasting time.

In one heartbeat, everything that had happened in the past few months fluttered into view, memories flashing faster than her mind could process. Her father was there. Her mother. Leoa. Maniuk. Janu. And now Rhen.

Eyes narrowing, lips pursing, anger brimming to the surface, Jinji dove for the queen's arm and wrapped her fingers firmly around her thin wrist.

As soon as they touched, Jinji's eyes rolled into the back of her head.

Her vision went black, disappeared.

All self-awareness vanished.

She didn't see the queen stumble back, blinking rapidly, eyes clouded over with confusion but color returned to normal. She didn't hear the windows above their heads shatter, fall into the dining hall, and crash into a thousand pieces. Jinji didn't feel the lightning bolts pierce her skin, bend her back almost in half, and lift her off the ground.

She was beyond that. Beyond the world. Beyond feeling.

Trapped within the confines of her own mind, back in the shadow dream, Jinji was drowning. Claws gripped her skin, her teeth tasted blood, large wings pushed against the water and stretched for the surface. Jaws gripped her neck, tightening her airway, making her lose all breath. Her talons stretched out, fighting, tearing thick skin with their razor-sharp edges.

This was the moment in the nightmare where she always awoke, the endless struggle, this battle.

But this time, her eyes didn't open.

No awareness came.

She was no longer Jinji. No longer an Arpapajo. No longer even a human. Jinji had left her body behind, to lay deathly still on the palace floor. Now she was pure spirit.

This time, it was not just a dream. There was no waking up. And if she did not escape, she would die here—in this otherworldly realm her mind had been catapulted into. An ether between the spirit and shadow realms.

All she needed to do was break the surface of this dream water—to return to the spirit realm, and leave this endless, death-enshrouded abyss. One gulp of fresh air and she would live.

But she was not strong enough. The darkness overtook her, removed her strength. Jinji was being pulled under, below the water, deeper and deeper, until the world changed, warped, and twisted.

She had entered the shadow realm, a different plane of reality.

No light pierced her eyes. No life.

Limbs weakening, she forced tired muscles to keep fighting, refusing to let herself drift away in this eternal midnight where even stars refused to shine. Still, they sank farther. The shadow pulled her slowly, steadily down.

Her last reserve of energy gave out.

What more could she do?

Nothing.

But she would not die without seeing her home one more time. She could not die in this lifeless place, this place that her soul rejected, this place where the elemental spirits seemed untouchable.

So Jinji released her hold, let her claws ease apart, her long jaw release. She closed her eyes and envisioned her home—the spirit realm that she had brought to life.

Wind caressing her gliding wings. Great, white mountains disappearing into the startling blue sea. Green land sprouting, stretching as far as her eyes could see. Glittering gold sunlight hitting red-walled cliffs, making the earth spark and flame.

As she imagined, she wove the elemental spirits. Life suddenly sprang into being in a place where it didn't belong, a place of death and destruction that had never before seen the beauties of her world.

The shadow released her, fell away, blinded by the images of a realm it couldn't imagine. It jerked, covering its scaled face with ebony wings, pushing away from the light.

Moving on their own, Jinji's wings flapped against the water, pushing her higher and higher, climbing closer to the surface.

Unable to wait any longer, Jinji's eyes drifted open. The water was no longer black, but blue, shimmering with sunlight.

It lightened. And lightened. Her eyes were drenched in ivory.

And then she was free, breaking through the surface to breathe in fresh air, floating through the sky, wings light without the heavy weight of water.

It felt good to stretch her muscles. To dip and glide and soar. To weave through trees, rise over snow-capped peaks, plummet into crashing rapids.

The longer she flew across the spirit realm, her otherworldly home, the more she forgot.

Forgot the body left cold on the floor in the human world.

Forgot her human self.

Forgot Jinji.

But remembered other memories, of lives gone by, of pasts being reawakened.

The spirit dragon had returned.

Reborn for the first time in millennia.

20

RHEN
~RAYFORT~

Rhen fell to the ground, hand pressed tightly against his stomach, trying to hold in the blood forcing its way out.

He looked up at his mother, desperate, pleading for mercy.

She stepped back, lifted the knife to her own throat. And suddenly, something clicked into place.

This was the shadow.

Jin had tried to tell him, to warn him, but Rhen had never really believed the boy until that instant—looking into his mother's empty, soulless eyes. Something had taken control of her body. Something had ripped away her will.

That same thing wanted Rhen dead.

And it might have succeeded, he thought, pushing harder against his weak muscles.

His mother looked up sharply, eyes widening at something over Rhen's shoulder. The knife dug into her throat, pushing deeper, trying to break through delicate but sturdy skin.

"No," he tried to say. It came out softer than a whisper.

In a flash, someone had jumped over his body, crying out. Rhen recognized the bronze armor of the royal guard, the red leather overcoat. Pride surged in his chest at the sight of the rearing stallion of Whylkin, still charging into battle, still strong.

The man reached out, stretched for the queen's hand, for the knife.

The instant they touched, time stopped.

The guard's skin rippled, trembled. It grew in size, inflating, swelling larger and larger. The colors on his jacket seemed to melt, to mix together. They dripped down into his flesh, spinning and turning, separating into individual strands.

Rhen watched with widening eyes. The man was a monster. An aura sprung to life around his person, dragging his image wider and wider, until the man's body was encased in a glowing shell, white with veins of color intermixing, weaving together, and pulling against each other. It brightened, whiter and whiter, growing, expanding, becoming more vaporous, until it burst.

The man fell.

The queen stumbled back, blinking. Her eyes, green and so like his, had returned to normal—mulled over with confusion but vibrant and full of life.

Rhen looked at the guard. But he was no longer a guard.

He was a boy, wearing dark leather boots and a fine white shirt that was splattered with dirt. Looking closer, Rhen spotted fingers, copper toned as though kissed by the sun, glowing despite being indoors. It was the only bit of exposed flesh Rhen could see, but it was enough. Even presented with his back, Rhen recognized his friend.

"Jin," he said, hoarse, pained.

Of course Jin had come to fight the shadow, to save Rhen yet again. It was no surprise, and yet his heart felt just a little bit lighter, a little more able to hold on.

Reaching out, Rhen extended one hand, keeping the other firmly planted against his wound.

"Jin," he repeated, softer. But the sound was deafened by the crack of splintering glass.

Rhen arched his head up, peering at the windows so far overhead just in time to see them burst apart, shatter, rain down with sparkling fury. He tried to look away, to shield his eyes, but they were glued to the spot. Blinding flashes followed, crackling through the empty windows, half a dozen bolts of light, maybe more.

Faster than his mind could process, they dropped to the floor, meeting at the same exact spot—Jin's lifeless body. Immediately, the boy was lifted off the ground, catapulted feet into the air as his body bent almost in half from the electric shock coursing through his veins.

Rhen's bones chilled.

It wasn't the lightning. It wasn't the gruesome curve of Jin's body. It was his silence.

Racked by pure elemental power brought down by the sky, yet Jin was quiet. Unmoving. Not a single sound escaped his body. It was eerie, and it made Rhen's skin crawl with unease.

The entire banquet hall stilled, enraptured by the scene. No one moved. No one stirred. The only sound was the sizzle of heat.

And then it was gone.

The lights relented, disappeared, and zipped back up into the sky. Jin fell to the ground. The entire room paused...then dove into action.

Rhen inched his way forward, using his one free hand to pull himself closer to Jin, wincing at the pain it caused in his gut.

When Jin's hand was in reach, Rhen grabbed it and latched on. Waiting, praying, he felt for a pulse.

There.

It was there. Ticking, thrumming rapidly, as though the boy were running instead of lying still.

Rhen tugged.

Jin flipped over, falling onto his back, head rolling to face Rhen…

He sucked in sharply.

It couldn't be. It wasn't possible.

But his eyes met full lips, wide and defined cheeks, long closed lashes framing elegantly angular eyes.

A woman.

It was undoubtedly the face of a woman.

Yet as he looked closer, Jin was in there too, like one face altered just enough to become something, someone entirely new.

Reaching out his hand, Rhen ran his fingertips over her soft skin, thumb brushing the curve of her jaw until it reached the bottom edge of her lip. A memory came unbidden, one of a golden-veiled face looming over him, worriedly caressing his brow. He recognized her now. It was never the princess. It had been Jin all along.

Since the day they had met, Rhen had known Jin was hiding something. And now he knew. Jin could change his skin, could appear to be someone else. It was impossible—but some would say no more impossible than a prince who could walk through fire unscathed. Minutes ago, she had appeared as a royal guard, but somehow touching the shadow had caused her true self to be revealed.

A pain sharpened in his chest.

At first, Rhen thought it was his wound, but then he realized it was something entirely different. The white-hot sting of betrayal.

He had shared everything with the boy. Had opened up, revealed secrets he had never told anyone before. Rhen thought he had finally found a confidant, a true companion, a real brother.

But it had all been a lie.

All of it.

False.

Jin was a woman, and that changed everything.

Hands slipped into view, grasped Jin under the shoulders, pulling her roughly off the ground. She didn't stir. The only movement on her person was the constant flick of her eyes behind their lids.

"Take the girl to the dungeons with the others," Rhen heard Whyllem command, saw his brother step into view, and kneel down over him.

The guards pulled Jin away, her boots scraped along the floor as they dragged her by the arms. Rhen remained silent. Not one protest stirred on his lips as he watched them take her away.

"Rhen," Whyllem swallowed, voice catching as he lifted Rhen onto his lap.

For his part, Rhen tried to answer, tried to respond, to ease the worry in his brother's face. But it came out as a gurgle. His tongue felt heavy and fat. His lips would not obey.

Whyllem reached down, pressing his hands against Rhen's stomach. But Rhen found he couldn't feel them. Couldn't feel anything, not even his own fingers. Panic made his heart race, but his muscles would not respond—they felt disconnected from his brain.

"I will not let you die, brother," Whyllem said, voice thick. "You cannot leave us." He looked up at the sky, back down at Rhen. His eyes were moist, darkening over and growing wilder by the second. "I," his voice cracked, "Rhen, I cannot do it alone. Without father. Without Tarin. I need you."

Whyllem's head bent down. He started shaking against Rhen's chest. Silent cries racked his body.

More than anything, Rhen wished he could lift his arm, wrap it around his brother's shoulder, and assure him it would be okay. But the harder he tried, the weaker he seemed to feel.

Vision spotting, his eyelids felt heavy. Drowsiness muddled his mind.

"Get him to the apothecary, immediately." A voice commanded, but Rhen could no longer recognize it. He seemed to be floating, drifting through darkness, dreaming of endless night.

He was gone.

Hovering.

Sinking closer and closer to a world not of the living.

21

JINJI
~RAYFORT~

Jinji woke with a start, gasping for air, eyes opening wide as her entire body came alive in one single second.

She blinked. But the scene remained the same. Eyes open, eyes closed—she was drenched in ebony, drowning in it.

"Rhen!" She called. There was no answer except for the echo of her own scratchy voice. Jinji tried to stand, but she couldn't—she was restrained.

Heavy iron weighed down her hands, encircled her feet. Every time she moved, the clank of metal on stone scraped her ears. Shivering from the wet cold air, Jinji pulled her legs into her chest. Gradually her eyes began to adjust, to faintly make out bars lining the walls around her, bars and stone.

"Rhen," she whispered. But no one would hear. That much she knew. The last Jinji remembered, she was leaping for the queen, touching the shadow, falling into her nightmare. And then nothing. Blank. Until waking up here.

Cold.

Hungry.

Helpless.

But not alone.

Someone else had woken up with her, inside of her. Even now, Jinji could feel it crawling through her thoughts, exploring her senses, stretching out as though awakening from a long sleep.

New memories were blossoming like flowers in the back of her mind, growing, spreading, taking up space. But hard as she tried, she could not access them. Could not touch them. Could not remember them.

You will.

A voice that was not her own whispered across her mind.

You will.

Don't miss

THE
SPIRIT
HEIR
A Dance of Dragons #2

Coming in 2014!

Sign up at the below link to be notified the morning it goes on-sale!

TinyLetter.com/KaitlynDavisBooks

ABOUT THE AUTHOR

Kaitlyn Davis graduated Phi Beta Kappa from Johns Hopkins University with a B.A. in Writing Seminars. She's been writing ever since she picked up her first crayon and is overjoyed to share her work with the world. She currently lives in New York City and dreams of having a puppy of her own.

Connect with the Author Online:

Website:
KaitlynDavisBooks.com
Facebook:
Facebook.com/KaitlynDavisBooks
Twitter:
@DavisKaitlyn
Tumblr:
KaitlynDavisBooks.tumblr.com
Wattpad:
Wattpad.com/KaitlynDavisBooks
Goodreads:
Goodreads.com/author/show/5276341.Kaitlyn_Davis

17580495R00164

Made in the USA
Middletown, DE
02 February 2015